THE BATTLE

OF THE VILLA FIORITA

THE BATTLE

OF THE

VILLA FIORITA

Rumer Godden

New York: The Viking Press

To Ceril, who made the dream real

THE BATTLE

OF THE VILLA FIORITA

I

THE HEDGES of scented whitethorn on either side of the villa gates had the longest fiercest thorns they had ever seen. The gates were iron-barred and high, the bars set close. Obviously people were not meant to get in. The villa was firmly shut away from the little village that straggled up the mountain, more of a hamlet than a village, having only one hotel, the Hotel Lydia down by the road, a few houses and farms, a camping ground in an olive grove and a *trattoria* beside the lake. Notices on the gates said *"Attenti al cane,"* which conveyed nothing to Hugh and Caddie. "Who would ever have thought it meant 'Beware of the dog'?" said Caddie afterwards. *"Proprieta privata"* was clear: "Private property." But *"I contravventori saranno puniti ai termini di legge"*? "Can that mean 'Trespassers will be prosecuted'?" asked Caddie.

The villa was on Lake Garda in northern Italy, "But it doesn't matter where it was," said Hugh afterwards. It might have been anywhere; it was simply a place where two opposing forces were to meet, as two armies meet on foreign soil to fight a battle. "The battle of the Villa Fiorita," Caddie called it afterwards and always with an ache of guilt.

Now, looking through the bars they could see an olive grove, cypresses, a walk of grey stone flags winding away beside a cypress hedge that shut off a further view; there were glimpses of tumbling flowers, of honeysuckle and wisteria—they had seen that in clusters all along the road —of small yellow roses climbing up a cypress tree. They could hear bird songs coming from that cool green and, faint and far beyond, water lapping. It was another world from the hot white road along which they had trudged, with cars driving past so fast that wind and dust had stung their faces and Caddie's legs.

Hugh had put down the grips that had wrenched his arms all the way from the bus stop at Malcesine but Caddie still carried their raincoats, the belts dangling, and the netted bag, limp now, that had held the sandwiches, or-anges, and a bottle of lemonade they had bought at Vic-toria. On the gate were gilt letters, VILLA FIORITA. They had arrived, but could they push open those heavy bars, walk past those notices into that private green and shade? "We have come so far, we must," said Caddie and she opened one gate a few inches and slipped through; she had a feeling that she was stepping where she should not but Hugh had followed her. Once inside he was drawn by a curiosity that, these days, was becoming his familiar. What did he expect to see? He did not know but he felt on tiptoe with expectancy.

Set back from the gates was a garage, with terra-cotta walls. On one a painted Saint Christopher took up the whole wall. Outside it was a car, a dark green Mercedes open coupé, left there as if someone had just driven in. They looked at it, almost sniffed it, as cautiously as two dogs. The hood was down and on the seat was a scarf, white silk patterned with brown flowers. Mother's scarf? thought Caddie. She had not seen it before. Beside it was a pair of driving gloves. His? They both noticed that the car was glitteringly clean.

A path led away through the olive grove, a wide belt of rough grass and old, old trees with twisted trunks, some lichened, some split halfway up their length, showing wood dried to paleness; their roots made humps and coils in the grass but each of them had a crown of leaves, blowing now green, now silver in the light wind. They were circled round with stocks, purple and white, growing wild. By common consent, Hugh and Caddie had kept off the path and walked quietly on the grass; to get into the garden beyond they had to step onto the path with its rough worn flags, but here they were in the shadow of a hedge. The evening sun drew a warm spiced smell from the clipped cypress and with it a drift of scent from the stocks, a scent that grew stronger as they came out into a hedged garden. Sunk behind the villa, it was out of the wind, still and hot in the sun, and filled with a tangle of flowers: lilacs, japonicas in bushes of red and salmon pink; narcissi, pansies; a jasmine falling from a terrace above to which a flight of worn pink steps led up with, on every step, pots of geraniums. "We have to go up there," whispered Caddie, but she wanted to stay, still, where she was. She and Hugh were both gilded in sun; the things they held, the grips, coats, and net, had edges of light as had Hugh's bare head, Caddie's panama. Light bathed their tired dusty faces, their clothes which were crumpled and dishevelled as only clothes that have been slept in all night can be; it lay on their hands and legs, their dusty shoes, a light more warm and gold than anything they had known but, "It's Italian," said Caddie as if suspicious of it. All the same she would have liked to shut her eyes and let it rest on her eyelids that felt brittle as paper; on her neck and shoulders and hands, on her aching legs but, looking up, they could see above the terrace a tiled roof, dark yellow walls, with painted eaves, cream arches like the cloister arches in the print of the Fra Angelico Annunciation that hung in Caddie's bedroom at home in Stebbings, and, "That's the villa," she whispered.

Timidly, she followed Hugh up the steps. Now they could see that the terrace had a roof of vines; on the right a long walk trellised with wisteria led down and out of sight. From somewhere came a shrilling of birds. The terrace made a forecourt under the vines whose tendrils were just budding—"Funny," said Caddie, "I never thought that vines had flowers." It led to an open porch with a floor of black and white tiles; an iron table and chairs were set there and the front door was open. It was from here that the shrilling came; they saw that the house wall was covered in cages, each a few inches square and holding a bird that hopped from floor to perch, perch to floor, sometimes opening its wings, and, "Oh! Oh! Oh!" cried Caddie.

"Ssh!"

"But . . . They're wild birds, shut in. There's a chaffinch."

"Ssh!"

"Those tiny cages . . ."

"*Ssh!*" Hugh's fingers pinched Caddie into silence. "You clot! Do you want someone to hear us?" Why this imperative need for silence, he did not know. Their crêpe-soled shoes had made no sound, even on the gravel, and the birds' voices had drowned Caddie's.

It seemed a place of birds; swallows nesting under the roof flashed dark blue and cream-coloured as they flew in and out. "The poor caged birds have to watch them," whispered Caddie in misery. There seemed no human about. Then, from behind an arched door on the left, they heard singing, loud, almost raucous but abstracted, the abstracted singing of someone who worked as they sang. "Italian," whispered Hugh, and he looked at the arched door again. Outside it were a basket with a hoe and a string of onions "That must be the kitchen. Should we knock there?" asked Caddie. Hugh shook his head. He did not want to knock.

The singing went on and Hugh, with Caddie tiptoeing after, went to the front door. "Can we go *in?* Shouldn't we ask?" But Hugh only said, "Ssh!" That compulsion of secrecy was still on him.

He listened again. "It's all right. Come on." In the hall he stopped. A coat they recognized was hanging there. Fanny's, their mother's coat. A man's short sheepskin-lined duffle hung beside it. Below on a rack were shoes; their mother's walking shoes and a man's shoes, brogued and laced. "His feet are not as big as Father's," whispered Caddie. There was a Japanese sunshade of oiled paper, lavender colour. "She didn't have that before." Again they seemed to sniff its unfamiliarity, then, quietly, they slipped into the room beyond.

It was a dining room. They noticed immediately that the tablecloth on the round table was all of lace with a branched silver candelabrum in the centre. More candlesticks were on the sideboard, a stand of pink hydrangeas in the window. There were Persian rugs in soft colours. "Well, we had Persian rugs at home," said Caddie.

"Not like these," said Hugh.

A trolley of drinks had been wheeled by the door. "Dozens of bottles," said Caddie. The room smelled of flowers, wine, and food, and Caddie's hungry stomach gave a loud rumble. Glass doors divided this room from the next, a drawing room, bare and cool, with more Persian rugs on a polished wood floor. Caddie left a dusty footmark when she stepped on it and hastily withdrew her shoe; they did not go in, but stayed just inside the doors, looking. Cream paint and double windows, their shutters half down, gave the room a look of the rooms they had seen in Switzerland but the furniture was—"Italian?" asked Caddie in a whisper—certainly antique; polished wood chairs, upholstered in cream brocade; a low table covered with crystal, silver, and enamel boxes and ornaments. There was a great carved chest, an inlaid writing table with gilt legs, its top holding rows of miniatures, a tapestried stool and, "What is that thing?" asked Caddie.

"I think it's a prie-dieu," said Hugh. "You kneel at it to pray."

"In a *drawing room?*" asked Caddie, astonished.

There were tapestries on the walls and paintings in gilded frames. At one end a fireplace was made of the same pink stone as the steps they had climbed from the garden; it was laid with olive branches, and perhaps the faintly pungent smell in the room was of olive smoke. It mingled with the scent from the azaleas and begonias grouped on the window sills. Each side of the fireplace were book-

shelves, reaching to the ceiling and, above the fireplace itself, two carved angels almost as tall as Caddie held sconces;
their gilded wings shone in that dim end of the room.
French doors opened on to another terrace, "Which must
be on the lake side of the house," whispered Hugh. They
could catch a glimpse of the wisteria trellis beyond but did
not dare to cross that shining floor and look.

The dining-room floor was of tiles, patterned with flowers, and from it a staircase curved out of sight. "Is it marble?" asked Caddie, awed. It was of white marble and,
"Can we go upstairs?" asked Caddie, shrinking. Hugh listened again; there was still only that singing and, "Come
on," he said, sounding bolder than he felt, but, when gingerly they trod on the smooth whiteness and came up the
first few steps, they saw the staircase was closed off from
the upper flight by a door of rose brocade. A brocade door!
That seemed to lift the house into undreamed-of luxury.

When it was opened, they stood again to listen; then,
stepping silently on the bare marble of the treads, they
went up the short flight to a landing. It was here that the
arched Fra Angelico cloisters guarded a balcony that
looked down over the sunken garden they had walked
through and over the olive grove. On the balcony a towel
horse was spread with a towel on which vests, stockings,
and socks were laid out to dry. A hanger held a shirt, open-
necked, dark blue; a woman's slip, white and threaded with
ribbon, and some white briefs hung over a line. "We
shouldn't look," said Hugh suddenly.

"Why not?" said Caddie. "It's only washing."

The landing had four doors. Greatly daring, Hugh
opened the first, but it was an empty room. They saw a bed-

room where the shutters were down so that its light was dim. They could make out boxes on the bed, a chair covered by a sheet, a gleam of mirrors. The next door was of a dressing room. Its green shutters were only half closed and, standing in the doorway, they looked at a dressing-gown thrown down on the day bed, a row of shoes, ties hung over a chair on which a pair of binoculars were slung. Ivory brushes were on the chest of drawers, with a litter of ashtrays, packets of cigarettes, a handkerchief, bottles, jars, some with their lids on crookedly, while a Penguin lay face downwards on the floor. "He's not very tidy, is he?" whispered Caddie.

At the end of the landing, a small door led into a room that was . . . "Queer," said Caddie. She meant it was a mixture. Cupboards filled all one wall so that it, too, looked like a dressing room but the other three walls were hung with tapestry. There was a large painting of the Madonna in deep blues and pinks, a vividly rosy Madonna. Inlaid chairs were pushed back against the wall and in the middle was a wooden kitchen table, heavy, rough, with a wooden kitchen chair. The window sills were heaped with books, there were more books on the floor with a big waste-paper basket, while the table itself was covered in papers, more books, blotting paper, clips, a typewriter. A red crystal goblet held pencils and pens, and on top of it all was a notice printed on a piece of cardboard in English and Italian. *"Non toccare.* Don't touch!" For the first time Hugh smiled. "I bet Mother tries to make *him* clear up his table."

Next door was the bathroom, big and white-tiled. "Look!" whispered Caddie. "Big towels and little towels and a bathmat all to match." Someone had just had a bath; the air was heavy with steam, "And scent," said Caddie, wrinkling up her nose, "but Mother doesn't use scent."

"She does now," said Hugh.

Fanny, if it were she who had had the bath, seemed to have caught the untidiness; underclothes were thrown down on a stool; the bathmat, still damp from wet feet, was wrinkled on the floor, powder was spilled; it might have been their seventeen-year-old sister Philippa, not a responsible woman, a mother. Caddie picked up the box of powder with its large puff. "Jicky Guerlain," she read.

"Put it *down*," said Hugh. "Come out." He looked even paler than he had on the road and his forehead was clammy. It seemed too intimate, there in the empty villa. The swallows flew round it, making a rush of wings in the height; a shutter, loose on its catch, clacked gently; the singing sounded from below. These were the only sounds but the house was filled with two people, Fanny and—"Mr. Quillet," whispered Caddie and, caught unawares, spied on like this, they seemed not enemies but vulnerable. It was like putting one's hand into a nest and finding it still warm.

If the last door had not been open they would not have looked in. As it was, Hugh stopped short on the threshold and Caddie had to reach up and look over his shoulder. "Mother's bedroom," breathed Caddie. She felt Hugh's arm quiver against her. She quivered herself. This was even worse than seeing the furniture from Stebbings in the new London flat. Mother's room. At Stebbings it had not only been where she slept—and their father when he was home—it had been where anything serious, or private, in the family had happened or was discussed. Talks took place there and what Fanny called reasoning; punishments were given, temperatures taken. Doctor Railton did his examinations in it, and ill children were allowed to spend the day there in bed. Hugh and Caddie had both been born in that room. It had been the core of Stebbings, though they had not known it. Now, this pink and cream enamelled furniture, the wide bed that had a bedhead of brocade in a gilded frame, the tiled floor, and shutters were Italian, foreign, but still there on the dressing-table were their photographs, as they had always been: Philippa, Hugh, Caddie; under the glass of Hugh's was a brown curl of baby hair. There, too, was the apple pincushion Philippa had made and painted at school, the wooden pinbox Hugh had made in carpentry with Fanny's initials burned in its top: F.C. They won't do now, thought Hugh. There were a great many more bottles and jars than there used to be and the brushes were new; perhaps the old silver ones with cherubs' heads on them were too battered to bring to this villa. These matched the blue and gold of the clock on the bedside table. "Is he fearfully rich?" asked Caddie.

"Shut up."

As if holding to a thread of Fanny, Caddie was glad to see by the clock a shopping list, written in Fanny's sprawling writing, and beside it was the little green leather book, the *Imitation of Christ* that had been by Fanny's bed since they could remember. Its corner had been chewed by Danny as a puppy and it had a ring on the binding where Philippa had once put down a cup on it.

This room too was untidy; someone had dressed and thrown things down. Caddie gave a "tchk" and picked up a petticoat; it was fine, gauzy with net and embroidery. "Is it Mother's? It doesn't look like hers."

"Shut up. Put it down," said Hugh even more fiercely.

They looked through to the dressing room they had seen before; the door was open as if he and she came in and out, talked while they were dressing. The bedside table on the other side of the bed was heaped with books, there were cigarettes on it, an ashtray, and, "She lets *him* smoke in bed," whispered Caddie. "She wouldn't let Father."

The *Times* had had only a paragraph: "Colonel Darrell Charles Clavering was granted a decree nisi in the Divorce Courts yesterday because of the adultery of his wife Frances Clavering with Robert Paston Quillet (the film director) on the 12th of October and subsequently, at Mr. Quillet's flat in Lowndes Square, S.W.1. The suit was undefended. Colonel and Mrs. Clavering were married at St. Michael's, Chester Gate, in 1945. There are three children of the marriage. Custody of the two younger was awarded to Colonel Clavering, who was also awarded costs."

The other papers had been less reticent. A few had headlines: "Queen's Messenger brings suit." "Well-known film director named as co-respondent." "Rob Quillet (of *Diamond Pipe* and *Haysel to Harvest* fame) named in case." "Colonel Clavering awarded costs against film director."

Philippa and Hugh had been told at half term—"But Darrell should have let *me* tell Hugh," Fanny had cried.

Caddie had not known until the end of the Easter holidays. "When the case is all over, and it's all settled," Darrell had told the others. "It will be less painful like that."

"Was it less painful?" Caddie might have asked.

She had been bundled off out of the way to Devonshire for the Easter holidays. "Not bundled, you wanted to go," said Philippa.

"It was a riding course," said Caddie as if that settled it. Even now, in the midst of this shock, her face had shone when she thought of it. "I learned an immense lot," she said, "and so did Topaz."

"But didn't you suspect?" asked Hugh. "Didn't you think Father was being extraordinarily kind? Paying those fees and boxing Topaz all the way to Dartmoor after the fuss he kicked up when you won him?"

"I thought he was beginning to believe in him," said Caddie.

"Oh Caddie!" They could not help laughing. "It was just to distract you, my poor infant," said Hugh.

"Only too easy," said Philippa.

"You must have had *some* inkling, heard gossip?"

"How could I?" asked Caddie. "I never listen."

"We know that," said Philippa. "But all the same . . . Mother being away all that time up in Scotland at Great Aunt Isabel's?"

"But Aunt Isabel was dying. She *died*."

"Then us going so suddenly with Mother to Switzerland for Christmas?"

"I hated that," said Caddie.

Those had been Darrell's terms. "Terms?" Fanny had asked when Rob came back from that one interview.

"He can make terms," said Rob. "It's only just."

Fanny had waited that late November morning in the sitting room of Rob's bachelor flat. Because of the block's central heating it had been over-hot, the air stuffy and stale after the English coldness of unheated Stebbings, and she had pushed up the window and sat by it. Outside in the Square, traffic came and went; there was a perpetual roar of it from Knightsbridge; cars pulled out from the parking spaces round the Square gardens, voices floated up; Christmas shopping was already in full spate; throngs of women were going into Woollands, Harvey Nichols, as a year ago she would have been going. Everything was busy, crowded, rushed, but here in this room was stillness, silence: only the ticking of the clock, the beating of her heart. Beside her had been a bowl of chrysanthemums, small, curled, bronze, that Rob had bought for her that morning; in his distress for her he had gone in and out buying her things. The glow of their colour and their pungency filled the room but, as Fanny waited, she had fiddled with them cruelly, jerking them, uncurling the petals until her fingers had smelled pungent too. When Rob had come in, quietly closing the door, coming to her and sitting down beside her, she had known by his gentle protectiveness that his news was harsh—but what could I have expected? thought Fanny.

Only a few of Rob's sentences reached her. He said them as if he had learnt them by heart. "Darrell is thinking of the children, naturally."

"Naturally." That came stiffly through Fanny's lips.

"He was quite fair."

"He always was," said Fanny.

". . . not time now before their Christmas holiday to make arrangements. He asks that you go back to Stebbings to meet them. He will guarantee to keep away. He wants no one to know until they need. I think he is still hoping you will change your mind." Fanny bent her head over the mutilated chrysanthemum, jerking it, pulling it, and after a moment Rob went on, "To save gossip when he doesn't come home for Christmas, you will take the children to Switzerland."

"We can't afford it," she had said automatically.

"He says his mother will help," said Rob.

"Lady Candida!" said Fanny. "Must she? Yes, I suppose so."

"He will start proceedings at once. After the holidays you can come out to me in Africa, or have this flat until I can get back. The case should come on in the spring. By that time he will have found somewhere to put the children."

"Put the children!"

Darrell had been awarded the children as he had been awarded costs. "It makes them seem like chattels," said Fanny, and, "One must hand it to them," Hugh had said that day of Caddie's return. "They are clever arrangers. Everything went most smoothly and all behind our backs." His hands were in his pockets when he said it and then he tried to whistle, the clear blackbird whistle that always filled Caddie with envy—she could never make more than a breathy squeak—but the whistle jarred and was jerky, just as Philippa's talk was offhand. Caddie could tell they were both quiveringly hurt and she ached for them. "The worst of Caddie," Gwyneth often said, "is that when she does think of other people, she thinks too hard." Gwyneth had been the Claverings' daily woman since Philippa was a year old and she knew them, "Inside out," said Gwyneth.

She had come to London to housekeep and look after them, closing her own cottage, but the life seemed to have gone out of Gwyneth; she no longer sang the chapel hymns the children had loved and her step was heavy. "Well, she worshipped Mother," said Philippa.

"More fool she," said Hugh.

To the whole of Whitcross it had come as a shock.

"Fanny? Fanny Clavering?"

"The Claverings? Darrell and Fanny? Impossible."

"I can't believe it."

"It's there—in print."

"But *Fanny!*"

"With all those children!"

"She never said a word," and, "I thought we were friends." That was Margot and Anthea, Fanny's best friends, "Well, my oldest friends," said Fanny.

There were other, humbler voices about whom Fanny cared even more: people like Prentice, their old gardener, and Mrs. Derrick at the shop; George Glossop at the garage, post-office Emily; the travelling fishmonger who had always let the children ring up the cash register on his van when they were small, and Patrick Aloysius, the milkman.

"Mrs. Clavering? Up at Stebbings? Never!"

"But she wasn't that kind."

"Well, you could knock me down!"

"Mrs. Clavering!"

No one could believe it, yet it was true. All her life Caddie was to remember Darrell telling her in the taxi on the way from Paddington: in the flat Philippa and Hugh had confirmed every dread thing he had said.

Lady Candida had found the flat, on the fourth floor of a great modern block of "cement shoe boxes," as Hugh called them, and it was true that the rooms were all the same though fitted in differently. It depressed Caddie and Hugh to think of the hundreds of other rooms round them: it made them feel like rabbits in hutches instead of people. On the ground floor were shops, "Very convenient," said Lady Candida but, "Wickedly expensive," said Gwyneth; she always went to the shops in the poor streets round the corner. There was a swimming pool and a restaurant. "Your father can go there when Gwyneth is away. You and Hugh can go to the snack bar. You will like that," said Lady Candida, but Hugh and Caddie did not like it; the snack-bar soup came out of tins, as did its meat, while the bread of its sandwiches looked and tasted like thick white flannel: it was, too, always crowded with people, "Who look at us," said Caddie quailing; she and Hugh might have been a pair of new and peculiar rabbits. "Oh Gwyneth, don't go away," prayed Caddie.

The flat had, too, a nightmare quality because it was furnished with bits of Stebbings so that one came across the nursery armchair in the kitchen, dining-room chairs in the hall, the oak chest from Stebbings hall in the new sitting room, the grandfather clock telling London time. Stebbings itself was empty, left with only Prentice to keep an eye on it. Presently it would be sold. *"Sold!"* Caddie had cried.

"Naturally. Father can't run it without Mother. She worked like ten men." For a moment a quiver came even into the airy Philippa's voice. Fanny herself had gone to Italy. . . . "For the present," Darrell had said.

"How long is the present?" Caddie asked Hugh.

"We don't know. Perhaps the summer."

"But she can't," said Caddie aghast. "The second of August is Risborough Show. Topaz is entered."

"Caddie, haven't you taken *anything* in?"

"And don't you ever think of anything but that blasted horse?" asked Hugh.

"Pony," said Caddie mechanically. "He's under fifteen hands," but she did not dare at this moment to think about Topaz, boxed trustfully back from Dartmoor to Stebbings. Darrell said Prentice had met him and taken him to Mr. Ringells' farm and stables, where they kept ponies at grass. Caddie's mind took refuge as it so often did with her dream Topaz. "Miss Candida Clavering's Topaz made a perfect round, in the Juvenile Jumping." "The Fitzherbert Cup was won by Miss Candida Clavering's Topaz for the third year in succession, a record for this show." "Miss Candida Clavering's Topaz won the fourteen two showing, then this grand little pony went on to win the Supreme Championship."

"Not ambitious, are you?" Philippa would have said if Caddie had said this aloud and, "Yes, I am," Caddie would have answered, but she did not say it aloud. She was used to the fact that no one saw Topaz as she did. "Dog meat. Knacker," Hugh called him, which was near the bone because everyone said that no pony would have been given as a prize by a girl's magazine unless he had been bought cheaply. Caddie had won him with an essay called "My Pegasus." That had amazed her family. That Caddie had cut out the coupon, filled it in, bought the five-shilling postal order for the entry fee, was almost as incredible as that she had written the essay. "I wanted a pony," she had said as if that explained it. There was one fact that she and Hugh had kept to themselves; he had helped her with "My Pegasus."

Once upon a time, long long ago—"Well, six years," said Caddie, which after all was more than half her life-time—she and Hugh had been companions, inseparable. They had gone to school together, the little day school where most of the Whitcross children went. They played to-gether though not equally—Hugh of course was the master, Caddie the slave—but played, shared. They had had a house in the big apple tree, Hugh had hauled Caddie up it, a secret harbour by the stream. They had slept together in the night nursery. Caddie could remember it quite well; after all she had been nearly six when Hugh went away to his first boarding school. She could still see him in his new grey flannel suit, shorts with pockets, jacket with more pockets, a striped school tie, a new blue cap with crossed keys embroidered on it. Hugh had had a wooden playbox with iron hinges and clamps, a trunk of his own, both lettered: "H. D. Clavering." Hugh went to school and Caddie was left behind forever.

For years she had been still attached, still tagging on, as Hugh said; and there was always a hope far ahead of an enchanted time when they would both be grown up; then the two and a half years that made such a difference would not be the chasm it was now, nor the fact that she was fe-male. "There are too many women," Hugh had often

cried of Stebbings, and certainly there were many of them:
Fanny, Lady Candida, Gwyneth, Philippa, and Caddie herself, if she could be counted as a woman: five of them to
balance, if Darrell were away, one boy. No wonder he
was spoilt as Darrell always said he was, but Hugh could
still be kind, still share with Caddie, and sometimes he
lent her a little of his slipperiness. "It says you must write
the essay yourself," she had said.

"You will write it," said Hugh. "I shall only tell you
what to say." Yet mysteriously, when Topaz came, Caddie
was freed of Hugh.

"But why call him Topaz," Philippa had asked, "when
he's the colour of a mole? Topazes are yellow."

To Caddie it was because of his eyes, though she did not
tell anyone that. His eyes were a pony's, dark, lustrous,
lashed, but Caddie had a private idea that they were gold.
Now, "It's his first show," she said. "I have been training
him. He . . . He . . ."

"Why cry?" asked Hugh. "It's perfectly normal. Thousands of couples get divorced every year."

"Think of parents at school," said Philippa.

"Yes, but not ours," said Caddie.

"It was all because of that film," said Philippa.

"What film?" asked Caddie.

"You know perfectly well. *Haysel to Harvest*. The film
Rob Quillet was making. It was nearly all shot in the village. It has just come on in London." Sometimes Philippa
forgot and talked as if they still lived in Whitcross. "It's at
the Empire, with Gail Starling and Mark Bennett."

She had made capital out of the film at school. "Gail

Starling, walking down our village street, Mark Bennett
going into the post office. Both of them staying at the Red
Lion," she had told the other girls.

"Did you meet them? Actually meet them?"

"Of course," said Philippa.

"We saw them," muttered Caddie.

"They were shooting in our park," Philippa explained.

"It's not our park. It belongs to the Big House." Caddie
had not been particularly interested in the film until the
Big House children's ponies were used in it. "They are
not a quarter as good-looking as Topaz," she had said.

"They were there all summer," said Philippa now.
"That's how Mother met Rob Quillet. I must say I don't
blame her. He's attractive. Dark, thin, rather melancholy."

"How do you know?" said Hugh.

"I cut his photograph out of the papers."

"You did," said Hugh with distaste.

"Yes, and I kept all the clippings," said Philippa.

"You . . ." Hugh began, but Caddie interrupted.

"What was Father *doing*? Why did he let her go?"

"You wouldn't want him to make her stay, if she wanted
to go," said Philippa, but Caddie certainly would.

"In a gipsy marriage," said Philippa, "the husband and
wife only stay as long as love is in their hearts. I think
that's beautiful."

"This isn't a gipsy marriage," said Caddie.

"To think it all happened when we were at school and
we hadn't a glimmer," said Philippa. There had been no
doubt that she was excited. Her eyes seemed to flower into
a brighter blue and she kept tossing her hair back, in its
fan of fairness.

It was all very well for Philippa. At seventeen she did not rank as a child and was going to Paris to the Sorbonne, "Only for the course *La Civilisation Française*, that all the foreign girls take," said Hugh, and then to a secretarial college. "But I may stay in Paris and train as a model," said Philippa loftily.

"With those legs?" said Hugh. Philippa, though exceedingly pretty, had inherited Darrell's stocky legs. "Which is better than being stocky all over," said Caddie. Now not even her legs could stop Philippa and she swept on, "English girls are tops for models in Paris." Philippa could escape, but, "I work it out I have twenty-three months in custody," said Hugh. "As for you," he said to Caddie, "you have years."

"Custody? That's what they say when they take you to prison," said Caddie, her eyes alarmed. "Will Father keep us in custody from Mother? Won't we even see her?"

"Don't be such a goose, Caddie," said Philippa. "Mother has access."

"Access?" Caddie could only repeat these terrifying new words. "What's access?"

"It means that we can be posted about like parcels," said Hugh, "To Italy or wherever Mother happens to be, when Father says we can visit her."

"*Visit* her?" The full meaning of this extraordinary conversation had at last reached Caddie and she sat appalled until Gwyneth came in to call them to tea. "I have put it in the kitchen. I thought it would be more cosy."

The kitchen was the most homelike room in the flat, if any of it could be called homelike; in it, and the slit of a bedroom next door, where Gwyneth's things, though they too were jerked out of their right context, the cottage where Caddie had seen them all her life; here, transported to London, were the chalet musical box Fanny had once brought Gwyneth from Austria, the framed photograph of Mr. Morgan, her husband killed in the First World War, the red tablecloth worked with Welcome in each corner, the crocheted antimacassar on the armchair. They gave Caddie a wrench each time she saw them, but not such a wrench as the things from Stebbings, and Gwyneth had brought Thomas. "Cats don't mind London," she said, and indeed his tabby paws had not had to be buttered; he was there as usual, stretched out, making a hearthrug on the hearthrug, as Gwyneth said, but, "Where's Danny?" Caddie had asked at once.

"In kennels," said Gwyneth.

"Mother has taken him," explained Philippa.

"Taken *Danny?*"

"Dearie, he was her dog," but two tears had squeezed then from Caddie's eyes and trickled down her cheeks onto her chin.

The days on Dartmoor, in wind, sun and rain—"Lots of rain," said Caddie—had given her more freckles than ever; her hair needed washing and hung limp in its "ginger," as Hugh called it. "And it has probably got hay in it," said Philippa. Caddie's face was lumpy with distress, and she looked so plain that her brother and sister found it difficult to be patient with her.

"For goodness' sake!" said Hugh.

"Can't you stop?" said Philippa.

"It's no use, Caddie dear," said Gwyneth. "We all know what we think and feel but we have to face it. It has happened, and in two months now, Mrs. Clavering will be Mrs. Quillet."

"We have to accept it," said Philippa.

"Put it in our pipes and smoke it," said Hugh. "On our needles and knit it," but Caddie still sat at the table, and it was then that she had spoken.

"What if we won't?" asked Caddie.

At first it had been Hugh who had hung back. "What, crash in on their honeymoon?" he had said.

"They shouldn't be having a honeymoon." said Caddie, unconsciously as moral as any elder of the church.

"But they are, and they won't want us."

"If we go, they will have to have us."

"We shall spoil it."

"All the better," said Caddie and for the first time Hugh had looked at his small sister with respect; but now, in the villa, far from the flat in London, she was not so certain, and, "Perhaps we oughtn't to have come," she said.

Shaded by the shutters so that the evening light was mellowed and made rich, this villa bedroom with its feminine colours seemed small and close, again too intimate. The same delicate scent was in the air and Hugh felt a tingling in his stomach that he had come to know. It was like a shiver, but can a shiver be hot? he thought. This was always strangely hot. Raymond, a boy at school, older than Hugh but in the same class, had some secret photographs. Like everyone else Hugh had looked at them and, having looked, had this same tremor. Nor could he forget them; indeed, he seemed to be attached to them by an invisible cord that kept jerking him into remembrance. They "visited" him, he might have said. They were shown only to a chosen few. "This is Mirabelle," Raymond would say, watching for his effect. "That's Coral. This is Darleen," and even Hugh had been startled into saying, "Do you *know* girls like that?" which had sounded like Caddie, but he could not help it. "Do you mean to say you know girls who . . ." and, "Aha!" said Raymond. "I don't believe you," Hugh had said, but he would not have put it past Raymond and, though Hugh had treated him in a lordly fashion, if the truth had been told, his whole being shrank away—until this curiosity had begun and disclosed another Hugh. Now he looked at his own curl of baby hair. Every boy hair of him felt erect and he was irritated as a young stag is irritated by the velvet on his antlers, combative— but there was only Caddie to combat. "We shouldn't have come," she went on saying.

"Shut up."

"We didn't know it would be like this."

"Shut up. Shut up. *Shut up!*"

Suddenly he turned and ran lightly down the stairs and out of the front door to the forecourt. Caddie ran after him but she kept her eyes away from the bird cages.

To the right a path led from this high forecourt, down behind the villa and back to the olive grove. Noiselessly they followed it and, on the level again, came to a little walled orchard of peach blossom and figs, then to a vegetable patch, neat in plots of carrots, onions, lettuce, celery. It was sheltered by the rock ridge on which the villa was built, a ridge that ran in a long spine across a peninsula jutting out into the lake. Peering through the olive trees, they could see another entrance from the road, open, not barred, and leading to what seemed to be a boathouse, coloured terra-cotta like the garage. Smoke coiled upwards from its chimney—so somebody lived there—and its back veranda was hung with fishing nets; oars were propped against its wall and beyond it they could see a small harbour, the mast of the boat, and they could hear someone hammering. They had turned to go back when Caddie froze, her hand clutching Hugh's arm, "Look." In the grove a man was stretched under one of the olives, his back against its trunk, a beret half over his face. He seemed all brown; brown overalls, patched brown shoes, brown face and hands, dusty brown hair, straggles of brown beard; only the beret was dark blue. He was asleep.

"Now? It must be six o'clock. A funny time for a grown-up to sleep," said Caddie.

"You don't know Giacomino," Rob was to tell them. "He sleeps at any time. And drinks at any time," he added. Beside the man was a straw-covered wine bottle. He looked so peaceful, so comfortable and happy, almost at their feet in the olive grove, that Caddie felt reassured and she asked an idiotic but hopeful question. "He couldn't be . . . Mr. Quillet?" After all, Rob Quillet is a sort of artist, she argued to herself, and artists can look like that, but, "Don't be a super clot," said Hugh and led the way up, back to the villa. Round it, on its other side, another paved path led to the lake front of the house, passing the French doors of the drawing room, outside which was a table, again of pink stone. "A *stone* table?" asked Caddie. There was a stone bench too, both sheltered from the lake by another clipped cypress hedge too tall to see over. Then, in front of the house, Hugh and Caddie stepped out on a terrace with a balustrade over which more of the yellow roses cascaded, and, "Oh!" said Caddie. "Oh!" not in a cry as when she had seen the birds, but in a deep breath. This was the first time they had seen the whole width of the lake.

They had glimpsed it already from the bus, sometimes close beside the road when it ran along the shore but they had been too shaken—litcrally—and too anxious to look; they had trudged along beside it but now, from the height of the villa on its ridge, the command of its peninsula, they looked at a blue that stretched as far as they could see, disappearing to the north into far folds of mountains, and to the south widening into a pale haze. Directly opposite them, it was bordered by high mountains.

The mountains reared along the lake on both sides; some were capped with snow; the biggest was behind the villa itself. Their flanks were scattered up and down with villages, hairlines of roads criss-crossed them and, as Caddie and Hugh stood there, the sound of bells floated down to the terrace, some so faint they hardly seemed like bells, only a half-heard quivering in the air. Then, from somewhere nearer, a single deep-toned bell rang out. It was just six o'clock, and though Caddie and Hugh did not know it they were listening to the ringing of the angelus.

"But it's beautiful! Beautiful!" Caddie was saying.

"It's only a lake," said Hugh but Caddie could not say that. She had not his and Philippa's ability to shut their eyes to, or gloss over, what they did not want to see. "Like a postcard," said Hugh scornfully but even with a pigmy steamer crossing it, a little white steamer on that painted-looking blue, it was not like a postcard. Waves lapped the rocks; their reflections threw waves of light across the villa walls, round which the swallows swooped and flew. With the mountains, the dark cypresses, the sun, it took Caddie's breath away and she could not pretend that it did not. "It's a giant of a lake, and beautiful," she said.

Below them a grassed walk was bounded by a low wall; steps went down to the water and a jetty ran out into the lake; it had painted pale green railings that matched the house shutters. This was the villa front jetty, there was another, humbler, by the boathouse; at this one's head a boat was moored, and, "What a boat!" said Hugh. Even he could not cry this down; its brown polished hull was half decked, it gleamed with chromium and glass and its seats were covered in blue and yellow and an Italian flag floated from the stern. They could even see its name, *Nettuno*.

"He must be *fearfully* rich," said Caddie.

All at once they heard voices. Voices? A voice. Fanny's! Caddie gave a sound like a little yelp. She would have rushed headlong but Hugh caught her by the back of her dress. Through the trellis he had seen a glimpse of dark blue, a dark blue shirt, twin to the one they had seen drying on the balcony. Fanny was not alone; this Rob Quillet was walking up under the wisteria with her, and, "Wait. Hush," hissed Hugh. "Wait."

The two came into view. He was carrying a jacket, lightly over his shoulder; Fanny was wearing a white dress —"She *never* had a white dress," said Caddie—and held an unfamiliar pale pink jersey, a bag and scarf. "They are going out," Hugh said warningly.

"Out!" Caddie said that as if it were treachery.

At the top of the walk they stopped, dazzled by the sun after the shade. Because of the brilliant light, and because his eyes were so tired, Hugh could not see them clearly; the whole garden and the lake had become a blur but, standing in that flood of evening light, framed against the green leaves and the spirals of mauve flowers, they looked illuminated, glorified. "A couple," Hugh thought before he could stifle the thought, not his mother and Rob Quillet but a man and woman close together.

As Hugh and Caddie watched she looked up at him and laughed; his arm was round her shoulders, now his hand touched her neck, caressing it.

Hugh and Caddie had seen their father kiss Fanny's cheek or forehead often enough, pat her head or shoulder, but this was the first time they had surprised a grown person in a moment of real tenderness—and a tenderness of ownership, Hugh could have said. He and Caddie seemed to swell to giant size. "Crash in on their honeymoon." "They oughtn't to be having a honeymoon." But what could anyone do against this? and Hugh had a wild desire to punish them, wipe that look of private bliss off their faces; holding Caddie as if she were a prisoner, he stepped boldly out onto the path.

"Good evening," he said with icy politeness.

II

A s H u g h spoke, Caddie burst into a loud wail and tore herself from him to go to Fanny. Fanny's jersey, bag, and scarf dropped to the ground and in a moment she was crying too, Caddie gathered close in her arms. "But . . . how," Fanny kept saying incoherently because she was laughing and crying together. "How?" Then, as Hugh still stood by the stone table she freed one hand, holding it out to him. "Hugh? Hugh?" At the pleading in her voice, Rob abruptly bent and picked up her things, dropped them on the table and went to the balustrade, where he lighted a cigarette. Only the way he flicked the ash continually, showed he was in any way concerned. "Hugh, darling." He watched Fanny, her arm round Caddie, come across to the table.

Before she reached Hugh, there was an eruption from the back of the house, shrill cries, voices, a babel of Italian, and round the corner came a big woman in a flowered apron, a woman of a big bust, big forearms, small snapping eyes with, behind her, a pretty girl, big too, with red cheeks and a mane of curly black hair; she was wearing a black dress, a short white apron, and carried the grips and raincoats. They must have found them on the terrace, thought Hugh—and found your disgraceful bag, he said silently to Caddie—and indeed the big woman was panting out, *"Signore! Signora! Schurten! Schurten! Dei turisti. Dei gitanti sono entrati.* They get in. *Malgrado tutti gli avvisi!* So many notice. *Ecco quanto Giacomino ha cura di voi!"* Behind them, still lazy but with his beret now on the back of his head, came the man who had been asleep under the olive tree, and she turned on him, *"Fanullone, buono a nulla!* Good-for-nothing." When she saw Fanny's arm round Caddie, Hugh by the table, the cries and scoldings stopped. "Children, this is Celestina," said Fanny, "Celestina and Giulietta, and Giacomino, Celestina's husband," and she whispered, "Shake hands," but Caddie was too broken with tears and Hugh only gave a curt nod. *"Mio figlio, mia figlia,"* said Fanny and from the balustrade Rob spoke in quick Italian. Celestina, when she understood, broke into cries of admiration. "From England. England!" She translated for Giulietta and her husband. "From England." Then, taking in their dirt and tiredness, *"Poveri bambini!* Poor childs! *Devono aver viaggiato tutta la notte."*

Fanny detached herself from Caddie and went to Hugh, turning him towards Rob. "Rob, this is Hugh." The pride in her voice made Hugh scowl.

Rob was a man, Hugh only a boy, and Rob with kindness held out his hand, but Hugh kept his in his pockets. "How do you do?" he said, and Fanny could guess that his hands were clenched; for all his whiteness, tiredness, and tenseness, there was all Hugh's old insolence in the way he looked at Rob.

Hugh was not tall for fourteen but he looked tall—until

he stood beside a man; it was the way he held his head, the smallness of his thighs, waist, and shoulders. "His shoulders are too slim," Darrell had said lately. "It's time he broadened out," but Hugh refused to broaden out. His head looked big because of his mop of hair; Darrell must have been at him to get it cut, which is why he wouldn't, thought Fanny. Caddie could have told her this was true.

"Quanto è bello il giovanottino inglese!" Giulietta murmured to Celestina. *"Che carnagione! Così chiara e rosea!"* and it was true that Hugh's skin was pink and white, disgracefully pretty for a boy, almost like apple blossom. "How unfair that it shouldn't be the boy in the family to have the freckles," Caddie often said. Hugh's eyes were a darker blue than Darrell's or Philippa's, and his had none of the blandness of hers; Philippa could tell lies so that everyone believed them—except her nearest and dearest. Hugh only told them to be difficult or quip people. Caddie never lied. "I'm not clever enough," she would have said. To her it was an inconvenient defect.

Now, in this scene with Rob and Fanny, she knew she had little importance, it was Hugh who mattered. *"Bello, proprio bello il signorino,"* Giulietta murmured to Celestina. "Beautiful." Standing on this alien sunlit terrace, Caddie looked small, stocky, and very English, a little English bullock, thought Rob. He alone had looked beyond Hugh to her, until Fanny, quick to him, looked too. She saw the crumpled school dress and blazer, Caddie's dirty knees, wrinkled socks, and brown walking shoes white with dust; the locks of ginger hair, the panama askew, face blotted out with tears. Not very attractive for Rob, Fanny thought wincing, but here she was wrong; Rob knew real grief when he saw it, and watching Caddie he began to sense what this journey had been and what lay behind it. Caddie had not a glance to spare for him, or for Celestina or Giulietta, and in that torrent of feeling there was no anger or jealousy, only grief. What was more, he saw Fanny in Caddie; in the brown eyes, the hair whose ginger held a promise of Fanny's bronze, and just so had Fanny often wept. The boy doesn't feel like this, thought Rob.

"Stop it," Hugh said now through stiff lips to Caddie. "Can't you stop?"

"No, I can't," said Caddie.

"Put her to bed," said Hugh. "For God's sake! Just because we have been up all night."

"You must both go to bed." Fanny's own tears had dried and she was brisk. "Baths first. You look as if you needed some hot water. Have you had any food?"

"We had some s-sandwiches we b-bought at Victoria and c-coffee this morning," said Caddie between sobs.

"Only coffee? Nothing else?"

"C-couldn't buy anything in Italy." Caddie was becoming incoherent.

"We had a ten-thousand-lire note," said Hugh, clipping his words as if he hated to speak at all. "Couldn't change it on any of the stations. We changed it in Desenzano but then we had to stay at the bus stop for the bus."

"Where in the world did you get a ten-thousand-lire note?"

"From Father."

"F-Father d-didn't know," said Caddie.

"You must be starving," said Fanny. "Rob, will you tell

Celestina? Hot baths at once. No, I won't hear anything until you have eaten and slept. Hugh, your eyes are bright red." This was a Fanny Rob had not seen, brisk, dictatorial. "Rob, will you tell Giulietta to take their things up and Celestina must make up two beds. Can Hugh go in your dressing room, on the daybed there? Are the sheets aired?" asked Fanny, her forehead wrinkling. "Then a hot soup—omelettes perhaps, and . . ."

"Fanny," said Rob.

There was something in his voice that made Fanny stop. He had not moved but was sitting on the balustrade, smoking. "Fanny."

"Yes, Rob?"

"We were going out to dinner," he said quietly.

"Now? When Hugh and Caddie . . ."

"Now," said Rob. "The *Nettuno*'s waiting. Celestina will look after them."

"We can look after ourselves," said Hugh quickly but Rob's Italian cut across that as he gave orders to Celestina. "*Sì*," said Celestina. "*Sì, sì, senz'altro.*" Her eyes were bright. She loved an occasion. Then Rob got up and put on his coat. "She will show you your rooms," he said to Hugh, "and the bathroom. The hot water runs very slowly but see that your sister has a bath. Then there will be something to eat."

"But what sort of something?" asked Fanny.

"They were not expected," said Rob. "They must take what there is. Fanny, I have ordered dinner at San Vigilio. They won't keep it if we are too late."

"But, I must just take them upstairs. . . ."

"Very well." Rob looked at his watch. "I can give you

ten minutes." Was it the children who had brought that echo of Darrell's voice? "Ten minutes, then we must go."

Upstairs, Caddie quite innocently let off the first shot as Fanny conferred with Celestina on the landing, "Yes, Signorina Caddie in the big bedroom, the piccolo Signor in the dressing room. You can keep your things with Caddie's, Hugh, then you won't disturb Rob too much." Caddie, looking down at her mother's hand on the banister—the *marble* banister—said, "That's a new ring."

It was a ring with a great dark red stone. A ruby? wondered Caddie, set in a circle of diamonds. Behind it Fanny wore a thin gold wedding ring. Caddie tried to think what Fanny's wedding ring had been like at Stebbings; she must have seen it hundreds of times yet could not think; it was not like this one, Caddie decided and, *"Two* new rings," she said.

Fanny abruptly took her hand away, but, "Gwyneth told us you had to wait two months," said Caddie and, because she had to know, she blurted out, "Are you Mrs. Quillet now or . . . Mother?"

On Fanny's first day in the villa there had been a package on her dressing-table. She remembered how she had followed Giulietta upstairs, the powerful brown legs and strong back bounding up before her, as Giulietta carried the heavy cases. "Shake hands," Rob had whispered to Fanny—as this evening she had whispered to Hugh and Caddie—"Shake hands," when Renato Menghini had introduced Celestina and her niece Giulietta. Giulietta had opened the bedroom door, carried the cases in, and stood back invitingly, but Fanny had not gone in; she stayed in the doorway, drawing her gloves through her fingers.

"Come in. Come in. *Entri, entri pure, questa è la sua came-ra,*" said Giulietta. "It is your room." How attractive she is, Fanny had thought, not pretty but healthy, ripe with that glowing rose-brown skin, and those white teeth. In a few years she would, this young Giulietta, become like Celestina, worked into coarseness. Would Giulietta, too, marry a Giacomino about whom Rob had told Fanny? Perhaps she, too, was in love but now Fanny did not want her. She had to be alone in this room. "*Grazie,*" she said, which was the only Italian word she had known then. "*Grazie. Grazie,*" and Giulietta had understood. "*Prego.*" She gave Fanny her wide smile and went out past her. In a moment she had shut the door and Fanny had walked slowly into the room, her heels clicking on the tiled floor, and sunk down on the dressing-table stool. She was alone in their bedroom.

Rob had scarcely looked at her or spoken to her since he met her at the airport barrier. He had brushed her cheek with his lips, taken her small case, and waited impatiently, jingling the coins in his pocket while the porter put her luggage in the Mercedes. Driving he had looked steadily ahead, driving too fast and jerkily. Again he did not talk to her and this neglect filled her with content.

It had been the same after each of their partings, partings whose anguish had augmented rather than lessened as they grew accustomed. Rob had grown even thinner in this month she had not seen him, the month of the divorce, of the children's Easter holidays, when she had not seen them either. She, the guilty one, had not had to go to court but she had kept vigil up in Scotland, packing up Aunt Isabel's house, alone with Danny; the big collie was

the only one of the family she had left. "But why?" Rob
had asked of the vigil. "Why, there alone, when it isn't
any use?" "Somehow I should feel better," and he had let
her have her way. I was selfish, thought Fanny seeing him
now; his fingers were stained with the cigarettes he lit and
threw away; but it was the same each time, until we were
alone. Now we are alone for the rest of our lives and, in
the bedroom, Fanny's heart began to beat as it always beat
in those times of meeting Rob.

This room of delicate colours, with its windows on the
lake—though I must take down some of those dozens of
little curtains, thought Fanny—its wide bed with its silver
and peach-coloured brocade and coverlet of lace belonged
to them now.

There were flowers, and Celestina did not arrange those,
thought Fanny, lily of the valley and white roses. They
were Rob's, and on the dressing-table was the small package tied and sealed from curious eyes—servants, thought
Fanny—and addressed to her. It unwrapped to a small
blue case. Fanny opened it and saw the wedding ring.

The day the decree was given Fanny had taken off Darrell's wedding ring. "In honesty, I had to," she had said.
His diamond engagement ring had gone to the bank with
her other jewellery for Philippa and Caddie and, when
she had come down from Scotland to spend a few days in
London before she had flown out to Milan, her hand had
felt curiously bare; it increased the feeling of a dream in
which she herself was suspended, without status, without a
name.

"How many rooms? How many beds?" Celestina had

asked when she had been told Rob and Fanny were coming to the villa.

"Two," Madame Menghini had said, then hesitated. "Yes, two, my bedroom and its dressing room."

"Then it will be Signor and Signora Quillet?" Celestina had asked. Madame Menghini had hesitated again, then put it differently: "Signor Quillet and the Signora."

Rob had given Fanny the ruby, months ago, on the day this became irrevocable, though she had not known that then. It was one of the days when they had been starved for one another and she had been so restless that she had come up to London and telephoned Rob.

"Fanny! You are in London."

"Yes. Are you free?"

"For you."

"Could we lunch?"

"Chirico's, one o'clock. Or shall I come and get you?"

After lunch Rob had had to admit there was an appointment, "Almost unbreakable," he had said.

"It doesn't matter," said Fanny, "I have seen you and I can walk in the park until it's time for my train." I walked miles in those weeks, thought Fanny; it was the only thing that steadied her but, as they came out of Chirico's, it had started to rain and, "You can't walk in this," said Rob.

"I can—or look at the shops."

"That's ridiculous. I won't have you getting wet and tired. I will drop you at my flat and you can wait there."

"I have never been to your flat."

"It's empty," said Rob, watching her face. "Empty and harmless. You can even make some tea."

They went to Lowndes Square. Rob took out his key. "I shall need this, so I will just let you in." He opened his front door, glass fluted and set in gilt as were all the doors in these expensive flats. In the hall he stepped past her to switch on the fire. "The bedroom's through there, and the bathroom." He opened the doors to show her, bent down to kiss her ". . . and it happened," said Fanny.

They should have known. On the first evening they had been alone, in the drawing room at Stebbings—"When you came to fetch me that first time"—as Rob handed her a glass of sherry, his fingers had brushed hers. Soon they had only to be near one another for this current to begin, any time, anywhere. If he rested his hand on the back of her seat at the theatre, leant across her to shut the car door, touched her hand, it began; but, that moment we were almost innocent, thought Fanny afterwards and over and over again. We were thinking of other things; Rob had his meeting, I thought I would look round his flat—of course I was curious—and leave when the rain stopped, but he kissed me and we made love. Fanny knew now that most women only have a mirage of love. To her it had been a revelation. I suppose, in spite of Darrell and having three children, I was untouched, virgin to love. Afterwards I could have knelt to Rob and he to me. How crooked the world was. This, that she ought to have felt for Darrell, she felt for Rob. Yet because of Darrell over it, each time, there was a shadow. Well, with a sacrament, each time you come near it, you bring the shadow of your sins, thought Fanny. Sin seemed a hard old-fashioned word to use, an Aunt Isabel word, but it was true, and for Rob and Fanny, there must always be, not far off, never out of mind, inevitably, the shadow.

She remembered how Rob had lain with his eyes shut. "Fanny."

"What is it?"

"Nothing else. Only Fanny."

Perhaps she ought, then, to have thought of Darrell, but he never crossed her mind. This was Rob's. Anyone else was an outsider. Then, lying beside him, she had gone to sleep. Presently she felt him kiss her eyelids. "I'm going now. Ring Gwyneth and tell her you will be late. We will have dinner and then I will drive you home. Chirico's at seven."

He had gone and Fanny woke, "Not from sleep, from it," she said.

She did not know afterwards where she went or what she did. It was panic. "What a fuss." She could imagine Margot's or Anthea's cool voices saying that. "Do you think this doesn't happen, every day everywhere? Why most women . . ." "But I'm not most women," as Fanny so often had to say, "I never managed to be as slippery." That sounded priggish but she knew it was because she was inept—and because things that happen to me mark too deeply.

The panic had stayed. It was still raining, the day turning to a dark cold evening; rags of cloud blew across the sky that showed between the houses. People passed her, hurrying with umbrellas. She was bumped into, knocked and pushed—I must have been in the way—but she still walked on, soaked and cold. Yet she had had a burning thirst and somewhere, in a poor street, she had gone into a little brown-painted café where, on an oilclothed counter above the cups and tea urns, globes of orange and lemon squash turned under a celluloid orange and lemon. She asked for a lemon squash and when the woman had poured it from a stop-tap underneath, Fanny found she had no money. Her bag was in Rob's flat. The men in the café stared as she had to come out and the woman's indignant voice sounded after her down the street.

She went into a church. Somewhere in the back of her mind was "a cup of cold water"—I suppose I was a little delirious, thought Fanny—but there was, of course, no water in the church, not for the public. She had knelt down in the first pew, but not to pray, her mind was too numb. Then she had felt faint and had to sit down; her whole body was dizzy and bruised; Rob had hurt in the fierceness of that ecstasy. She was tired, and satisfied as she had never been satisfied before and, I fell asleep again, thought Fanny.

When she woke it was dark. Only the sanctuary lamp burned by the high altar and its jewel-red warmth made her think of Rob.

As she came out of the church—and for a moment she had thought she was shut in and had battered on the door, only to find it open—under a lamp post she looked at her watch. "Chirico's at seven." It was half past eight.

Before I see him, I must tidy and wash my face, thought Fanny. There was a public lavatory in the next tube station. Having no money, she had to use the free cubicle and could not wash, only rinse her hands under the tap; but, using a square of mirror, she took off her hat and tried to re-do her hair—but I hadn't a comb. She had been watched by the young West Indian attendant, and, "I can't tip you, I haven't a penny with me," she wanted to say but she could not speak. Outside again, she took a taxi; the doorman at Chirico's will pay, unless Rob has given up and gone.

He was there, sitting, watching, waiting. When he saw her he came quickly across the room to her, steering her between the tables to their own; in these last weeks it had become theirs, part of us, thought Fanny. He took her hat and gloves, undid her soaking coat, and gave them to the waiter, gave her her bag—"I found it in the flat"—and ordered brandy in a voice she had not heard him use before. Is it the one he uses on the set? she wondered.

"Did you think I wasn't coming?" She tried to smile but her voice was so cracked and dry it frightened her.

"I knew you couldn't not come now," said Rob. He did not ask any questions, only made her drink the brandy and every now and then he took her hand and cradled it in his. "Don't talk. Don't think. Drink," he said. That was the first time I had ever drunk brandy, thought Fanny. With it and the food Rob made her eat, not asking her what she wanted but ordering for her, and with the slow warmth that was beginning to creep into her bones, tranquillity fell upon her. "I have known joy," she could have said, "joy complete. Not many women can say that. Rob will go away. He must. It's in the nature of things. He has this new picture to make in Africa I . . ." And here she flinched as she thought of Darrell. He, her husband, had turned into an intruder, almost into a thief. Poor Darrell. What had he done to deserve this? but she would not think of him now, not yet, thought Fanny. I don't know what I shall do, but I have had my joy. Nothing can take that away from me.

When the waiter had brought their coffee and they were left alone, Rob had put his hand in his pocket and brought out a case, twin to the one on the villa dressing-table. "I couldn't go to the meeting and I had to do something, so I went hunting," he said and he opened it and held it out to her. On the white velvet she saw a deep sparkle—no, not a sparkle, a glow, the colour of the sanctuary lamp, deep red, Rob's colour, as it became for Fanny. "I wanted a ruby," said Rob and he put his hand over hers, "I would say heart's blood but they call it pigeon's blood!" he said.

"But Rob, what is it?"

"Your ring."

"My ring?" Fanny was dazed.

"Men usually give a ring to the woman they are going to marry."

Chirico's panelled walls, its prints of travellers, the pink-shaded lamps, the tables with their white cloths, carnations, plates, glasses, bottles, the black and white of waiters, the white coats of the boys, seemed to tilt together into a blur and run away from Fanny; their table tilted and blurred, there was a loud buzzing in her ears, then it steadied as once again Rob's hand came over hers. "It has to come to that," said Rob, "hasn't it?"

In this new bedroom at the Villa Fiorita Fanny had sat looking at the two rings in her hand until, "They are to wear," said Rob behind her.

He had come in so quietly that she had not heard him and, for once, not sensed him. "Put them on."

"You mean . . . because of Celestina?" said Fanny.

"Because of us." Rob had blazed at her so fiercely that she shrank. "I'm sorry," said Rob. He knelt down beside her. "But sometimes I think you will never understand. I have waited nearly a year," said Rob. "Each day was a year. This last month was twenty, and then this interminable day."

"The day's nearly over." She tried to speak lightly. "Look, the sun is going down."

"I don't want it to go now," said Rob. "It's just beginning." He had his face against her hair. "Your hair smells like a child's, honey and satin."

"It's beginning to be grey."

"Then it isn't a child's, thank God," and sensing her trouble he moved to look into her face. "What is the matter?"

"Rob, shouldn't we keep the wedding ring until . . ."

"Until?"

"We really are married." She knew he would say what she would say herself in strict reasoning: "Can some words that a little man will say over us make us any more married than we are?" They should not, but mysteriously they will, thought Fanny. Rob was laughing at her—because he refuses to be disturbed, thought Fanny, and she freed herself from his arm. He stood up, taking out a cigarette. "It's a little late to be conventional, isn't it?" he said but Fanny looked up at him in the mirror, still troubled.

"Wouldn't it be more honest?"

"No." The laughter had gone, leaving his face and eyes purposely expressionless, a mask that she had seen him

put on for other people. "Honest?" he asked smoothly—
and when Rob was smooth it meant he was angry. "If you
are thinking on those lines, honesty has gone."

"How gone?"

"If a public promise, before witnesses, to put it at its
least, makes all that difference to you, I have to remind
you, you have already given that promise to Darrell."

"This, this is my Hugh," said Fanny, her face lit with
happiness and triumph.

She and Rob were on the veranda of the hotel at San
Vigilio, finishing their dinner.

The *Nettuno* was moored at the jetty and in the dusk
small fishing boats were moving out, each with its search-
light shining down into the water, to make a pool of luminous green through which the fishes moved. A man stood
in each boat moving the oars, while another knelt to cast
and draw in the nets. The veranda was dimly lit, its
orange-red walls seemed to glow; they made Fanny's skin,
so much browner now, look warm, her hair a deeper
bronze. She had a flush on her cheeks. Rob had never seen
her look prettier.

"What was Mother like?" In the flat, Caddie, wrinkling
up her forehead to try and remember, had asked that.
None of them were sure, though Philippa began to em-
broider. "Her hair is nut-brown," she had said.

"Nuts can be all kinds of brown," said Hugh. He did
not want to discuss Fanny.

"I mean red-brown. Her eyes are the colour of sherry."

"Sherry can be anything from dark brown to pale gold."

"Her eyes are not pale gold," said Caddie. Only Topaz's eyes were gold.

"She has dimples." Philippa was developing a new admiration for her mother.

"She's big and soft," said Caddie.

"You make her sound like a sofa or a pillow," but Fanny was soft, soft to lean against, and Caddie's eyes had stung so that she had to trace out the pattern of the chintz on the armchair, to stop tears spilling over. "Caddie is always brimming," said Hugh.

Fanny had thought she knew what she was like—like any of the others who lived in Whitcross, she would have said. It seemed to her now that they had been almost identical, "Peas in a pod," she told Rob. "I, or Anthea, or Margot, or Molly Ferguson, Pam Winter, or Charmian. We dressed the same, in tweeds, a cardigan or jersey jacket, a string of pearls, cultured or very small—except Anthea's; we wore good stockings, a little thick, and flat shoes. We talked the same," she said. "But you never had that high-pitched carrying voice," objected Rob. "We lived the same, in houses a little shabby but gracious, with Regency wallpapers or panelling, chintzes, bowls of flowers. Our children went to much the same boarding schools, the younger ones to the same small private day school. We drove them there and back and those of us who hadn't two cars drove our husbands to and from the station; in fact we were perpetual chauffeurs. We all had dogs, most of our children had ponies. We had accounts at Harrods, Debenham and Freebody's, a few of us at Fortnum's. We gave the same parties, mostly children's or for drinks, but

Anthea's and Margot's were more ambitious; for instance I should never have thought of asking you to dinner," Fanny told Rob. "In the holidays we were so busy we scarcely had time to exchange a word and the driving was really hard work. Children are supposed to keep you young," said Fanny. "I know often at the end of the holidays, I felt old, almost worn out. We were critical of each other, especially behind one another's backs, but if any of us were ill or in trouble, we all helped as a matter of course. We were almost sisters, which is why . . ." And Fanny broke off. Then, "Anthea was the most important," she said. "You saw that when you were shooting in the Big House park." They always called Whitcross Park the Big House. "Anthea went to the Palace, did things the rest of us couldn't. Margot was the clever one and the most sophisticated. She really knew about the theatre and films."

"God deliver me," said Rob.

"Charmian had a tongue. Pam was a darling. Everybody loved her."

"Didn't they you?"

"I was separate, even then," said Fanny slowly. "Quieter. Perhaps it was that I had to do things by myself with Darrell so much away. I was usually odd woman out. Besides I wasn't interesting. Everyone knew everything about me and I suppose I didn't think much about myself. That's not being virtuous," she told Rob. "It's just that there was nothing to think about until . . ."

She had lost that unconsciousness. Nowadays she was always looking at herself in the mirror, but perhaps not as much with vanity, as with questioning wonder. "I am forty-three. I have had three children, one almost grown up. My waist will never be truly slim again. I have wrin, kles at the corners of my eyes"—she could have called them crinkles, but, "Wrinkles" said Fanny firmly, nipping off all illusions. "My eyes still look like Caddie's and my nose is straight, and I have kept my skin, that's from what Margot would call innocent living, but I am large, my mouth is too wide and my forehead is wide too, rather than high, which is supposed to be unintelligent—Lady Candida often said that—and I haven't any presence," but, "I saw you in your village shop," said Rob, "and I thought you were sweet."

If Margot had said that it would have been derogatory, but Rob meant sweet as a good apple is sweet, sweet and sound. "That's the kind of wife I want," said Rob.

"But you could have had someone exciting."

"My work is exciting," said Rob, "I need rest."

He loved to dine with her like this, to look at her across the table, but tonight there was a change. She was not alone with him, absorbed, content, as she had always been. There had always been other people in the room, of course, people round them, beside them—but not between us, thought Rob. I suppose it was too much to hope that this could last. They say a female animal changes completely when she has young; perhaps humans do as well. There was an air of quiet management about Fanny that irritated him. Silently he poured out her wine.

"It hurts that they had to do it at all," but Fanny did not sound hurt, she sounded happy and gratified. "Darrell can never say again that Hugh hasn't guts. For a boy just fourteen to plan and face all that."

"He had Caddie with him," Rob pointed out but Fanny was intent on Hugh. "He always took my side," she said, triumphant again.

"Did you take sides?" asked Rob. "That strikes me as disloyal."

"Darrell didn't understand Hugh," and Rob remembered how her eyes had shone with pride and love as she had turned Hugh towards him on the terrace. "Rob, this is Hugh." "I knew Hugh wouldn't stay with him. I knew it," said Fanny.

"He has to stay with him," said Rob. "It would be wrong to encourage Hugh to think anything else."

"Encourage him?" There was a distinct bristling in Fanny's voice. "How encourage him?"

"Making them feel too welcome. I know it's hard but . . ."

"Is that why you rubbed it in about not being expected?" The bristling was unmistakable now. "I thought that was unkind."

"Not unkind, it was sense."

"But of course I welcomed them," said Fanny. "Children are always welcome, where their mother is. Always."

"At any time?" asked Rob.

"At any time." Fanny lifted her chin at him in a way he was beginning to know. "Does that sound wrong to you?"

"It sounds false," said Rob. "No one, however near and dear, is welcome at any time," and he said roughly, "Be yourself, Fanny."

"I am myself. This is me."

"It's not. It's a kind of play-acting."

"Thank you," and there was pricking silence between

them until she began to talk about San Vigilio, its famous old hotel keeper, and the chapel that was open once a year in the count's villa. Rob knew by the lightness of her voice that he had hurt her and presently he leant over, took her hand, and kissed it. The forced talk stopped at once, but with the coffee he had to go back to it. "You know, dear, no matter what our feelings are, they must go back. We must telegraph Darrell. It's only fair."

"Yes, but not tonight."

"Tonight. We can call in at Malcesine. We have to, Fanny dear."

When the *Nettuno* turned into the small walled harbour, Fanny stayed in the boat watching the waterfront lights while Rob went to send the telegram from the little café that was the town's public call office. When he came back he looked at her as if he thought she might hold this against him, even be sulking but, as he sat down next to Salvatore, the young boatman who owned and drove the *Nettuno,* she moved closer and slid her hand inside Rob's arm. The children are not to turn into an argument between us, they are not to, thought Fanny.

The lake had never been more beautiful; it was still as a pool, its mountains dark against the sky; only their snow glimmered, as the foam glimmered in the wash behind the *Nettuno.* The lights in the villages and towns had been put out, only a few were strung out along the shore, or one shone here and there like a firefly on the mountain. The *Nettuno*'s prow broke up the reflections of the stars in the water—because they are only reflections? asked Fanny and caught herself back. She would not think any more contentious thoughts tonight. Indeed, she felt blessed more than she deserved; to have Rob and this warm triumph in her heart: "They ran away. They ran away to me."

The *Nettuno* circled in a sweep to the jetty; the engine died and in the sudden lull Salvatore sent the rope flying; it fell neatly round the post and they came alongside. They were back at the sleeping villa.

III

I T W A S N O T Rob's villa, nor was the *Nettuno* his. "Great Jehoshophat, I'm not as rich as that," he would have said, though for Hugh and Caddie he remained immensely rich forever. The villa belonged to Madame Menghini, Renato Menghini's aunt.

The Menghini were, it appeared, an even bigger clan than Celestina's, whose relations peopled the village, let the camping sites, ran the kitchen of the Hotel Lydia, owned the trattoria and many of the farms up the mountain. Celestina's cousins and uncles and aunts were in almost every shop in Malcesine, "Every shop with which we deal," said Rob, but, *"We* are a cadet branch of the famous Menghini," Madame Menghini liked to say. "They have a palace in Riva."

Renato Menghini had been the producer of the last three pictures Rob had done. "Think of it, he came to Whitcross," said Fanny. One of Renato's uncles and his grandmother had helped to finance *Haysel to Harvest* and in this crisis Rob, between pictures, had asked Renato if he could find a house somewhere in Italy where he and Fanny could go. "We are better out of England for the next three months." Renato had immediately delved among his relations and come up with this aunt. "She is French-English," he said, which, now she was a widow, was why she liked to be called Madame Menghini, not Signora Menghini.

"But . . . turn her out of her house?" Fanny had said.

"She has three," said Renato gently. "One on Garda, one in Genoa, one in Milan." He had driven out from Milan to see that everything was in order and to greet Rob and Fanny. His bright brown eyes slid away from Fanny and looked at her again, in a way he could not help but which embarrassed them both. "She often lets one or other of her houses," he explained.

The Villa Fiorita was her holiday home. All the villas on these north Italian lakes, Garda, Como, Maggiore, Iseo, had been built for holidays; for mountain air, sailing, sun-bathing, relaxation, peace. Renato told Fanny that Garda, because of its winds, was never as sizzlingly hot as most of Italy can be; every morning brought the *tramontana,* "the wind from the mountains" that the people called simply, the *vento;* in the afternoon it changed to the *ora,* which blew from the south but in early spring could be so fierce that it was deadly to the orange and lemon blossoms. Because the lake was so far north, Garda was not as popular—"Thank God," said Renato—as the more flowery and accessible Como and Maggiore, though tourists came to it all summer long, driving down to Riva over the Brenner pass, coming in from Milan, Verona, Mantua, Venice. It had its riviera too, stretching from Gardone to Salo on the western side, and famous Sirmione's narrow peninsula under the ruins of Catullus's villa. Here were the big hotels, the Excelsiors, Grands, Imperials, and

Splendides with their Edwardian-sized rooms, marble pillars, and marble floors.

At the north end of the lake the villas and gardens were smaller, hotels more modest with more modest names: Hotel Alpina, Primula, Claudia, Lydia. Here were camping sites in the olive groves—campers were far more profitable than olives—with little pebbled beaches and wooden jetties; there were canteen bars, communal washrooms, trattorias. In the villages the stands of oranges and lemons were smaller, most were sold from the road wall, by children. The steamers, so busy down the southern end, and the *aliscafo,* that lifted out of the water on two red wings, did not call anywhere on the eastern shore after Malcesine, but went straight to Riva at the head of the lake or across to Limone. In the harbours there were only fishing boats and none of the fishermen wore yachting caps as they did in the tourist towns; none of them had clubbed together to buy a *Nettuno.* There were no gift shops until the road reached Torbole.

The villa was on this quieter shore, two kilometres above Malcesine. Madame Menghini, Renato told them, had bought the land and built the house long ago when land on Garda was cheap. Now a small camping site in a lakeside olive grove sold at four thousand pounds. Then, the roads were not built, the *occidentale* and *orientale* roads that bordered the west and east sides of the lake, cutting less lucky villa gardens in two, running behind the little fishing towns and tunnelling under the mountains where these came down sheer to the shore. "We have no railways here," said Renato. "Once the only way between

most towns and villages was by boat. The people were prim-
itive then, as they still are back in the hills. They lived off
their fish, fruit and vines and olives; now they live off the
tourists. They are cannibal," said Renato, his brown eyes
twinkling.

"We are not tourists, we are staying," said Fanny.

"All the English like to say that," said Renato.

Malcesine was one of the smaller towns, almost a fishing village, topped by an old red stone castle that went
back to the thirteenth century. The castle was deserted
now, Malcesine had grown but it had kept its small harbour and its steep cobbled streets. They were so narrow
that the house roofs almost met overhead, with hardly
room to hang a line of washing across, or a string of peppers, or put out a birdcage. Firewood and the wicker
damigiana of wine, loads of vegetables and groceries, had
to be taken up or down on wooden-runnered sleighs,
drawn by mules.

All the streets ran down to the lake; its blue could be
seen at every turn and they teemed with life. Besides the
grocers and wine shops, the bread shops, confectioners,
and the green grocers that this time of year sold pots of
azaleas and arum lilies with their potatoes and salads,
there were gift shops hung with scarves and ties from the
silk mills at Como; they had copper from Toscana, Venetian glass, Austrian embroideries, model galleons carved
from horn, and everywhere, in every shop, postcards. Every
ferry boat brought crowds; the café tables under the oleanders were always crowded. Every half-hour a speedboat
backed out of the little harbour where the fishing boats
knocked against the old stone walls, and took a load of

tourists out onto the lake. Though they paid several million lire for their boats Salvatore and his friends made a
golden harvest.

To the tourists, the great blue lake probably seemed a
place to be looked at rather than lived in; the villa, if
they passed it on the lake, seemed a façade with its yellow
walls, painted eaves, and tumbling roses. If, in the evenings, they strolled as far as the gates, all they could see
were the old olives in their grove, a glimpse of flowers beyond, cypresses, the painted garage, and the hedges of for-
bidding prickly whitethorn. "If they were not there," said
Renato, "you would have Germans picnicking in the garden, or on the front steps." The open back road only led
to the boathouse. "Villa Fiorita," they would read, in the
gilt letters. Fiorita would have been a usual name on
Como or Maggiore, where azalea and camellia bushes
grew as large as trees, where every flower was lush; here,
in the Garda winds, it was a struggle to grow flowers at all
but Madame Menghini, with her English strain, had been a
gardener; she had sent down as far as Naples for rare
bushes and flowering trees, to England and to Paris. In
the old days when she could keep the villa up and had two
gardeners, not Giacomino asleep under the olives or sun-
ning himself on a wall, with only an occasional hand from
Mario, who was boatman, handyman, chauffeur, fisher,
the garden had been famous up and down the lake. Now
creepers and blossom trees were unpruned, roses had
grown into tangles, bushes been choked and Celestina's
chickens had scratched up the beds. "But it is still Fiorita,"
said Fanny. "Flowering peace and stillness."

It was strange that it should have felt so still because the first few days were cold and stormy. Fanny had always thought of Italy as sun-drenched, warm, hot, lazy, but now rain and wind hurled themselves across the lake, the vento blowing all day long. "Two metres of snow on the Brenner," said Rob, "and it's nearly Easter!" The villa on its point caught the full force of the wind which shrieked down the chimney; every room was filled with the clattering of the shutters as they shook and rattled. Though there were double doors and windows—"Now we know why," said Rob—draughts whistled across the floor, lifting the rugs and turning feet to ice. Outside in the garden, the flowers were dashed headlong, and lay in soaked masses; the olives threshed themselves to a sea of silver green, made more silver by the rain; rain dripped from the hedges, and the cypresses bent and twisted into such loops that Fanny thought they must snap. The mountains were hidden in cloud, and the lake as far as they could see it was white with breakers. Yet under the waves, the water still kept its blue, as mysteriously intrinsic as if the lake were a jewel that held its own colour. How, when the sky was grey? "That is Garda fame," Celestina told Fanny. Celestina had once spent a year in England. "When me young," said Celestina, "*come* Giulietta. Very good England. *Molto bella l'Inghilterra.* Oxforrd Street. Peecadilly." She spoke a little English but often German words crept in and she did not know which was which. Celestina was, she said, shamed by the weather. "*Aprile, Maggio,* bestest munths. *Schön. Schön,*" she said regretfully but, to Fanny, the tempest outside only shut the villa further into peace.

Rob, Celestina, and Giulietta were united in worrying

in case she was uncomfortable, cold, depressed. Here Fanny was first and for years she had always been last; the last to be served—"Because I did the serving"—the last to go to bed, unless Darrell were at home, but first to get up in the morning, she thought wryly. She was last on every list and automatically the one to give up everything, to stay behind, to go without. "Well, mothers are like that," she would have said. "Some mothers," said Rob.

Now Rob made her stay in bed for breakfast and Celestina panted up the stairs with relays of coffee, while Giulietta, strong and nimble as a goat, carried up the breakfast table so that Rob could eat with Fanny. In the sitting room Giulietta built a big fire of olive wood that gave out its warm incense: Rob and Fanny sat by it, reading, talking—or dreaming, thought Fanny, and idling. "I'm not going to do any work for three months," Rob had said. They had drinks before lunch which always began with one of Celestina's pastas, gnocchi, cannelloni, ravioli, or with shrimps, fresh caught in the Adriatic or the new season's asparagus. Afterwards Fanny rested, Rob wrote letters and then in raincoats, scarves, thick shoes, they would walk down to Malcesine to buy stamps and get English papers, or up the mountain into the storm, past dripping terraces of olives and vines and steep peach orchards where the pink blossoms shone in the rain. The farms seemed to be of goats and bantams. "I haven't seen a sheep or a pig, scarcely any cows," said Fanny. Perhaps the cows were not let out yet to graze in the meagre pastures. Fanny and Rob came in soaked, battered, but glowing, and Fanny made tea; there was no kettle in the villa but she went into the kitchen and used a strange little electric pan of Celestina's that held only a cupful of hot water at a time. Rob, she discovered, was fussy about tea. It had to be China, his special brand of Lapsang Souchong; she began to appreciate its fine and smoky taste.

At teatime the post came and this was a dangerous moment; there was scarcely ever a letter for her but Rob read his aloud. "You must begin to understand," he said. Now too they read the papers, "From a far-off world," said Fanny. Then Fanny went up for a bath; the hot water trickled so that she had to allow half an hour for it to run in but she would fill the tub, add the pine and balsam essence Rob had bought for her, and lie soaking. She would dress leisurely and come down to find the fire heaped up, drinks ready on a trolley and she and Rob would talk again until Giulietta, who was as sudden as Celestina, would burst open the glass doors and call, *"A tavola,"* and they would dine at the round table, with its bowl of stocks, "And eat far too much," said Fanny.

The villa had no radio, television, or telephone. "You will have absolute quiet and peace," Renato had said, and after dinner Rob read aloud. He had bought a case of new novels and biographies but now he read Fanny a fifteenth-century manuscript he was bewitched with, a story of Saladin that he hoped one day to make into a picture. "I see it as a film opera," he said—Margot had told Fanny he always wrote his own scripts. "I have been trying to get backing, and so has Renato, for three years."

It had always been Fanny who had read aloud, endlessly she thought; now she sat idle, gazing into the olive fire, listening to his voice against the storm.

The dark came early and they went early to bed, leaving

the fire burning. Its warm smell would drift up the stairs, seeming to warm the bedroom if they left the brocade door open. In the night the wind and rain, battering and shaking outside, only lulled the house further into sleep.

The Villa Fiorita had opened a new world to Fanny with its chosen antique furniture, the tapestries and brocades hung on the walls. "I didn't know everyday houses had them," Fanny said as Caddie might have done. There were endless bibelots; glass bowls, goblets, and tear bottles; snuff boxes, family portraits, two especially that Fanny loved, a man and woman, Huguenot in their primness, with dark clothes and ruffs. There was the pair of angels that were to impress Caddie. Fanny's bedroom with the gilt and brocade bed, the pink and cream furniture, was for someone feminine, loved, thought Fanny, and precious. She had never thought of herself as precious before. It was as if the frontiers of her old world had been opened, giving a bigger view of a wider world, at the same time more cultivated and more careless. "But . . . isn't there an inventory?" she had asked bewildered. All this valuable china and glass, pictures, silver left to strangers.

"My aunt either leaves everything or puts everything away," Renato had explained. There was a compliment in that but he did not add that, in any case, the inventory was there, in Celestina's head. Every article in the villa was listed there and who would dare to dispute with Celestina? Not even the German generals who had occupied the villa in the war, not even the Egyptian prince whose servants had been light-fingered. "Twenty thousand lire compensation they had to pay," said Celestina.

Madame Menghini's bookshelves made Fanny feel a

school girl, books in French, German, Italian, English. Many of them were written in by the authors, some of them were dedicated to Madame as well. There was a rich abundance of books as there was of flowers: pot plants of begonias, crimson, salmon, lemon yellow, white; begonias by the dozen, azaleas, hydrangeas. There was a new vista, too, in Celestina's cooking, the meals arranged with grace, and simplicity, thought Fanny and she thought of all the years she had spent in endless, and what seemed here needless, cooking; porridge, bacon and eggs for breakfast— though, as she soon learned, no meal is more envied in Italy than English breakfasts—but all those puddings, thought Fanny, daily potatoes, cakes and scones for tea and all the other tea: early morning tea; kitchen elevenses, tea for workmen come into the house, tea, tea, tea; no wonder at Stebbings there was never any time; but, though the villa was a revelation, Fanny was still Fanny and a subtle change began to come over it; the chairs no longer stood stiffly round the centre table; two were by the fire, a rug moved between them, a table of books pulled out beside them. Fanny would pick up the cushions and throw them back in the chairs after Giulietta had set them in careful triangles. Papers and books were left undisturbed and the flowers were grouped, not set in rows. The small gauze curtains that had been stretched across every window, shutting out the view, had come down, and the crocheted mats that Celestina felt should be under every vase, ash- tray, and ornament, disappeared. It was as if Fanny had shaken the villa into comfortable living, and Rob looked round and said, "I don't know what you have done, but it's different—as I am."

That was true. How could such a difference come in so short a time? But it had. Rob looked as if he had been . . . crowned, thought Fanny.

"Well, this is the first time I have ever had a woman of my own," said Rob.

"Someone on every picture," Margot had said. Fanny could disregard, now, the pang that that had given her. She knew it was not true. "Most film people are very much family men," Rob had said. "I was the exception."

"You had Lucia," Fanny said, remembering that far-off girl wife, whom Rob had only talked about once, and briefly.

"Lucia was a child. She made me feel guilty." The moodiness came back, the look that had made Philippa say Rob looked melancholy and Margot declare he was unhappy, a hollow look. Then his face cleared. "I ought to feel guilty about you but I don't. I can't." The hollowness had gone; he looked fulfilled; his eyes had a spark, not only of amusement but of a happiness that spilled over. And I have done that, thought Fanny.

They had been ten days in the villa when they woke to a new silence. For a moment they did not know what it meant; the wind had dropped; there was no blustering round the house; the shutters were not rattling and from the garden came only the sound of waves lazily lapping. Fanny jumped up to open the windows; the lake was a deep iridescent blue, the mountains so clear that every town and village showed; their blue and pumice heights were lit with sun, their caps of snow shone. Now, so early in the morning, the sky arched pale; presently it, too, would be that postcard Italian blue and soon the sun was streaming across the lake. It was now, when they could have been outside all day, that Rob started to work.

It began with a telegram from Renato: "Telephone me, Milan 22306." "I can guess what that is," said Rob.

"A picture?" asked Fanny.

"Yes, but I can't do anything about it."

"But Rob, if it's *Saladin*, you must."

"It won't be *Saladin,* and this time belongs to us. I deserve a rest," said Rob. "Eleven months on *Haysel to Harvest,* seven in Africa and Rome with *Diamond Pipe,* and more to come on that. It's slavery. I am spending this time with you, and *only* you."

"But you can't if it's something interesting."

"Indeed I can."

"You said that in your life you have to take what comes when it comes," said Fanny. "You said one can't dictate to work. We are going in to Malcesine to ring up Renato."

The café public telephone was behind the harbour in a narrow busy street, where the traffic made it difficult to hear. The woman behind the bar dealt with the numbers; she put Rob through, while he waited by one of the booths, patiently, but tapping his foot and talking to the café children while Fanny sat at one of the tables. She avoided all children: indeed she had asked Rob to tell Celestina that the trattoria children were not to play in the garden. *"Proibire ai bambini di venire qui!"* said Celestina. The Signora, so kind and gentle, not to like children! Not to want Beppino and Gianna!

But now in the café she could not help watching these

two. The eldest was a boy of Hugh's age, proudly playing with his tiny sister. Fanny watched his rough head bent over the little dark one as he teased in a voice that squeaked suddenly on a high note and went down; a breaking voice always made them seem more vulnerable, thought Fanny, and hastily turned away. Even the little girl had shades: Philippa at that age had none of the melting sweetness of this little Italian, but had been direct, fierce, with a fall of golden hair, clearly marked eyebrows and an imperious mouth. She still had them. My beautiful Flip, thought Fanny. Hugh . . . The thought of him followed though she tried to shut it out. Often to her, Hugh was still at the fledgling stage that little boys go through when they have big downy heads, skins more delicate than a girl's, long lashes; but Hugh was as old as this boy now, at the thorny, unmanageable stage. She could imagine how difficult he was being and Fanny hastily turned to think of Caddie. Caddie was always her right age more or less, more or less because she was in the nebulous incognito of ten to thirteen when a girl might be any age—or anyone, thought Fanny—and Caddie was surely more nebulous than most because she was so hopelessly shy, as I was, thought Fanny. Yet Caddie was braver than her mother; she had not been at all shy over Topaz, for instance. She was to have ridden him in Risborough Show, thought Fanny. The letters from Dartmoor had been all about that, nothing of Caddie, only of Topaz. His first show . . . Here Fanny had to tell herself to sit up straight, drink her coffee. How absurd, with all the major things she had left undone, to feel such a pang over Caddie's pony. It was better, much better not to think of the children, not to look at the café children. She got up sharply and went into the booth with Rob.

She listened to the short sharp sentences. "No, I can't. I told you. Nothing at all for three months. Damn it all, we agreed, Renato." She could hear the loud Italian voice crackling and talking on the other end, it sounded both urgent and excited.

"It is *Saladin,*" said Rob to Fanny.

"*Saladin!* Oh Rob!"

"Yes, I *know,*" said Rob into the receiver. "Yes I did. I have always wanted to. I went over it all with Herz last year, as you know. Does it have to be *now?* Then it's 'no.' "

"I am going to spend this time with you," he said again to Fanny.

"You have wanted to do this for years, and I won't run away." Fanny was calm and decided. In spite of everything Rob was saying, she could feel his excitement and she took the receiver from him. "Signor Menghini."

"Yes. Is that . . ." He doesn't know what to call me, thought Fanny, nor did she know what to call herself. "Yes. This is Fanny," she said. "Signor Menghini, Rob *is* to do this picture."

"You say so?" There was approval as well as amusement in his voice.

"Yes," said Fanny.

"They want a breakdown by June," said Rob. "That's almost impossible."

"You can do it," said Fanny and down the telephone to Renato, "He is standing beside me waiting to talk reasonably to you," and she gave the receiver back to Rob.

The call went on. "No, I'm not coming to *them*. No, of course they can't come here. They can wait. It will take a month at least, to get an outline. No I won't. Not even to Milan."

"And he went to Milan and stayed three days," said Fanny.

Rob took the small south bedroom as his study; shut away behind the *loggia* that led from Fanny's room, it made a cell, sunny and quiet. "Don't you want a view?" asked Fanny. "No, I want four walls," said Rob. "A desk?" Fanny had looked round Madame Menghini's furniture. In the drawing room there was a desk of walnut inlaid with painted wood and gilt. It did not look a desk for work, but, "There isn't another," said Fanny.

"I don't want a desk, I want a table," Rob had said, and had taken the kitchen table that was to shock the children. It shocked Fanny too. "Because it looks incongruous?" asked Rob.

It was not that. To take the kitchen table was, for Fanny, to upset the whole order of a home. "Quite hopelessly domestic," Margot used often to say of Fanny. "I like being domestic," Fanny had countered unperturbed and now, "What will Celestina do?" she asked wide-eyed.

"Buy another table," said Rob. It was part of the new carelessness; order, as Fanny knew it, had vanished. "Don't call me for lunch," said Rob.

"But you must eat."

"I will have something when I have finished."

"You could go on after lunch."

"I couldn't," said Rob. "To start once is bad enough. To start twice would be murder."

"But don't you *want* to work?"

"Of course," said Rob. "Why not?"

"You must have something to eat, all those hours."

"Giulietta can bring me a *panino*"—a *panino* was an Italian sandwich, a cut roll with ham or salami clapped inside it. "Giulietta, not you," said Rob.

"That's not very flattering."

"It is. I don't notice Giulietta. Fanny, if you love me, leave me alone."

It was the first time that Fanny had come to be closely bound with work that was first, before anything; before eating or drinking, before sleeping. She had thought Darrell, in the Army, and as a Messenger, had worked hard; but he had hours, defined times, time when he left off, was free—though of course he had sometimes to fill in for other people, leave unexpectedly. Often Rob would work the whole day through shut in the study, though sometimes he was restless and needed to rove; he would spend an hour standing on the point, looking into the ripples, or sending pebbles skimming across the lake; he would pace in the garden. Fanny learned not to speak to him or notice him. She kept herself apart.

"But what about you?" Rob had asked when he started on the breakdown, "What will you do alone for hours?"

"What you told me to do," said Fanny, "nothing."

She had all this time flagged behind Rob; she could not get over her tiredness. "Well, I have been packing ever since Christmas," she might have said. First the children to school, packing them for the last time; I knew that though they didn't. Then Stebbings, when only Gwyneth understood the reason. "Giving up Stebbings? For a flat in *Lon-*

don! Fanny, you are mad," Margot and Anthea had cried. They knew now what lay behind Fanny's quiet, "It will be easier for Darrell." Then up in Scotland packing up Aunt Isabel's cottage, the small bleak grey stone house with its dark yews. It was strange that it should all have come together, thought Fanny: Aunt Isabel's where I had lived as a child, that was my home up to my marriage; Stebbings, and the children. I was packing my whole life away. No wonder I am tired.

Rob had been shocked by her thinness. "I was shocked at yours," said Fanny.

"I have always been thin. You should be plump, and I haven't dark hollows under my eyes."

Every morning before he went up to work, Rob would carry out a long chair and cushions onto the terrace and Fanny would spend the morning there, lying in the sun, growing together again, thought Fanny, as one can grow no matter how one has been torn.

After Renato had left them in the garden that first evening, Fanny had gone across the grass and wonderingly touched one of the old olive trees. Its roots had lifted lumps of earth in the grass; it was split halfway up its length, twisted out of shape, the trunk showing dry and pale where it was holed, but it still bore its crown of leaves, the olive leaves that blow now green, now silver in the wind and that she would come to love. The old damaged tree would have a crop of olives, year after year, silently fruiting, and—I have been making a clamour, thought Fanny suddenly.

The only sounds that came here were from the road or lake and none of them were anything to do with Fanny:

oars were dipped as Mario took his boat out, wet clothes were slapped on wooden washboards from the villa's own beach or from the hotel foreshore as Giulietta or the village women or the hotel's two maids did the washing. "We don't have many laundries in Italy," Renato had told her. There was a spluttering, now and then, from an outboard motor, the grander rush of a speedboat and, every hour or so, the distant churning of the steamers on their way from Riva to Limone, Limone to Malcesine. Sometimes greetings were called across the water; Celestina's voice rang out as she shouted to Giacomino or to Giulietta, or the postwoman or the butcher in his white apron with his napkin-covered basket, or to the old milkwoman who wore the black and brown striped skirt, black shawl, and kerchief of the peasant women and brought the milk in old wine bottles, "Open to all the dust," said Fanny. "Not very hygienic," said Rob, "but Madame Menghini has been drinking it for thirty years and is still alive and well."

At Stebbings everything had concerned Fanny; here she could not even understand what was said and she was concerned in none of it. She had not ordered the meat, or the milk. Celestina did the housekeeping.

Traffic on the road made a continual hum. Rob complained that there were too many cars but to Fanny it was only a distant drone; the olive grove lay between and even the maddening scooter explosions sank to a faint whine. With the advent of the little cars there were, Rob said, far fewer scooters. The bus horn made its two notes every four hours, but Fanny need never catch that bus.

Morning, midday, evening, if the wind were not too fierce, she heard the bells. Each village had its fine church with a turret roofed with brown tiles, a wide piazza, an interior of paintings and marbles. The churches seemed too big and grandiose for villages, but, "See them on Sundays," said Rob. Sometimes the bells were only that faint quivering in the air; sometimes she heard only the one from Malcesine but they seemed to measure off the hours into peace and stillness.

When they sounded at midday, Celestina would send Giulietta out to lay Fanny's lunch outside on the stone table. The pink stone bench was sunbaked by twelve o'clock. Often Celestina would bring the coffee herself and stay to talk in her broken English, German, in the midst of much Italian and dramatic mime. Fanny could have learned a great deal about Celestina's family, about Celestina's life in the war, Celestina's marriage, but as she listened with one ear she let it slide out of the other. Celestina was not Fanny's business.

After lunch she would sleep, often on the grass under the cypresses that made another private little garden above the villa's beach. She would listen to the lapping of the waves until she fell asleep.

"You look as if you hadn't slept for months," Rob told Fanny.

"I didn't."

"You can sleep now."

She could not have enough of sleep; there had been so many nights spent penned in Stebbings, or pacing the floor of her narrow old room at Aunt Isabel's, or unable to sleep because of the stuffiness of the London hotels, and Fanny slept as if she were drugged.

When she woke, often she would go out in the car. It was

a new delight to drive Rob's Mercedes after years of the old Rover. At first Rob had been anxious. "Will you remember to keep on the right? And Italians drive fast," but Fanny had laughed. "I have been a chauffeur more than half my life."

"Far too much of a chauffeur," said Rob. It was a new experience for Fanny not to be allowed to drive when she was tired.

In those afternoons she drove up the lake to Riva, the little town with its mountain-locked harbours where weeping willows swept their fronds into the water, and roses even climbed up the lamp posts. It had good shops in the streets around the big cream church. Fanny would go to the cleaners, the *tintoria* where a row of young girls stood at their ironing boards, ready to press clothes while the customer waited, and the doors were kept open because of the fumes of the dry-cleaning machine, so that the chatter of voices came out into the street. She would drive down to Malcesine to buy newspapers or go into the post office for Rob, then sit outside one of the cafés on the quay side, drinking coffee or eating an orange ice and watching the steamers come in, the slow and the *aliscafo* with its two-note horn. The motorboatmen, headed by Salvatore, grew to know her as they already knew Rob; she talked to his favourite waitress, Rita, little and swarthy in her black, with a tiny immaculate apron that hid the cloth pouch of change money. Fanny knew the hotel porters, who were always outside their hotels, bowing invitingly to every car; she knew the car-park man, whom Rob called the Bandit, as she knew the police, the *carabanieri*, in their dark blue coats and trousers with a red stripe, their cocked hats, swords, and snow-white gloves. Now and again she would come on a procession of toddlers, little boys, pale-faced, in blue pinafores and peaked caps, from the *Colonia Infantile* to which children were brought from the slums of Milan; every day they paraded solemnly down to the harbour, walking two by two, each child holding on to the tail of the pinafore of the one in front. Fanny always walked quickly past them, as she walked past the children playing in the piazza, the babies feeding the pigeons on the steps of the church.

Sometimes she would drive farther, right down the lake, past the little harboured towns with their pink stone or stuccoed houses, their olives, cypresses, and oleanders, their stalls of oranges and lemons: Torri, Bardolino with its vineyards, Lazisc with another old red castle, Garda, so much smaller than one expected of the lake's name town, right down to Peschiera.

"Wouldn't you like to see Verona, Mantua, Cremona?" Rob would ask, but Fanny seemed held to the lake; she had a feeling she would break the magic of their contentment if she went out of sight of its blue, and no matter where she had been, she was always back in time for Rob, and it was always with a quickening of her heart that she came round the last bend of the lake road and saw the villa cypresses serried above the water, the lights on in the kitchen and in Rob's window above. She would drive in through the gates, turn behind the flowering thorns, leave the car for Mario to put away, and go silently up to her room to bathe, change, and wait in the sitting room or on the terrace until Rob came down.

This was the time she loved best, to sit, or walk with

him in the twilight, when the mountains opposite grew dark, their edges sharp as black-green paper cuts against the sky. Clouds, still bright with sunset, were reflected in the lake which slowly withdrew into stillness and turned colourless except for a faint silver. There would be an occasional light, red or green, from a passing steamer; or a fishing boat's headlamp would make a spark, small and lonely on the lake's width. There was always one star, directly opposite, as if it were hung there for the villa. "It's the evening star," said Fanny, but it seemed their star. It shone with such intensity that a spear of light was thrown across the water almost to their feet, but the star always dropped below the mountain with extraordinary swiftness. Then the familiar beaded lights began to appear along the shore, and in clusters on the mountain. Car headlights made white flares in and out of the tunnels on the *occidentale*, the lake road opposite, or came on unknown twisted ways down from the mountains. "Time to go in," Rob would say. "I'm starving—and burning for a drink."

It was a pattern of sun, quiet, work, and slowly Fanny began to unwind, as if the tight thread that had held her—cutting my heart in two, thought Fanny—was loosening. One day I might even be whole again, almost, thought Fanny.

When she lay in the garden in the sun and shut her eyes, the light shone through her lids and it was scarlet. Was that symbolical? "But it was *not* like that," she could have cried. She had only to open her eyes and the light was clear, gold, warm, "And that is reality. I can't go on being haunted forever," said Fanny.

"Men don't like tears." She could imagine Madame Mcnghini saying that. Women, in Edwardian days, may have been hypocrites but they kept their faces and they had backbone; "And so must you," Fanny told herself sternly. "Now you can do this: untangle the thread of all this, follow it through for the last time. Then wind it all up in a ball that you can keep hidden in your hand or in your heart, and not talk of it any more. You can tell it all out," said Fanny, "from the beginning."

IV

I T   H A D   B E E N the last Sunday in May—nearly a year
ago, thought Fanny, only a year, for all this!—she had
dropped in at the Davenants' house in Whitcross to take
back a book; Margot had most of the new books and was
generous in lending them. "Anthea's here," Margot had
said. "She has brought some of the film people. They have
a scene about a poacher and they wanted Sydney's advice."
Sydney, Margot's husband, was a Justice of the Peace.
"They are in the garden now. Come out and you shall
meet Rob Quillet."

She spoke as if she were conferring a royal favour but,
from the French doors that led out from the drawing
room, Fanny looked at the thin dark man talking to Sydney, and, "Is that Rob Quillet?" she asked. "I have met
him."

"Met him? Where?" and, "Where could *you* meet him?"
asked Anthea. The surprise was as unflattering as was the
emphasis on the "you" but Fanny was used to Margot and
Anthea, and, "I met him in Derrick's shop," she said. "You
remember Geoff Derrick had his tonsils out."

"What in the world have Geoff Derrick's tonsils to do

with Rob Quillet?" "Everything," Fanny could have said now.

It was one of those chance winds—or not "chance," thought Fanny. Geoff did the deliveries for Derrick's shop all over Whitcross, and, "While he was in hospital, we had to fetch our groceries ourselves," said Fanny. Hers had made two large boxes on the counter. "Can you manage?" asked Mrs. Derrick and a stranger looking at the stands of flower seeds had turned and said, "Those are too heavy for you. Let me carry them."

"That was the first time I heard your voice," Fanny told Rob.

"Those are too heavy for you." She had given Rob a fleeting smile, said, "That's very kind of you," and led the way to the Rover. "I can remember your hand, stroking Danny," Danny's gold and white head where the dark-tipped ears fell over; it was a thin hand, olive brown, with long fingers. "Your hand and your eyes," she could have said. Before she drove off she had looked up and met the stranger's eyes, brown, oddly thoughtful and gentle in a face that was—sardonic? asked Fanny, but that was not quite right; it was not bitter or scornful, only aloof. "But it still did not occur to me he was Rob Quillet," she told Margot.

"With the whole village buzzing about the film for weeks? Didn't you look at his clothes?"

"No," said Fanny. "What about them?"

"My dear innocent. Don't you know a suit like that and handmade shoes when you see them?"

"For a guess I was wearing a sweat shirt, jeans, and

espadrilles," said Rob, when she told him this but, "No," said Fanny to Margot. "I just thought he was nice."

"Nice! He's Rob Quillet, probably our best director. They say he will be a de Sica or a Renoir," but, when Fanny repeated that with pride to Rob, it made him angry. "I'm a beginner, not halfway there, nor ever will be. Renoir! He has a humanity none of us will reach and he's never afraid."

"Are you afraid?"

"Yes. Blast me!"

"Ask anyone," Margot had said but Fanny did not ask anyone. She kept her usual reticence. "You weren't interested," Rob teased her.

"I wasn't then. I hadn't really seen you."

"I saw you," said Rob, "and I went straight back into the shop and asked who you were."

Most lovers, thought Fanny, ask each other, Where? When? Why? I shall never know why, nor could she exactly say when she had first known the stirrings of this strange, unreasonable, satisfying, never satisfied love. I suppose one day I shall settle down with it, it may even become humdrum, thought Fanny, but she knew that it never could. It was too piercing. No, she did not know why, or when, but she could, a little, trace out where; Margot gave a dinner, thought Fanny.

"Odd of Margot to ask you when Darrell is away," Lady Candida had said.

"She needs an extra woman."

"And there are no single women living in this village of single women, I suppose?" but Fanny knew why Margot had asked her. She could be trusted not to get in the way.

Margot had got Rob. She talked of "getting" people as if she were catching butterflies and, "I have got Rob Quillet," she told Fanny on the telephone. "But you were unkind," Fanny told Rob. "Margot thought you were really interested. She knew enough to know it wasn't likely you would dine out when you were in the middle of a picture."

"I came because she said you would be there," said Rob. "I wanted to look at you again."

"And you did look at me, all through dinner."

Fanny had always been ashamed of how far behind she was with books and plays and fashions, "and facts," Darrell sometimes said, though kindly. "You dream too much." At that dinner, Margot had talked of the new Swedish film *Skärgård, The Archipelago.*

"I haven't seen it," Fanny had to say.

"But Fanny, *everybody's* seen it!"

"Who is everybody?" asked Rob, but Margot did not hear.

"It's the religious conflict *after* the abortion that makes it so topical," she was saying earnestly. "That superb shot of the girl *racked* with pain on the edge of that pretty little bed that had been hers as a child." Fanny knew enough now to burn for Margot; after all, we were brought up, at least Aunt Isabel brought me up, not to talk to a doctor about illnesses, to a judge about his trials, but Margot had not been worrying Rob, he had simply not been listening; he seemed curiously abstracted and fidgety, twisting his wine glass, shamefully maltreating Sydney's splendid Chambolle Musigny. Sydney must have been thinking that film people were vandals, and that Margot's party was not being the success she had hoped, and Fanny had wondered what was the matter with this dark stranger. "Dark stranger" sounded like fortune reading in a teacup, but it was as she thought of him. Why was he abstracted? His hand had left the wine glass and was playing with the roses in the crystal bowl lit with a green light, when, suddenly interrupting Sydney, he had leaned forward across the table that Margot had arranged so carefully—crystal candlesticks with black shades, black porcelain salt cellars and pepper pots, black plates, the lit roses—and he asked, "Is there a rose called Fanny Clavering? If there isn't, there ought to be."

"That was all over the village by the morning," Fanny told him. "Sarah Ogilvie was in the room. We could never have a party without Sarah Ogilvie to help us. She went to each of us in turn and it was in turn," said Fanny, "a kind of tit for tat; 'I asked you. It's your turn to ask me'; dinner for dinner, drinks for drinks."

"For heaven's sake!" said Rob.

It had been all over the village. The voices could not reach Fanny in the villa; though she had shut her ears and her mind to them for a long time, all this last year they had always been there; not, to begin with, anyone outside, not even Anthea or Margot—because they did not really know, thought Fanny, until I left Stebbings for good—but there were important voices, intimate, that had ruled her life; Darrell, Aunt Isabel, Lady Candida, and suddenly she thought, I shall never have to listen to Lady Candida again.

There was one voice Fanny could not shut out, her own. "I know now," said Fanny, "that people do have a voice of conscience." It had spoken clearly, steadily, all this time; she had not been able to stifle it, only refuse to listen as she had not listened to it that morning after the dinner, when Rob had telephoned.

"Rob Quillet here." His voice had sounded curt, almost clipped. "Will you have dinner with me?"

"I?" Such complete surprise had showed in Fanny's voice that, Rob told her afterwards, he had not been able to help smiling. A pause, then; "I think perhaps you are confusing me with Margot Davenant," said Fanny gently.

"I most certainly am not. Will you come?"

There had been a longer pause before Fanny answered him. Clearly and insistently that voice was saying, "No. Don't go," and, "There will be trouble," but instead of listening she had scolded herself: "You are being ridiculous. Are you turning into one of those middle-aged women who imagine that any man . . . It's simply that he is bored in Whitcross," she told herself, though that did not seem likely in the middle of *Haysel to Harvest,* and the voice still said, "Don't go." Fanny went.

It had been another Sunday and, as Rob waited for her in the hall—she had run up for a handkerchief—idly he had looked at three letters ready for the post on the table. "H. D. Clavering, The School House, Strode, Wiltshire." "Miss Philippa Clavering, St. Anne's School, Bentry, Kent." "Miss Candida Clavering, St. Anne's School . . ."

"My children," Fanny had explained.

"Do you write to them every Sunday as if you were at school too?" Rob had asked.

She had not thought of it that way, as if she too were bound by a set of rules, yet I suppose I was, thought Fanny. Even then, by that first going out with him, she felt as if she were breaking one. Children bound one into a rule, thought Fanny, and, "If you hadn't sent us to boarding school, this wouldn't have happened," said Caddie.

Rob never came to Stebbings again. "It wouldn't have been fair," he said. "Though none of it was fair, of course. At least it made me feel a little less guilty when I had you on my own ground."

"But we didn't have any ground for a long, long time," said Fanny. "Not until you took me to Chirico's and we made it our own. All those out-of-the-way places where we knew we shouldn't meet anybody." Those little inns, restaurants where Rob was not known—I wasn't known in any, thought Fanny. Cheap ones sometimes: there was one in the Fulham Road with red plastic lampshades on the tables, and a little Spanish one where the waiter thought we were married. "It had the quince jelly I liked and you didn't," she reminded Rob.

"Tasting of sour soap," said Rob.

Some of the restaurants were so exalted that they were safe too. Only Rob's producers might have haunted them; Fanny might possibly have met Anthea there, certainly no one else she knew. "You must have spent a fortune in those days," she told Rob.

She could not put them into chronological order, tell the dates, the days of the week, but it went on all through May and June, into July she thought. It was too big for arithmetic, thought Fanny.

Rob was shooting *Haysel to Harvest* every day of those long dry months, though dogged by the cold winds. "Trying to work in England!" he said. "How can anyone get a halcyon hay-making scene in a June north-easter?" and, "We must finish here by mid-July," he told Fanny. "We are booked at the studio." He had, too, rushes to see every day, sometimes at Technicolour—Whitcross was handy for West Drayton—sometimes at Pinewood; now and again in Wardour Street. He had evening conferences, script changes, meetings, and all the time, behind *Haysel to Harvest*—a small picture for Rob—was looming the big one, *Diamond Pipe,* that would take him to Africa.

"Why *Diamond Pipe?*" asked Fanny.

"Diamonds come out of pipes, not mines," and Rob explained. "Over billions of years, the heat at the earth's core has made vents, like long tubes or pipes, from deep, deep down to near the surface. No one knows how or why, but some of these vents have solidified into a sort of blue clay, and in that clay, rough stones, diamonds, are found. A pipe might be half a mile in diameter and *Diamond Pipe* is about one of these huge ones."

Still he found time to meet Fanny, once, twice, three times a week, though she never knew where she must go, by car, by train. Her comings and goings in the Rover were too familiar to be remarked; Whitcross was used to her driving up to London, or to the airport, to meet Darrell. And it was my business, thought Fanny. Margot had often called Fanny an oyster—why is an oyster always derogatory? wondered Fanny—and all that time she said not a word to anyone. She even succeeded in evading Lady Candida, who thought she was giving talks to Women's Institutes. "She knew Anthea had asked me to." What Gwyneth thought Fanny did not know.

Each time she and Rob met they grew more tense, a tenseness that became unbearable, thought Fanny. If she had come by train he would be waiting for her on the platform, so many platforms, thought Fanny, and they would walk away, not touching one another, we had not touched then, and get in a taxi or Rob's car. Sometimes I came in the Rover, thought Fanny. Cars tell no tales.

"I suppose we were so furtive," she said to Rob, "because we thought it would pass."

"It was never that," said Rob, "it was just that we decided to be private."

And strangely enough we succeeded, thought Fanny, until Charmian saw us at the theatre. Charmian, of course, told everyone, but because it was Fanny no one believed there was anything in it.

"I didn't believe it myself," said Fanny. Even in those days, her trust and belief would suddenly ebb. "It can't be true. He can't mean it," but it became obvious that Rob did mean it. He was in love.

Only in Margot and Anthea a small antenna lifted. Fanny, Anthea reminded Margot, had met Rob Quillet before either of them; Margot reminded Anthea about the dinner party and they came to see Fanny. It was the day after Charmian and the theatre and Fanny had been making apple jelly. Then it must have been October, thought Fanny, puzzled. She seemed to have skipped over a hiatus of time, but, yes, the children had gone back to school, been back several weeks. Then it must have been the end of October, after Rob and I . . . Then why was I making jelly? asked Fanny. Force of habit? Or had it been an excuse not to think?

Now, across the villa terrace drifted the smell of Celestina's cooking, tomato, garlic, peppers, chicken, sizzling in oil. Apple jelly is very English, thought Fanny. Very far away. Had anyone eaten that batch, or was it sitting, labelled, "Stebbings, October," on that London larder shelf? Gwyneth would not have thrown it away, thought Fanny.

Fanny had been straining the apple juice when Anthea and Margot had walked in. Gwyneth, sweeping down the front stairs, had told them where to find Fanny. Their faces were portentous. "We want to talk to you."

"Do you mind if I go on?" Fanny had asked.

"It's something that may be . . . important," said Anthea.

"That *is* important," said Margot.

"I can listen while I sieve."

"Gwyneth might come in. Anyway she's in the hall. Can't we go up to your room?" And Fanny had known what was coming.

Margot sat in the armchair, Anthea on the dressing-table stool, Fanny on the window sill, facing them; Anthea had leaned over and pressed her hand. "You won't mind what we say?"

"How do I know until you have said it?" Fanny smiled at Anthea.

"It's not funny, Fanny," said Margot. Her eyes were harder than Anthea's. Well, Margot was piqued, thought Fanny, so piqued that she was angry. It was not that she, Margot, had been prepared to be serious with Rob, but she had undoubtedly been ready to be flattered, marked out, and, yes, perhaps ready for more. It must have been an unpleasant shock to find unintelligent ordinary Fanny preferred to herself, and it was very gently that Fanny had said, "Let me hear what it is. Say it."

"Charmian saw you at the theatre last night with Rob Quillet."

"Yes, he took me," said Fanny. She found she could keep her voice level. "We saw Charmian." Fanny seemed to see Whitcross in a new perspective now. "She must have rung you both up this morning? I knew she would."

"It's not funny," said Margot again, and, "He seems really attracted to you," said Anthea.

"It was clear at my dinner," said Margot.

"That's ages ago," and, "In another life," Fanny might have added.

"He was attracted then. You knew it, Fanny. Everybody knew it."

"How did they?" asked Fanny. "Unless you told them? You or Sydney."

Margot coloured at that but she retorted, "Sarah Ogilvie was there, and then he saw you home."

"Wasn't that courtesy?"

"Perhaps, but the next night . . ."

"The very next night," said Anthea.

"He came here again."

"Yes," said Fanny. "He took me out to dinner. I thought that kind."

"It may not have been kind," said Anthea.

"I took it that it was. He knew that I was lonely. I have been sometimes."

"Oh, Fan dear, don't be such an innocent."

"What exactly," asked Fanny, "are you trying to say to me?"

"This . . ." said Anthea but Margot broke in, "You are a darling, Fanny, but not very worldly wise."

"You are afraid I might lose my head because a man takes me out to dinner and the theatre?"

Are we all such hypocrites when people give us advice? thought Fanny now. "She deceived us," Margot and Anthea must be saying now. "I didn't deceive you," Fanny answered silently. "People need only be told as much of the truth as they are entitled to know. You were not entitled to know about Rob and me."

She let them talk and said nothing more.

Anthea, sensitive compared to Margot, had been disturbed by Fanny's silence. "Forgive us, Fanny dear."

"We are old friends," said Margot.

"And we don't want you to get hurt."

Fanny almost betrayed herself then; it was this new vanity, she thought, but this was after Rob and I . . . Under her blouse she had been wearing Rob's ring. It had become for her a jewel in the deepest sense, a talisman, the red of the sanctuary lamp that had shone in the frightening gloom of the church, the deep red of heart's blood as Rob had said—and he had bought it on that afternoon, gone straight out to buy it, never wavering as she was so piteously wavering, even at that moment. "What makes you so sure," she had asked, "that I should be the one to get hurt?" She saw Margot and Anthea exchange glances: so Fanny is vain after all.

"Shall we," she had said, getting up, "shall we have some coffee before I get on with my apple jelly?"

"But we did try to stop it," said Fanny in the villa now. From the beginning she had known that it ought to stop. "Aunt Isabel had brought me up too thoroughly for me not to know that," she could have said, "but I had told myself that it was to be nothing. Nothing but a little light amusement, something to while away the time for him, for me a peccadillo, and I had never had a peccadillo in my life." To be simply a wife and mother can blot you out, thought Fanny. I had had no fun or flattery for years and I was tempted, but Aunt Isabel and the moral books are right when they tell you, you are playing with fire, tasting goblin fruit. All those clichés are true, thought Fanny.

But she had tried. There was a day—it must have been far back in June, before these months that she had skipped —when she had gone up to London to lunch with Rob, and it was only lunch, thought Fanny, as defiantly as if she could have told that to Margot, Anthea, Charmian. Rob drove her back to Marylebone and as they turned into the station yard, had said, "The same time on Friday?"

"No, Rob."

"No?"

"I'm not coming again."

He had glanced down as he slowed the car. "Do you think that will do any good, my darling?"

"My darling." Fanny's heart had begun to beat in a strange suffocating way, and she looked quickly out of the window to hide the tears. "I must try," she had said. "I must try to stop now."

Rob had said nothing.

"I must be frightfully busy," said Fanny, speaking as slowly and deliberately as if she were dictating. "Too busy to think. I must do all the things I haven't been doing. That have been left, neglected. I don't know where I have been these last few weeks but I have been neglectful. I must do things."

"What things?" Rob's voice was nonchalant as he stopped by the curb.

"The holidays will soon be here," Fanny tried not to let the words tremble. "Philippa is going to a family in France. I should have written to the mother again. There are things to do in the house; the stairs to be painted. I must garden. None of my flowers are in for next year, wallflowers, pansies." It did not sound important and she gave it up. "All the same, I must try," and she had said desperately, "Rob, leave me alone."

"Very well." They were two such quiet little words that Fanny felt rebuffed. "I suppose I was surprised and piqued," she said now. The tears really came into her eyes and hastily she found the door handle and opened the door before he could get out and come round. "Good-bye, Rob."

"Good-bye."

"You might have made a show of minding," she told him afterwards.

"Why?"

"It would have been polite."

"You are not polite when you are in love."

"You didn't seem in the least perturbed or moved."

"I wasn't," said Rob. "I knew we couldn't stop, but I knew, too, it was better to let you try."

"I did try."

For more than a month she had lived in a vacuum, blank, somnambulant, "And nobody noticed, except Lady Candida," said Fanny.

"You look listless, Fanny. You need waking up," and I expect I did, thought Fanny, because I was sleep-walking; but Lady Candida had not the power to wake her, nor

Darrell, nor anyone, not even Hugh. Being without Rob was like being put back to sleep when you had been awake. For the first time in my life, thought Fanny, since I was a child, I was awake. What wisdom there is in the old fairy tales, she thought; "The Sleeping Beauty"—only I am not a beauty, thought Fanny and Rob did not even have to kiss me to shatter me awake; but the end of "The Sleeping Beauty" was pure fantasy; in real life even the heroine has to go back to sleep, "And in those endless few weeks," said Fanny, "I found out what that meant and how far I had gone."

"*We* had gone," Rob would have interrupted her.

"Yes, but I didn't know that about you then," Fanny could have answered. "I was sure, for you, this was a passing thing," and she went steadily on in her sleep-life. Oh yes, I could have stopped then, thought Fanny. Rob and I had barely touched one another, we were still finding out about each other, and ourselves, and I could have gone on with Darrell at Stebbings quite well, only asleep, only knowing with a vague and perpetual unhappiness what I had missed.

Then one day . . . was it in July? asked Fanny. It must have been because she was sorting the children's holiday clothes; towards the end of July, Darrell had come in and said, "The company is leaving."

"What company?" Fanny was feeling too dimmed to understand even that.

"The film company. The picture is finished, at least the parts they can shoot here, and they are giving a farewell. Anthea's lending the Big House and Margot is helping to organize it all." Anthea and Margot seemed to be the fates for us, thought Fanny. "Margot caught me up at the Club House," said Darrell. "She said she had been ringing here all afternoon. Didn't you hear the telephone?"

"Yes," said Fanny.

"Then . . . ?"

"I didn't answer it," said Fanny and Darrell stared at her.

"Are you ill?" he asked and he still looked at her. "You don't look very well."

"I'm perfectly well. Tell me about this . . . this . . . is it a party?"

"It's a *Haysel to Harvest* 'thank you' for all the locals. The village has been pretty good, helping and providing. The Red Lion will have a free night, and there will be supper—and champagne I gather—for invited people up at the Big House. All of them in the picture will be there: Gail Starling, Mark Bennet, and this Quillet man, the director. The producer chap's an Italian and he's over here. I must say it's decent of them," said Darrell. "I thought film people used you and forgot you as soon as they had finished."

"They must forget," said Fanny. "It's inevitable," but the words seemed to stick in her throat.

"Can't expect them to remember what happened on every picture," said Darrell cheerfully. "This is quite impromptu, and Margot wants you to help."

"I can't," said Fanny. "I won't," she might have said. She prayed Darrell would not probe but that was a vain wish with Darrell. "Why not? Are we doing something?" he asked at once.

"I am."

"What have you to do?"

"Something I promised." Fanny's voice was near breaking.

"You couldn't have promised anything very important."

"Important to me."

"You can put it off."

"I can't."

"It would do you good," said Darrell. "You have been in too much lately. That's why you are looking pale. Mother says you need a good tonic."

"Is a noisy party a tonic?"

"She says you are too quiet."

"I have always been quiet."

"She says . . ."

"Darrell! Will you *please* ask Lady Candida to leave me *alone*." Darrell stared at the exasperation on Fanny's face, the way she clenched her hands. "Please, Darrell."

"My dear Fanny! Very well, if you feel like that, we won't go."

"You go."

"If you won't, I should rather stay with you."

"No, go! Go! Go!" Fanny wanted to shout at the top of her voice but, "I shan't be here," she managed to say calmly. "So I think you should go. You don't get much fun out of Whitcross."

"I must say I should rather like to see Gail Starling at close quarters, and the grounds will be floodlit when it gets dark," said Darrell like a small boy. "If you are sure . . ."

"Quite sure," said Fanny. She had to fight the exasperation down again. "It had come upon me suddenly," Fanny told Rob afterwards, "that you were to be so near." The Big House gates and the park were only across the road from Stebbings. "I would hear the cars drive up, voices, laughter. Darrell said it was all to be in the garden. . . ."

She had thought, when the time came, she would do something onerous. When Darrell had gone, she would turn out the linen cupboard, tidy the attic, anything busy or heavy so that she should not hear or think, but as half past seven came, I couldn't do it, thought Fanny. I couldn't stay in so near. She had to get away. She went into the cloak-room and blindly took a coat. Gwyneth had come in— Fanny had forgotten to tell her Darrell was out for dinner —and called, "Are you going out?"

"Taking Danny for a run." Fanny slipped out through the door at the bottom of the garden, so as not to meet anyone, and up the side lane. It had begun to spot with rain. Poor floodlighting, thought Fanny. Poor Anthea and Margot with their tables in the garden, but the rain was cool as it hit her hot cheeks and aching eyes.

There was one walk where people seldom went, a path that led behind the park, up through the woods to the Cross that gave Whitcross its name. It was cut in the chalk of the hill and made a landmark for miles. Only lovers walked this way, to be alone, thought Fanny. She knew that they would be too shut away with themselves to notice anyone else. Her breath felt as if it were choking. Danny ran ahead.

The path made a green alley, closed like a maze as it came higher up the hill. I used to tell the children not to run along it in case they might collide with someone com-ing the other way, but they always ran, thought Fanny. I was walking fast, my head bent, rain on my face like tears, my hands clenched in my pockets—and she had come round the corner full tilt into Rob.

If it was not meant to happen, why did God let it? asked Fanny like a little girl. It was absurd to bring God into it, but, "We were avoiding one another," she said. Rob could not face the party either. "Not to meet you casually. I knew you were coming." "Fanny Clavering with her *husband*," Margot had said and had looked at him with her emerald gaze, and, "She could look," said Rob. "Her barb was more right than she dreamed. I knew I couldn't see you with another man, going away with him. I thought I would put in an appearance, I had to do that, it was Renato's party, and leave when you came. You didn't come —but I saw Darrell," said Rob, "Margot kindly pointed him out to me and I knew I had to go. I went through the park, like a tornado, I expect, and up on the Cross, and looked down on Stebbings, those tiles among the apple trees. I could have dropped a pebble down your chimneys. I wondered if you were there. I could hear the party and I thought I would go back to town. I started to walk down and you walked into my arms."

"It was literally into your arms," said Fanny. "Almost before I saw you, you were holding me. You were kissing me."

"It had been so long," said Rob. "I had almost taught myself not to hope, to make myself think you were right and we had succeeded in being good. I suppose it was 'good' officially. After all, I didn't *want* to break up a home where there were children. I was resigned, or very nearly. I was going to Africa and could try and forget you. *Diamond Pipe* was an interesting picture, I had always wanted to do it, then Margot pointed out your husband and I knew I was not resigned, nor ever would be."

"So we were both driven out on the hill," said Fanny. "I'm afraid I wept."

"I thought it was rain on your face," said Rob. "Until I tasted salt. When I knew they were tears, I knew too I could never let you go."

Fanny opened her eyes. She was not on Whitcross hill with the whitebeams blowing in the rain to show their underleaves, the smell of wet chalk and summer grass. She was in the garden of the villa; not chilled by the wetness— she remembered how Rob had run his hands up her arms under her coat and said, "You're cold." She was warm, sunned; not driven, tormented, but quiet and at peace. The sun, as it grew higher, was even too hot and she opened the Japanese sunshade Rob had brought her back from Milan; every time he went he came back with presents. "I hadn't anyone to buy them for before," said Rob. The oiled paper cast a cool glow over the chair cushions and on Fanny's dress, a lavender glow lit with sun. Now, when she had balanced the sunshade and lay back again and shut her eyes, the light did not swim red through her lids. I didn't feel guilty any more, thought Fanny, not after that day. I hardened. I had tried to stop it, quell it, cut it off, be good, "Officially good" Rob had called it, and it was no good being good. It seemed meant, thought Fanny and, "Why not?" she had said and told herself that other women had lovers—and Rob was not even my lover then.

"We hadn't consummated it," said Rob, "if that's what you mean, but I was your lover. I loved you, and you knew it."

"I knew it," and Fanny gave the secret satisfied smile of a woman who knows she is loved. All through that time the world had seemed to her lit, bright at the edges as if everything had a halo, as Caddie and Hugh were to see it that first evening in the villa garden. I have never been nicer to Darrell and the children, thought Fanny, valued Gwyneth more, been more patient with Lady Candida. She remembered Lady Candida's "You seem very happy, Fanny."

"Thank you. I am."

"Yet only three weeks ago I was telling Darrell you looked as if you needed a good tonic."

"Perhaps I am taking one," said Fanny. That led to "What tonic?" "Where did you get it? Not one of those iron things? You should take yeast. Brewers' yeast," and Fanny, without irritation, promised she would take yeast.

That had been perhaps their happiest time, or "Our only absolutely happy time," they could have said; afterwards she had been too well aware of the ruin, and it was fun, thought Fanny. To her that was surprising. In the puritan mind so carefully instilled in her by Aunt Isabel, fun was the last thing Fanny had thought an affair would be—in those days she still, conventionally, called this "an affair." Passionate, yes, breath-taking, but it did not seem suitable for it to be fun. That was an unexpected gift Rob brought her. It was fun to run up to town, be taken out to lunch or dinner—in places she had never thought she would see, with food such as she had never tasted; to be put into taxis, handed in and out of cars, bought flowers, taken to the theatre.

No one in Whitcross noticed what she did—except

Gwyneth. August was a doldrum time; most people were away but the Clavering young never wanted to stir from Stebbings, except Philippa and she was in France. Next summer we should have had Marie José Lefèvre in exchange, thought Fanny; poor Marie José, she would never come now. Hugh had been building a telescope and spent half his time going into High Wycombe or up to London to get parts. Caddie was absorbed; she was having riding lessons, beginning to school Topaz. Lady Candida was mercifully absent. She always went to Switzerland for August and September, to stay up in the mountains, "Far, far away," said Fanny. Darrell came and went; he was in South America for five weeks, she remembered, delayed. He was always being delayed. That, once upon a time had been exasperating; it had spoiled many invitations; often at the last minute I had to ring up and say he was not back, thought Fanny, which left me odd woman out, but now it opened the way to a halcyon time, filled only with Rob and herself and if any voice spoke or whispered in her, she stifled it at once. "It's all harmless," she told herself even after the warning of the sleep-walking weeks that had gone before. All harmless. What is it? A few lunches and dinners; a theatre, an occasional kiss. "We are friends—friends," Fanny tried to insist. "I can have a friend?" and when that was too palpably a lie—she had only to meet Rob's eyes, touch his hand to know it—"He is going to Africa," she would say. "Then it will be over." Rob was at the studios now, finishing *Haysel to Harvest*. In the evenings he was up in London, or at Technicolour. They could only meet desultorily, but even when they did not meet . . . "Why did Darrell and the children have so little power?"

whispered Fanny aloud. "Because Rob had so much. So much," and in spite of the sun shining down on the villa terrace, she felt as if she shivered. She was getting to the crisis.

All that time, Darrell had noticed nothing. "That wasn't his fault," Fanny defended him to Rob. "He didn't notice things, often not until Lady Candida pointed them out to him." It was not that he was stupid or obtuse. It simply would not have occurred to Darrell that his wife could fall in love with somebody else. He gave me all his trust, thought Fanny, and I was not trustworthy.

Darrell would not have betrayed her, she knew that. Not even if he had fallen as much in love with a woman as she with Rob. If he had not been able to resist it, and she thought he would resist, Darrell would have been able to . . . compartment it, thought Fanny. He would never have hurt her or the children. He was steadfast, thought Fanny, as he was steadfast with his mother, though Fanny had sometimes had an idea that he did not like Lady Candida any more than she did. Darrell was a disciplinarian— well, he is used to commanding a regiment; he expected people to come up to his standard, particularly his children, but he would never have hurt them, never, thought Fanny, and he was bewildered that she could.

"But what did I do wrong?" he had asked over and over again in the one time Fanny saw him. "What did I do wrong?"

"Nothing. Nothing ever."

"Then *why?*"

Lady Candida too, in Fanny's last meeting with her—I

had to see her for old enmity's sake—"You weren't on bad terms with Darrell?"

"They weren't bad," Fanny had answered wearily. "Not bad, not good, just terms." She could not tell Lady Candida that it had all . . . ceased, thought Fanny, if it ever had begun. She knew now that she had never been properly married to Darrell.

Some couples, for instance Margot and Sydney, are apart on the surface but cannot do without one another. Darrell and Fanny seemed to be of one accord, we were, yes, comfortable together, thought Fanny, but I did without him perfectly well. That was not his fault, she insisted again; he was loyal, faithful, kind; she had followed him unquestioningly, "Because I didn't know enough to question?" asked Fanny, yet now she saw that her happiest times had been since he was made a Queen's Messenger and was away so much.

"Clavering shouldn't have left her alone," they said at the Club House.

"Damn it all, if a wife can't be faithful while a man does his work . . ." She could imagine them saying that.

"But I was faithful, technically," Fanny might have said. That began to be the trouble. Restlessness set in. The holidays ended. The children went back to school. She remembered how Caddie begged to be a day girl again so that she could go on with Topaz's training. If it had not been for Rob, should I have persuaded Darrell to let her? asked Fanny. Lady Candida came back with her prick-needle eyes. "Do you *have* to be so fidgety, Fanny? What's the matter with you? First down, then up. You can't keep still a minute. I believe you have nerves. Darrell must take you away."

"If you worry Darrell, I shall never speak to you again." The fierceness was so unlike Fanny, that Lady Candida was more than ever convinced that she was ill. "Something *is* the matter," said Lady Candida firmly.

Fanny herself did not know what it was, any more than an adolescent knows; this strange heady excitement, at once miserable and sweet. Lady Candida was right; Fanny could not be still. She, who had always been peaceful, seemed on jerk-strings, who had been almost selfless, "willy-nilly," she might have said, thought only of herself. "I." "I." "I," struggling like a moth to break its chrysalis. She worked in the house and garden, "and hated the house and garden"; was as impatient as Hugh, silly as Philippa; could not bear to be with Rob, could not bear to be without him; rushed up to London to see him—and then did not telephone him but tramped about the streets and came home frustrated. Then driven, thought Fanny, that day I did telephone. We went to Chirico's, the rain came and it happened.

She sank her cheek into the long-chair cushions remembering that first time. She had said they were innocent, but was she? Wasn't I ripe? thought Fanny. It seemed to her now she had been like a girl, thin, big-eyed, with lust. Yes, lust, thought Fanny. One should call it by its ugly proper name because it creeps into love; but it cannot maim love, if it is love and, thank God, I was not a girl, thought Fanny, but a woman who can hide what she is thinking. All through that luncheon she could hardly take her eyes off Rob. Then he had to go to his appointment, and I said I would walk in the park, thought Fanny. Walking was the only thing that helped, to walk into exhaustion, but it rained. "Why?" Fanny, once again argued with God. "Why did you let it rain?" God sends the rain, they always say, not the devil, and there was nothing devilish in what happened that afternoon; it was more right, more tender, and beautiful than anything I had ever known, known or dreamed of, thought Fanny.

Rob had driven her home that night, too tired to think. "You are too tired and so am I," said Rob. "I will come and see Darrell in the morning," but Darrell was still away, mercifully, thought Fanny, or I could not have gone back to Stebbings, and even then, thought Fanny now, even then in the month—no, it was not a month—in the three weeks that followed, I hung fire, shilly-shallied.

Rob had argued. "I must talk to Darrell. It's only honest to leave, Fanny. Leave now. It isn't right that you should stay there," and all the while this passion burnt them; they could not bear to stay away from one another, could not have enough. There is a word "slaked," thought Fanny, when one's thirst is satisfied; we were never satisfied, never slaked. Yet Rob was patient. If I had needed any telling, I found out in those weeks how much he loved me, how he could go against himself for me. I didn't know what I was waiting for, or perhaps not waiting, only trying to keep everything together, not hurt Darrell too much, not hurt the children. Perhaps I thought that somehow I could have Rob *and* the children and Stebbings. Perhaps I could have had them, we could have stayed as we were. No, I was living in a fool's dream, thought Fanny, because Darrell came home, "And he noticed me," said Fanny.

It had dawned slowly. She had heard him talking to Gwyneth. "Is Mrs. Clavering quite well?"

"A little upset," said Gwyneth cautiously. Dear loyal Gwyneth.

"Upset? About what?" Darrell was honestly perplexed.

"It's been a trying summer and—ladies get moods."

"Moods?" He sounded more than ever lost. "Is there anything you think I could do?"

Gwyneth's advice was of the nursery, she had had a great deal to do with children. "I should leave her alone, sir, and she will come out of it."

"Leave her alone." It might be of the nursery, but it was sound. If Darrell had had the wisdom to do that, should I be here now? asked Fanny, but Darrell did not leave her alone; the opposite. He took more notice of me than he had since we were first married, thought Fanny and she wondered, does a woman, roused, give out an emanation, like a female moth?

It was after dinner, the third night he had been home.

When Darrell was at Stebbings the ritual was always the same. Changed, he and Fanny met in the drawing room for a drink before dinner. That always irked the children; they had an aloof disapproval but Darrell liked to sit, with a whiskey and soda or a gin, telling Fanny about the day, or his last journey. "And I liked it too," said Fanny. "It was adult. A change from those very children." Then they had dinner, which Gwyneth used to dish up for Fanny, after which they waited on themselves; it was a three-course dinner, the table properly laid, "With all the panoply," said

Hugh and the children were not allowed to leave the table for their private ploys, no matter what these were.

"Probably good for them," said Fanny, but again it was irksome. Philippa chafed while some boy who had called for her sounded his horn outside. "You can ask him to come in and have some coffee," said Darrell. "He doesn't want coffee; he wants *me*," and, "We have been sitting here an hour!" Hugh had once burst out. "A whole hour, or an hour and three quarters since you started drinking, and there is an important concert I need to hear." But Darrell had forgotten what it felt like to be young, to be passionate about things, thought Fanny. "Can jazz be so important?" he had asked, quite kindly, but it was almost with hate that Hugh said, "This is *classical* jazz."

The girls washed up or, when they were not home, Fanny washed the silver and glass, the rest waited until the morning. She brought coffee into the drawing room. Darrell read the paper or watched television, while Fanny watched too or wrote letters, or mended. At ten o'clock they went tamely to bed, usually to read, thought Fanny, each putting out their own light, with a kiss, usually on the cheek or forehead, only now and then something warmer, again not passionate but kindly. An ordinary harmless married couple, like any in the world, but that October night Darrell did not settle down with the paper, did not switch on a programme, he came over to her and touched her hair.

"You're looking very well tonight, Fanny."

"The same as usual." Fanny tried to speak lightly. Presently she got up and moved to the other side of the fireplace.

"Why go over there?"

"It's too hot."

"You feel beautifully cool," and he asked, "isn't it time for bed?"

"It's only a quarter past nine."

"Never mind. Why not go when we want to?"

"You go. I have things to do."

"Not now."

"Yes. I have to . . ." Fanny got up.

"Not now," said Darrell. He got up too. "Damn it all. I have been away for weeks." He put his arm round her and kissed her. "What would you say, Fanny, if we went away? Just you and I, for a few days. Mother says you ought to have a change and I think we deserve it. This job is brutish. You have been alone too long. We could go up to town, do some shows, or what about Madeira?" asked Darrell.

"No," said Fanny. "No," but she could not get the words out. He bent his head to kiss her again. She tried not to shrink, but she shrank. He held her firmly, closer. "Darrell, please don't."

"Why, what's the matter?"

This, thought Fanny to herself is where you use control. Other women . . . but it was no use thinking of other women. He was holding her closer still and before she could stop herself she had cried out, "Darrell! Please don't touch me."

"Don't touch you?" The blue eyes looked so astonished and hurt that Fanny fought again to control herself. This was not Darrell's fault and she did not want him to be hurt, any more than Danny, she thought, and caught herself back, but there was something as simple and noble as an animal about Darrell. "Not touch you? I'm your husband." She tried to be still but when that possessive hold tightened, the panic came up again.

"I can't." Now the struggling was growing frantic. "I can't. Perhaps never again."

"What *is* all this?" He was still holding her, but now not in his arms, holding her with his hands as he felt her struggling. "Fanny! You are not *afraid?*" I'm your husband. Your husband."

"Then help me." Now Fanny was clinging to him. "Help me."

"Help you? Why? How?"

"Just leave me for a little while. Leave me alone." In his grasp, the panic was coming up again. "Leave me. Then it may be all right."

"What may be all right? What's *wrong?*"

"Don't watch me like that. Don't probe."

"This is all nerves," said Darrell.

"It's not nerves. Darrell, perhaps I should tell you. . . ." but he was too sure of himself to listen. He was not angry; he still had not grasped what she was trying, though frantically, to tell him. "This is where, dearest," he said, "you have to let the man know best. It's only that somehow in the last few months we have lost one another a little, come somehow to be almost strangers." So he had noticed, thought Fanny. "It will be all right in a little while," said Darrell.

"No! No!" cried Fanny, but he turned her gently towards the door and into the hall.

"You go up to bed and wait for me."

"I knew then that I couldn't," said Fanny. "I had made love with Rob. Yes, that is what I had made, something binding, unforgettable, and 'private' is not a big enough word, a 'keep' between two people, made of minutes that last a lifetime, until death, perhaps past death, and for anyone else to touch me was desecration.''

It was hot under the lavender sunshade but again Fanny felt cold. Darrell had steered her to the stairs and stood in the hall, watching her go up. Then she heard him shutting up the house. In the bedroom she stayed still, listening, and as cold as this, thought Fanny, her arms goosefleshed . . . but my head and my temples felt as if they were burning, as if my heart had split and was beating there and in my throat. I heard Darrell come upstairs and go into his dressing room. I heard the sound as he threw his wallet and his keys down on the chest of drawers before he went into the bathroom.

She had stolen into the dressing room, picked up the keys, and quietly closed and locked the door that led into her bedroom. That would make him pause for a minute or two, poor Darrell. Back in her room Fanny kicked off her thin shoes, pulled on street ones and took a coat and scarf; her bag and gloves were where she had left them on her dressing table. As Darrell came back from the bathroom into the dressing room, Fanny ran downstairs, along the kitchen passage. Danny got up from his bed to join her but she hushed him peremptorily. She unlocked the back door, slipped through it, taking the key, and locked the door behind her. On the grass she ran to the garage; it was not locked and silently she opened the doors. Thank God the gate was open, thought Fanny and, thank God, the car was warm. It started at once and she drove out.

She thought she saw the lights go on downstairs; she

thought she heard a shout but it may not have been. She dared not look back. In a moment, she was on the road to London.

In January up in Scotland, the petition was served on Fanny by post. She had to sign the "acknowledgment of service," as her solicitor called it. "Do I need a solicitor as well as you and Darrell?" she had asked Rob. Mr. McCrae had been Aunt Isabel's solicitor and, for all his Scots disapproval, when Rob had said that indeed she needed a solicitor, Fanny had instinctively gone to him. Rob's "acknowledgment of service" had to go to Africa which caused a small delay. She, the guilty one, did not have to appear in court, and it was to Aunt Isabel's cottage that the telegram came to say that the case was on the warned list. It was heard on April the third and a decree nisi was granted. "In ten minutes flat," wrote Mr. McCrae. Ten minutes, thought Fanny, to undo eighteen years.

The law had disposed of the problem but it can't dispose of people, thought Fanny. Use them as chattels, not even children.

I was going to roll it all up, roll it into a ball that I could keep hidden in my hand, or in my heart. It was to be only Rob, Rob and I, together for the rest of our lives. I had accepted that, then . . . and across every plan and thought and feeling came this new triumphant song; "They ran away. Hugh and Caddie ran away to me."

V

"**B**UT HOW?" Fanny had not ceased to say that from
the time Hugh and Caddie had arrived. "How did it happen? How did you get here?" She asked it again, the next
morning on the terrace. "How did you come?"

"Train. Bus. Walked," said Hugh.

Breakfast was over. "If you can call it breakfast," said
Caddie.

She had slept round the clock, the drugged unrefreshing
sleep that comes with unhappy exhaustion; sleep crossed
with dreams, nightmare faces from the journey: the porters at Calais, the French girl who had talked all night,
a woman solitary on the platform at Dôle, they seemed
to have been cut into Caddie's brain. When she woke,
she did not at first know where she was, only that she
did not like being there. This last year there had been
many places where she did not like to wake; at school
where the sight of the white cubicle curtains and narrow iron bed made her feel an exile, the bedroom in
the London flat that smelled stuffy and stale and that
she had to share with Philippa, which meant that she
was squeezed into a corner. At Stebbings she had had the
old night nursery to herself and covered it with "a rash of

animals," as Hugh said: her collection of porcelain horses; a string of carthorse brasses, a lucky horseshoe; photographs cut from magazines of hunter trials and shows, of famous horses: and endless snapshots of Topaz, framed and unframed. Caddie's room, "Caddie's tack room," Hugh called it.

Now she woke in what seemed a shadowed cave, filled with the sound of waves, and it was some time before she remembered what she was doing there; she made out a high pink-washed ceiling, pink walls, bars of sunlight showing through the pull-down shutters. How strange to sleep with shutters down, closed in like a box, thought Caddie. The shape of a wardrobe loomed, a basin with a glimmer of china, a chair over which lay a shape that seemed to be a dress. Hers? There was a dressing-table with three mirrors and gleam of gilt, and she was lying in a large bed, its posts inlaid with flowers. When she reached up and touched one of them with her finger the flower was gilt. On the bed, pushed away, was a hard bolster, the bottom sheet still tucked immovably round it. She had been lying flat. Her pillow and bedclothes were on the floor.

From outside came the sound she had thought was waves, a steady splash splash of water; it was waves, gentle ones; the lake, thought Caddie. Yes, there was a chugging as if a boat passed. Down below in the house someone was singing again.

Caddie's head had a dull ache. She felt numbed and stupid, and in her mouth was a sour taste. Last night both she and Hugh had drunk the wine Celestina gave them. Presently she slid off the bed and padded over to the basin; there was no tumbler but she managed to drink from the tap; the water only trickled and had a queer strong taste; it was iron, Fanny told her afterwards.

Her eyes were accustomed to the dimness now and she saw that someone had unpacked her grip; clean clothes were put out. They had brought only vests, socks, and pyjamas but her dress and its knickers had been washed and ironed—already! thought Caddie. She dressed, leaving her pyjamas on the floor—"Caddie fashion," Fanny would have said—and brushed her hair; her school brush and comb looked childish on the big expanse of dressing table. She did not bother to put on her shoes. Then she stood listening. Still only that splashing of water, the singing, and, now, the sound of oars. The bars of light through the shutters fell warm on the floor, warm and deep gold. It must be quite late, thought Caddie and she went to the windows to try and push the shutters up but they were too stiff for her. Then she saw there was a glass door opening from the room. It opened easily and she stepped out onto a small loggia. It was the twin to Fanny's as Caddie found out later, its windows arched like the Annunciation picture again; its tiled floor was already warm from the sun, grateful to her bare feet after the cold of the bedroom. She leaned her elbows on the loggia sill to look.

The lake moved gently in the morning sun; near the shore its blue changed to a clear green and it was here that the waves splashed their freshness against the lower garden wall. In the top garden scents were beginning to warm; it was full of birds and even from here she could hear the shrilling of Celestina's caged ones; swallows flashed past the loggia; but after a moment, Caddie saw and heard none of these things; below on the terrace was Rob, Mr.

Quillet, in shorts and singlet, his bare arms and legs looking deep brown.

Caddie had not really been alive to Rob last night, only
been aware that he had sat on the balustrade smoking, that
he was dark, as Philippa said, dressed in the dark blue
shirt, and white trousers—she had taken in the trousers
because she had not seen a man wearing them in white
linen before. Yet, as if she had absent-mindedly photo-
graphed him, looking down at him now she recognized
him with startling distinctness. He was walking up and
down and he moved in a way that made other people look
stiff, stuffed, thought Caddie. He was not erect, like Darrell but he was . . . graceful? It seemed an odd thing to
say of a man. He was not exactly good-looking, his face was
too thin and, he hasn't very much hair, she thought. It grew
far back, giving him a high forehead.

Until the last ten days grown people had been to Caddie
no more than shades, nothing they said or did was in the
least interesting. "Your children are completely self-
engrossed," Lady Candida often told Fanny, to which
Philippa, Hugh, and Caddie would have answered that of
course they were; but Philippa and Hugh had at least been
conscious of what was going on about them, at any rate as
far as it affected them, but Caddie had been wrapped in
the snug cocoon she had woven for herself, the private
world of Caddie and Topaz. She had been stripped out of
it so suddenly that now she seemed to catch the slightest
mood or change and, standing at the loggia window, looking down on Rob, she knew he was more than a little disturbed—because Hugh and I have come? she asked.

"Children should keep out of grown-up affairs," Gwyn-

eth had said—but they shouldn't, thought Caddie now.
Already she and Hugh had made an impact and, with the
bright morning, she felt filled with confidence and a self-
importance she had had only in her Topaz dreams. Without giving herself time to think, she ran downstairs, down
those marble stairs, and out onto the terrace.

"Hullo," said Rob.

"Good morning," said Caddie. She had meant it to sound
as distant as Hugh's "How do you do," but it trailed off
into uncertainty. If Rob were disturbed, he was not going
to let anybody see it; his shoulders kept their quiet droop,
and his "Hullo" had been quite unperturbed. It brought
back the memory of his decisive voice last night when he
had put Hugh in his place—which is more than Father or
Mother can do, thought Caddie, and he had made Fanny
go out to dinner—when we had just come, thought Caddie,
which Darrell certainly could not have done. Caddie had
not believed it herself, until she heard the speedboat start.
She felt her new confidence ebbing; perhaps he was even
more formidable than he had seemed last night, and what
do we call him? she thought miserably. Mr. Quillet, or
Rob? What did people call Fanny now? No one knew what
to call anyone, thought Caddie. It was part of the uneasi-
ness and she walked past Rob to the balustrade and stood
with her elbows on it, feeling the sun on her neck.

Opposite the villa, across perhaps a mile of water, a
small town lay along the lake; round it, on the mountain
were strange encrustations that, from this distance, looked
like pale and elongated honeycombs.

"What are those?" asked Caddie.

"That's Limone," said Rob. "Limone, the place that

lemons are called after. Those are the lemon terraces. The lemons have to be grown in screened terraces because of the wind."

She and Hugh had seen lemons being sold all along the road; inviting-looking bunches, lemons and oranges, on their branches of glossy green leaves, sold from carts, and wooden stands in the towns and villages, some piled in pyramids on the road wall, with a tattered boy to guard them, but she said nothing more.

"Are you feeling better?" asked Rob, Rob Quillet, Mr. Quillet; Caddie nodded. "Coffee will be here in a minute. We are having it on the terrace this morning." He stretched and lifted his face to the sun. "Smell the lilacs," he said.

He did not, she noticed, talk to her as if she were a child, but levelly; the air in this strange garden was touched with fresh and dewy scent but all the same she was not going to give in to anything Italian. "The lilac would be out at Stebbings, too," she said. If she had been watching Rob, she would have seen that she had scored a mark. His face had tightened. "I wish I had never seen Stebbings," he had said once to Fanny. "It never ceases to make me feel guilty."

Fanny had had to try most of all not to think of Stebbings garden. That had been all hers, "I made it," while the house was Lady Candida's who had ceded it to Darrell and Fanny when they were married, "so it was never mine," said Fanny; but she had remade the garden, taking away the orderly laid-out gardener's plots and making a tangle of old roses, beds so thick with flowers that there was no room for weeds. "It wasn't a tidy garden," Fanny said, but filled with richness—"and intimate friends," she could have said. She had spent hours there working. Prentice had cut the lawns, clipped the hedges and he worked in the vegetable garden, "But the flowers were mine," said Fanny.

"The house felt comfortable," Rob had said. "Easy and content."

"It was," said Fanny. Stebbings had ample rooms, wide sills on which a child could sit, just as a child could sit comfortably reading on the stairs. Lady Candida's Edwardian furniture had given it heavy sofas and chairs, solid tables, brass beds. Its chintzes had been washed so often the pattern had faded to creams, faint pinks, and blues and browns. The bookshelves were filled with an accumulated jumble of leather editions, Penguins, books on cookery and gardening, children's books. Nobody knew where some of the pictures had come from. "Some of them were frightful," said Fanny. The silver was good but the china and glass often ran short, it was always being broken, and the linen cupboard was a disgrace; but there were always log fires, bowls of flowers, plenty of food for children's guests, plenty of children, "And rabbits, chickens, Danny, Thomas, and Topaz," said Fanny. It was a house that was thoroughly well lived in and Rob had said gloomily, "I can never give you that again. One can't buy a house like that."

"You can never buy a home," Fanny had answered. "You have to make one. We will make one," she said. The question was where. "Where would you like to live?" she often asked Rob. "Live when we are . . . when we leave the villa?"

They had often talked of it. "Somewhere beautiful," Rob would say. "Away but not so far that I can't travel backwards and forwards."

"Backwards and forwards to where?"

"Where I am working."

"But that might be anywhere," Fanny had objected. "Look where you have worked since I have known you. Whitcross. Africa. Rome. Now, if you do *Saladin* it will be the Holy Land or do you call it Israel or Jordan?"

"Which means we can live anywhere," said Rob. "New England is beautiful, or California, though I think Arizona's better."

"But . . . they are in America."

"One *can* live in America," Rob had said gravely. "But we could live in Paris, if you want to stay in Europe, or here, in Italy. We have the whole world to choose from," which was not the same thing, he knew when he was reminded of Stebbings, as having a world of their own and he was curt as he asked Caddie, "Is Hugh getting up?"

"I don't know."

"Well, tell him to get up and come down. After coffee, your mother and I want to talk to you."

There was no doubt about it, though he did not hector as Darrell did, when this man Rob—Mr. Quillet—told you to do something, you did it. Caddie went back upstairs and woke Hugh.

He did not want to get up. "You must. He says so," said Caddie. Hugh said he had a headache, a pain, and a bad taste in his mouth. Caddie, remembering the taste in hers, was sympathetic and brought him a glass of water but when he tried to drink it, he retched. "I have a hell of a pain. My inside's all upset."

"It's the strain," said Caddie, quoting Gwyneth.

"It isn't. I have eaten something."

There was one thing he had eaten that Caddie had not, a piece of pork pie an English woman had given him on the bus. There had been none left for Caddie—unfortunately, she had thought then. The only thing that helped Caddie was eating; she buried her sorrow in food as some people drown theirs in drink. In London she had "stuffed," said Hugh while he had driven Gwyneth to despair, but he had eaten the whole slice of pie. Now, "Can't Mother come up here?" he said with a groan.

"I don't think so," said Caddie, remembering Rob's voice, and Hugh reluctantly got up.

When Rob had said "coffee" instead of "breakfast" Caddie should have been warned, or remembered Switzerland. "Don't you have cereal, or porridge or eggs, either?" she asked when she saw the table.

"Not in Italy," said Fanny.

"They can if they like," said Rob. "They have only to ask Celestina."

"When they are in Italy they should do as the Italians do."

"I don't see why, when they are English."

Though Caddie would dearly have liked an egg, or better, egg and bacon, but did they have bacon in this barbarous country? she was not going to take sides with Rob and she ate doggedly through two rolls, though their crust was so hard that it almost cut her fingers. Hugh ate nothing at all.

"Hugh, have at least a roll."

"Don't pester him to eat if he doesn't want to."

"I'm not pestering."

There seemed an edginess between Rob and Fanny. It had begun when Hugh at last appeared. "Hugh, you're up?"

"I sent Caddie to call him."

"Oh, Rob, I wanted him to sleep it out."

"They can't do exactly as they like. There are things to arrange," and breakfast was silent. When Giulietta had taken the tray, Rob lit a cigarette and began: "Now . . ." and, "Yes, we must hear all about it," said Fanny, covering Hugh's hand with her own. She meant to make up for Rob's curtness but Hugh took his hand away.

"How did you come?"

"Train. Bus. Walked."

"Yes, but . . ."

"Oh, begin at the beginning," interrupted Rob. "How did you get away without being missed?"

"Where was—Father?" asked Fanny.

"He went the day before Philippa . . ." And even in the midst of his unwellness and antipathy, Hugh could not help smiling at the thought of Darrell's face when he came home. "He should be back today."

"But Gwyneth was there, and she was always so careful."

"She was," said Hugh and smiled again but Caddie felt a pang. Poor Gwyneth had not had a chance. The thought of her left alone in the flat to face Darrell's questions made Caddie ache. "It was all, all so dreadful," she said. "You don't know how dreadful it was."

The last straw had been the sandals, her school sandals. She and Hugh went to buy them the day after Philippa left for Paris, "And the flat was worse," said Caddie.

It was difficult to believe that it could have been worse because Philippa and Hugh had quarrelled incessantly. "It never used to be like this," said Caddie but then Fanny had been there. She must have been more of a shock absorber and buffer than they had known. In the flat there was continual jarring; Philippa was high-handed, even with Gwyneth; Hugh was rude and Caddie, babyishly tearful.

Another difficult thing had been that there seemed to be no room. At Stebbings Philippa had had the attic room which Fanny had converted into a bed sitting room, so that Philippa could have her friends up there. "Girls giggling, with the gramophone blaring its head off," said Hugh. "Girls kicking off their shoes, throwing chocolate papers about, girls always in the bathroom or on the telephone." They had been all over the flat; Caddie was ordered out of the sitting room and had to stay in the kitchen. Hugh, disgusted, had to go out. At Stebbings he had had a workbench in the garage, his room was his own, but in the flat the only place big enough for setting up his telescope was on the dining-room table. No sooner had he started work than someone wanted to lay the table. "But we must have meals," said Gwyneth.

"Why can't we have them in the kitchen?"

"The Colonel in the kitchen!"

"Yes."

Gwyneth said in that case she would have to eat off a tray in her bedroom. "Why can't you eat with us? Too high and mighty," said Hugh.

Gwyneth's eyes, that were the colour of her own Welsh peat streams, and as clear, looked hurt. "It isn't that, dear." She had never known how to deal with Hugh.

Nor did Darrell. "Darrell to rhyme with barrel," Hugh used to say, which was palpably nonsense; Darrell was stocky, but still, "A fine figure of a man," Gwyneth said.

"Especially in uniform," said Hugh. "Then you don't see him so much."

"He doesn't wear uniform now," said Caddie. "Not for his Messenging."

"He does for all those dinners—scarlet and blue and gold, all hung with medals. Bloody handsome," jeered Hugh.

That had been too much for Gwyneth's Welsh temper. To her Darrell was only one less than Fanny from the stars and, "I'm ashamed of you, Hugh," she said. "Your father's an officer and a true gentleman. I have never known anyone more . . . more upright."

"Oh, Father's upright, outside and in," Hugh had to concede that even in his bad temper. Caddie, and Gwyneth, knew too that Hugh was proud of Darrell, and fond of him as they all were. "He's us," as Caddie would have said, and, "Yes, upright, outside and in," Hugh had to say. So could he be when he wanted, but now he deliberately chose not to, "In every way," said Caddie.

"It would have been much, much better if Father had let Mother have Hugh," said Philippa.

He was, as Darrell said once when driven to lose his temper, both precocious and abominable.

"Sit up!" Darrell would rap out at last.

"Really. Really. You have just told me to sit down."

Yet Darrell had never been more kind, even indulgent. "Trying to be father and mother," but even Hugh could not mock about that. Darrell stayed away from his club, took them out to lunch to save Gwyneth, gave them tickets for matinées, tried to show them London. "He's trying to make up," said Hugh.

"He can't," said Caddie. Darrell knew he could not, especially when Hugh chose to stay in and work on his telescope. Then Caddie's heart ached for her father, as it had for Hugh and Philippa.

She tried to do things for him, creeping into his small bedroom; he had given her and Philippa the largest room. Every night she turned down his bed and laid out his pyjamas. He had come upon her looking at a hole in one of his socks. "Give it to Flip, to mend," he said, but Philippa, Caddie knew, was too busy getting ready for Paris. "I will give it to Gwyneth."

"No, don't. She has too much to do now."

"I can try and darn it, but I'm not very good."

"No, never mind. You have your own things. Tell you what," said Darrell. "I will buy some new pairs," and he had stuffed the socks into his pocket.

"You can't go out with socks in your pocket."

"It's only so that Gwyneth shouldn't see. I can drop them in a litter basket," and Caddie had suddenly flung herself at her father and hugged him.

Caddie herself had never been as rubbed up against her family. Day after day was bleak, angry, miserable, and empty. "She's missing her mother," Gwyneth said but it was not Fanny that Caddie missed.

"Father, may I speak to you? What . . . what is going to happen to Topaz?"

"Well, we can't keep him in London, can we?" The false heartiness in Darrell's voice made Caddie's heart sink like a stone.

"Do we have to live in London?"

"It's the easiest, Caddie, for the most people. I have to come and go. Soon Philippa will start training. Besides we couldn't manage Stebbings without . . . Mother."

"Couldn't you . . ." Caddie sensed where she was treading but she had to say it. "Couldn't you make her come back?"

"Because of Topaz?" Darrell tried to make his voice light but did not succeed.

"Topaz—and other things. *Everything!*" said Caddie in a burst of misery.

"I wish I could, Diddie, but . . ." He used her baby name and it was the first time Caddie had ever seen big, powerful Darrell helpless. He looked as if he, too, might cry. Father cry? thought Caddie, stunned. Indeed he could not look at her, he seemed to have a mist in his eyes, and he drew clumsy men with sticks for arms and legs on his blotting paper. "You have done very well with that pony," he said. "Do you know that Will Ringells says he will give you twenty-five pounds for him?"

"I don't want twenty-five pounds," said Caddie.

"Then one day, when perhaps I can arrange for you to be in the country again, you could buy an even better pony."

"I don't want a better pony."

"I see," said Darrell. "Well, we'll leave him where he is with Ringells for the present, shall we? He's happy there."

"It's three guineas a week," whispered Caddie.

"We can run to that for a little while, then we can see." Darrell's voice had been very kind but it was a knell to Caddie. "They will do it, sell Topaz, when I'm away at school."

School was getting near, only a few days, when Darrell had had to make one of his sudden absences. "An undivulged errand to an unknown destination," mocked Hugh.

"You ought to be proud to have a father who is a Queen's Messenger," said Gwyneth. They were proud, even Caddie often boasted about it, but the excitement had become familiar; it really only meant that Darrell was away, more often than not. "Conveniently, as it turned out," said Hugh.

There had been trouble over Philippa's going because she had wanted to travel in trousers. "Trousers!" Lady Candida had been horrified.

"Girls all do, nowadays," said Philippa.

"All girls don't, and you most certainly will not."

In the end Philippa had to give way because Lady Candida threatened to withdraw the twenty pounds she was giving her as a parting present. All the same Lady Candida would not come up to see her off—"She thinks that's a *punishment*," said Philippa—and there were only

Hugh and Caddie at the Paris train, "In a horde of girls," said Hugh.

"Not a horde, there were only eight," said Caddie.

"I never heard such a din in my life."

Hugh and Caddie had stood side by side at the carriage door, but Philippa had taken little notice of them, "Except to guy us," said Hugh.

"This is my little brother, Hugh. This infant with the freckles is Caddie."

"That's what we get for coming. Let's go," Hugh had said but Caddie insisted on staying. "Flip's showing off. You know she always has to show off," said Caddie, "and she must have someone to wave to. All the others have fathers or mothers, fathers *and* mothers," said Caddie.

They had come back to a flat that seemed darker and more desolate than ever and found Gwyneth worrying about their school clothes. "The Colonel asked me to do them but I just don't know," said Gwyneth helplessly. "I don't know. Your mother has always done this."

At Stebbings, three times a year, the house had rung with: "Has anyone seen my Larousse?" "Oh, *Moth-er!* Not name tapes even on *handkerchiefs.*" "Those tennis balls are *mine.*" "Caddie, only two pounds of sweets."

Packing for the summer term was particularly elaborate: thick things, thin things: cricket flannels and boots, white sweaters, white socks. Tennis shorts. Balls in nets, bathing dresses.

"Do you have to have *all* these things?" asked Gwyneth.

"Good Lord, no," said Hugh.

"Yes," said Caddie.

"If I could have gone for one week," Fanny had said to

Rob, to the solicitors, finally to Darrell. "Just to get them ready." But in his one interview with her, Darrell had treated her as a stranger. "Which is nonsense," Fanny had cried. "Guilty, yes, but I can't be a stranger." It was Darrell who was the stranger; Fanny had not known he could look as old and drawn. Rob had said, "Don't see him. It's kinder."

"I can't be kind. I must fight for the children."

"It's no good, Fanny."

"If he would let us have them, even half the time."

"He won't," said Rob.

"He must," but Darrell was adamant. "You chose," was all he said.

"I didn't. It chose me," but this new Darrell was deaf to anything that she, this importunate stranger, might say. "My children," said Darrell deliberately. "Philippa, Hugh, Caddie." Being Darrell he had to be fair, conscientiously fulfilling the judge's orders. "They can visit you sometimes. Short visits."

She had had a letter from Darrell, written in the midst of the proceedings, a letter she would never forget and could not answer. "If I had answered, I should have gone back," because there was not a reproach in it, only a desperate plea. "It's not only myself I am thinking of, it's of the children. No, I *am* thinking of myself," wrote Darrell. "You are my wife. This other man . . ." To Darrell, Rob would always be "the other man," the intruder. "You can't jeopardize a whole world." "It isn't jeopardized," Fanny wanted to cry. "It's gone." But, "Won't you come back? Can't you?" wrote Darrell. "I will try not to touch you. If I had understood . . ." and the letter ended: "Please. Please. Please."

Fanny did not know what had given her the hardness to tear it up and the hardness to carry on this fight.

"Philippa's over sixteen. You can't stop her," she had said.

"I think Philippa will decide to stay with me."

Will she? With Rob in films? Fanny wondered. She knew her Philippa, and she was sure that presently Darrell would be stabbed by Philippa too. Hugh? "Nothing— nothing you can do, can separate Hugh from me," she had flung at him. That was foolish. It gave him his opportunity. "Nothing *I* can do," he had said. "You forget something. They may not want to visit you."

Fanny could only try and comfort herself. "If I had died," thought Fanny, "they would have managed, and Gwyneth is there."

Unknown to Darrell, Gwyneth had come to the airport to see Fanny off to Milan. At the last minute, Fanny had put her arms round the familiar figure, though looking unfamiliar in a London coat, grey gloves, black handbag, and black straw hat with black hatpins, her face unrelent- ingly stiff. "Thank God they have you," Fanny had said as she kissed her and desperately, "Gwyneth, make Hugh take his warm pyjamas, it's still cold at the beginning of term. Tins of sausages and ham in his tuck box, not all sweet things. Send him a cake now and then."

Tears had run down Gwyneth's face. "I will do my best."

"Caddie's old enough to help sew on name tapes now. Hugh . . . "

"I will do my best."

"Write to me."

"I'm not much hand at writing," but Gwyneth wrote.

Now, "Three regulation gingham dresses," she read out from Caddie's list. "Regulation blazer . . ."

"Why does everything have to be regulation?" Philippa had always flared.

"Because girls have ideas," said Hugh.

"I have found the dresses," Gwyneth went on, "but they will need letting down. Oh dear! There isn't much time."

"I can wear them short," said Caddie miserably.

"And be all legs."

"Hush, Hugh. Two cotton dresses . . ." Gwyneth's finger came down the list as she faithfully read out every word. "Own pattern for wearing in the evening. Have you those, Caddie?"

"Grown out of them," Caddie muttered. She seemed in a state of growing out of everything.

"We must get them then," said Gwyneth. "You had better shop tomorrow."

"By *myself?*" asked Caddie in terrible alarm.

"We can ask Lady Candida if she could come up."

"Not Gran," groaned Caddie. "She talks about Mother to everyone. You come," she begged Gwyneth.

"I wouldn't be any use, not in shops like that. Philippa ought to have helped you before she went."

"Too busy with her own clothes," said Hugh. "One thing, about Flip, she won't try and be a little mother to us. No fear," and with one of his sudden turns of sweetness he had said, "Don't worry, Diddie. I will choose your clothes."

He had, and, "They were the prettiest dresses I ever had in my life," said Caddie, "and he helped me to buy a dressing gown and a bathing dress. He was nice to every-one and everyone was nice to us." It had almost been happy until it came to the shoes.

"Regulation summer sandals," said the list, and, "Good Lord!" said Hugh when they appeared. "Your feet can't be as big as *that!*"

"Not in your size," the assistant in the first shop had said. "Try Daniel Neal's. They go up to sevens there."

"I'm not a seven, I'm only a five," Caddie had wanted to say but even in fives the sandals looked like boats. "Boats? Barges! Flats!" said Hugh. It was not only their flatness, it was their childish shape. "Girls my age shouldn't be made to wear shoes like that," she had wanted to cry passionately. If Fanny had been there she would have found a way out, a compromise between Cad-die and the school, but Fanny was not there and Hugh was tiring. He certainly would not be dragged to any more shops and anyway, she, Caddie, was due at the den-tist's for a pre-school check up. "I will drop you," said Hugh. "You can come home by yourself, can't you? I want to get on with my telescope," and he had paid for the sandals, which were already in a bag. I shall have to wear them, thought Caddie. With them and the too-short uni-form dresses she would be what Hugh said she was, all feet and legs, knees, elbows, and freckles. Fanny would have shed a ray of hope: "It's only a phase. Your feet will shrink. Philippa's did," and the dresses would have been let down. Fanny would have gone with Caddie to the dentist and after it they would probably have had hot chocolate or an ice, but Fanny was in Italy and suddenly, there in Daniel Neal's, Caddie had rebelled.

It was such a violent storm of rebellion that it visibly shook her. It was hatred of her sandals, of the dentist, of going back alone to the flat, of Fanny's absence, of Mr. Quillet, Darrell, and all grown-ups; such hatred and despair, confusion and misery that she cast her parcels on a chair and, "Let's not have it," said Caddie in a choking voice. "Let's refuse."

"Refuse?"

"Absolutely refuse."

"My good child, what are you talking about?" Hugh had looked calm and slim, leaning back in the shop chair waiting for his change, in his grey flannel suit, his hair brushed, his shoes shining. Beside him, Caddie felt shabby and tousled. It was strange that while this impact with adult life had made Philippa romance and tell lies, it had thrown Caddie into truth, and the truth was very dreary, particularly about herself. "It's just that you are at the awkward age," Gwyneth tried to tell her but Caddie was convinced she was hideous. "Hideous!" she had said in despair. Now she was so angry that she did not care.

"Let's refuse to allow Mother to go away like this. Just not have it. Refuse."

"How?" But Hugh had sat up in his chair.

"Refuse to go to school," said Caddie. "To go to school

or stay in that ghastly flat. Refuse to live with Father alone."

"You can *say* refuse, but . . ." began Hugh.

"Not say it. Do it," said Caddie.

"But how do we do it?"

"We won't go back to school," said Caddie breathlessly. "We will leave. Run away," and then she had had her inspiration. "Let's go to this place in Italy and fetch her."

"But how did you find out where it was?" asked Fanny. "How did you know how to get here?"

"Asked," said Hugh but it had not been as simple as all that.

They knew the address. Darrell had given it to them; in fact it was then that Lady Candida had really "Clinched it," said Hugh.

"You must write to your mother," Darrell had said and printed for them: "Villa Fiorita, Malcesine-sul-Garda, Prov. Verona, Italy." "You can write to her there."

"No thank you, sir," Hugh had said. "I'm not going to write."

Darrell had looked astonished, even grateful, as if Hugh had given him a tribute, but he was always fair. "Don't think too hardly of your mother. It was my fault too. She was lonely."

"I do think hardly of her," said Hugh.

"And one can understand it," Lady Candida had put in. She tried to smooth Hugh's hair but he jerked away at once. "It's always the children who suffer most," said Lady Candida. "They are the victims."

"I won't be a victim," Hugh had said when he was alone with Caddie. "A victim" as if it stuck in his teeth.

"Then, don't," said Caddie. "Don't let's be. Let's go."

She had had some vague and Dick Whittingtonish idea of walking, of stowing away on a cross-channel steamer or pleasure boat, then walking again through France, though she was vague about this, cadging lifts, with their food done up in a handkerchief, Hugh carrying a bundle. She blushed now to think how childish that had been; Hugh, once he had accepted her idea, became a master planner.

"The plan was to leave the day we went to school," he told Fanny and Rob, now, on the terrace. "Luckily it was the same date for both of us." Piece by piece he had thought it out. "It didn't all happen in five minutes, as I say it," he told them. Telling about it, Hugh had almost forgotten his sullenness, his headache and pain. "I tell you, it took time."

"But not the telegrams," put in Caddie. "You thought of them in a minute."

"I think we should send telegrams," he had told her. "Writing is too risky. We could never make a letter sound like Father or Gran, or even look like them, even if we had it typed." Perhaps Hugh's strength lay in knowing his limitations. He was seldom naïve. "Yes. We will send telegrams."

"Saying what?" Caddie had asked and Hugh had reeled it off: " 'Regret Candida unable return today suspected measles writing signed Clavering,' the same for me, to Strode," said Hugh.

" 'Suspected' was clever," said Rob. "It kept them hanging about."

"Yes, I thought they would wait for news. . . ." Hugh caught himself back. He had almost called Rob "sir."

Gwyneth had played into their hands by asking Hugh to put Caddie on the train, "As you will be going off yourself, dear. She won't want me to see her off," said Gwyneth. "Not in front of the other girls."

Caddie's school train went from Victoria. "It was awkward being in the same station," said Hugh. "One of the St. Anne's girls might have seen Caddie and recognized her, even though our train left from another part. For Continental trains, one uses a different entrance," he explained to Rob. It had, too, been tight for time. "Caddie's school train left at a quarter past two, ours at half past. I had to run."

"Does she count you?" he had asked Caddie.

"Who?"

"The woman who takes you down to Bendry. There is a mistress with you?"

"Usually Miss Prescott. She has a list and ticks us off."

"Hell!" And Hugh exploded, "Girls' schools! At Strode we can arrive any time, anyhow, as long as we are there for call-over in the evening. She may not have heard about the telegram and if you are not there at the station, someone might telephone."

"Could you take a note?" Caddie had asked but a note held the same risks as a letter. "No. We will get to Victoria an hour early," Hugh had decided. He would deposit Caddie in the refreshment room on the Continental side. In the taxi, she was to put on a head scarf to hide her hair, "It's so ginger anyone would recognize it"—and hide her hat. She had to leave in her panama because of Gwyneth,

"And anyone could see that ghastly emerald band right across the station." "Dark glasses," Hugh had said, enjoying himself, "and you can hold up a newspaper."

He would leave her at a table—"You can have a drink and buy one or two sandwiches for us to eat on the train" —and he, himself, would arrive breathless on the school-train platform. "I can say Father sent me. Too late to telephone, and we're a bit disorganized. They are sure to know all the dirt," said Hugh bitterly and he rehearsed: "I'm Hugh Clavering. Caddie, Candida, my sister, is in bed. The doctor thinks it's measles. She won't be travelling." "I shall just have time to shoot back, and pick you up and get us on the train. And that's how it was," he told Rob and Fanny; but Hugh did not know how it was, sitting in that refreshment room on the Continental side for half an hour. "Half an hour! Half eternity!" Caddie might have said.

As Hugh had told her to, she held a newspaper up behind her glass of chemically brilliant orange squash, but she could neither drink nor read. She had more than a suspicion too that Hugh had overdone it; in the head scarf and dark glasses, crouched down in the chair and peering cautiously round the newspaper, she looked far more noticeable than a girl in a panama and school blazer, especially as the station was full of them, thought Caddie. Still, no one had looked at her or spoken; soon she almost wished that someone would, and could Hugh get back in time? What would she do if he didn't?

The hands of the refreshment-room clock crept round to a quarter past two. The school train would be moving off, the girls crowding the windows to wave as they were taken away to their safe enclosed world, as Caddie had been for three terms past, when the only ache had been leaving Stebbings and Topaz. Now the girls, Caddie herself in those days, seemed to her like children one sees in far-off, sunny pictures, unreal. This refreshment room was real, horribly real. Where was Hugh? Had Miss Prescott believed him, or had she snatched him off to telephone—but there would not have been time. Had she turned him over to the police? Caddie felt sick with fear; Miss Prescott, Gwyneth, a gentle couple, had turned into hunters, enemies; and Caddie was sick at heart; the numbness of her loss was wearing off, as it wears off from an amputation when pain begins to set in; and hers was an amputation that left her no reason for living that she could see. "If we do get Mother back, what use will it be to me now?" A terrible stifling lump was beginning to come in Caddie's throat. She had to take off the dark glasses because they were blurred with wetness, and her eyes flinched from the hard white light. We shall miss the train, thought Caddie. I don't care if we do. I shall never care about anything ever again. The lump was breaking into hurtful tearless sobs when Hugh's impatient voice sounded across the table. "Hurry up, slow coach. I have bagged two seats."

"But how did you know where Malcesine was?" asked Fanny.

"It was obvious," said Hugh. "We just worked backwards from the address. 'Italy; Verona,' That's a town," he had showed it to Caddie on the map. "Its province must be round it. Malcesine-sul-Garda; 'sul' means 'on,' I should guess, and Garda is that lake, see, near Verona, but Malcesine doesn't seem to be big, probably almost a village, and the railway doesn't seem to go there. We shall have to ask if we go to Verona or where."

Here Caddie had been of some help. "Remember when we used to go to Hamley's toy shop?" she asked.

"Hamley's?"

"When you collected trains." Like a red Indian or an elephant, she remembered every least thing Hugh had ever done and that always made him bad-tempered.

"My good child, what has that to do with Italy?"

"Only that, opposite Hamley's, there was an Italian travelling place."

"So there was," said Hugh. "How did you remember that?" Caddie had remembered it because in its windows were model painted carts drawn by little wooden horses with feathers on their heads. Every time they went to Hamley's she used to cross over and look at them. "It was an office only for Italy," she said. "We could ask there."

"You will be travelling alone?" They had stiffened. This is where we run into trouble, thought Hugh and Caddie's heart beat uncomfortably, but it seemed a routine question and when Hugh said, "Yes," in as chilly and grown-up a way as possible, the clerk had only gone on looking up the time table. There was no need, as Hugh had told her afterwards, for Caddie to say, "We are going to our mother."

"I see," said the clerk. "For Malcesine you must go by train to Desenzano."

"Desin . . ." That was a name that even Hugh had never heard of. "Would you write it down?" he said.

"Desenzano," the clerk wrote down and added, "It's one

of the only two railway stations on the lake. You can take the bus or ferry on from there."

Hugh had nodded, as if this were only confirmation of what he knew already but Caddie asked, "How do we get to Desenz . . . Desen . . ."

"Desenzano? You can go by air to Milan, the tourist fare is twenty-three pounds thirteen shillings single. Or by air to Paris, nine pounds eleven shillings, and catch the night express, ten-forty-four from the Gare de Lyon."

"Isn't there a through?" Hugh had asked to Caddie's admiration.

"Ah, yes, but that is slow. You leave Victoria at half past two in the afternoon, change at Paris. Leave there at midnight, arrive in Milan at one-thirty next day and on by the same train to Desenzano. You get there at three o'clock. The single fare is ten pounds, four shillings. As Miss, I think, is not fourteen, she would be half."

"That will suit us," said Hugh, and the clerk asked, "You have passports?"

"Naturally," said Hugh.

"They are valid?"

"Perfectly valid." As soon as Hugh had said that he knew it was the wrong answer, and Caddie once again had to blurt out, "Of course they are valid. They are new."

They had all three been given passports when they went to Switzerland for that Christmas holiday. Most children under sixteen travelled on their mother's, but for the reason that had not been divulged to them then, they were not on Fanny's. They had had their passport photographs taken; even one of those could not make Hugh look plain, though he was squinting, but Caddie's face looked lumpy and glowering. "Well, I didn't want to go to Switzerland. I wanted to stay at Stebbings and get on." She did not have to say "get on with what." Her hair was parted in a way that gave her an enormous forehead and she had hunched one shoulder up; "And that passport doesn't expire for another ten years!" said Caddie.

"But didn't anyone stop you? Ask you?" asked Fanny. "I thought children were not allowed to leave the country."

"They go backwards and forwards so much, to schools, service families, U.N.," said Rob, "that long ago they ceased to be remarkable. Children think nothing of it now."

"Some children," Caddie would have corrected him but this time Hugh could not help looking at him appreciatively. Here was one person who did not treat grown-up children "as morons," said Hugh.

The passports were kept in a pigeonhole in Darrell's desk. Here, too, were what Hugh had his eye on: envelopes in which Darrell kept the bits and pieces of foreign currency left over from his travels, not large sums but odd coins and small notes. "If we watched we could always know where Father was going by what money he takes," said Hugh.

When Darrell was away, he gave the key of the desk to Gwyneth, because it was here too that she kept the housekeeping money, the weekly cheques he gave her to cash, money for the children's school clothes, travelling money. Gwyneth was so afraid of losing the key, or having it stolen in this London she did not trust, that she wore the key on a cord round her neck day and night. How to get it without her knowing? The answer, with anyone as careful and staunch as Gwyneth, was nohow. "Though she would never suspect us," said Hugh.

That seemed to make it more their duty to protect Gwyneth and, "We must do it when the desk is open," said Hugh. "After all, it's only our passports and some currency we want."

Dear Gwyneth! It was a shame to trick her, "But we had to," said Hugh.

It turned out to be only too easy, which made Caddie ache for Gwyneth again. Easy and a little diabolical.

"I must pay the butcher," Gwyneth had said and went to the desk, Hugh and Caddie at her heels. Gwyneth unlocked the top and took out a small thickness of notes. "I cashed ten pounds," she said and carefully counted out three pound notes and put down the rest on the table. "Three pounds, four shillings," she said peering at the book. "It's much too dear, but there it is. That's London," and she took up her purse to find the silver. Hugh, standing behind Caddie, put his hand round, peeled off three more pound notes and slid them under the blotter. The next moment Caddie began to count what was left. "Did you say ten pounds?" she asked, not very steadily—"You are lousy as an actor," Hugh told her later—"You took three," called Caddie, "that should leave seven. There are only four here."

"Four!" Gwyneth's face turned mottled, then red. She snatched the notes from Caddie. "Four! But I'm certain. Look! Look in the drawer."

"Only a cheque," said Hugh, looking. "They must have fallen on the floor." As Gwyneth bent to look, Caddie saw him take the first envelope—each was labelled in Darrell's neat writing, "French Francs," "Pesetas," "Marks," "Kronen" and so on. Caddie lifted up the blotter for Gwyneth to search the desk top and lifted the three notes with it.

"Must be in my purse." Gwyneth was almost incoherent. She rushed to the kitchen, leaving the desk open. It was only a moment before Caddie again sang out, "Gwyneth, they are here. I have found them. Look. Under the blotter." Gwyneth came running back, her agitated steps shaking the flat, as Hugh, his pockets heavy, two flat shapes under his jacket, walked out of the study, whistling, but there had been no Italian small money, only the ten-thousand-lire note. Darrell must have put it there by mistake. "Ten *thousand* lire?" asked Caddie.

"It's only about six pounds."

"Then why couldn't they say so?" These thousands and hundreds that whirled round them in Italy—two hundred lire for an apple, a hundred and fifty for a roll with ham —seemed part of this twopence-coloured exaggeration that Caddie distrusted, "As much as Darrell would have done," Fanny said afterwards. Ten thousand lire, but, "It wasn't stealing," Caddie said now to Rob and Fanny. "We put our school money in to make it even. Hugh had four pounds, and I had two, which made it nearly right."

They would need, Hugh said, French and Swiss francs, Italian lire. "We had a few of our own Swiss from Christmas."

"How much did you have altogether?" asked Rob now.

"Nineteen new French francs."

"And sixteen centimes," said Caddie.

". . . in bits and pieces. Twelve Swiss francs."

"And seventy Swiss centimes."

"And we had some English," but Caddie was silent about the English money.

"Do we go through all those countries?" she had asked with dismay. Caddie, as Hugh said, had no sense of adventure. To her the many different countries only magnified her dread of going, and moments of that journey stayed with her forever. At Folkestone, for instance, when the long crocodile of passengers went down the covered way to the quay, it was a quarter-of-a-mile walk to the boat, they had had to pass the barrier of a man checking passports. In his tweed overcoat and string gloves, he looked to Caddie's imagination like a detective and she flinched. Hugh gave her a sharp blow in the back. "Go *on,* donkey," and, "If you look like that someone will think something is wrong and stop us."

On board the boat Hugh took Caddie to the cafeteria and gave her a cup of tea. He had a cup-cake and she had a fruit pie. It was disappointing, purple juice oozing through pastry that was grey, and inside it were hard cherries and chips of apple. The cafeteria smelled of rubber, steam, and wet people. Its decks seemed to swell and lift. "It's the sea," said Caddie.

"Yes. We have left."

"I wish I hadn't had that horrid fruit pie," said Caddie suddenly, and suddenly too, "Oh, I wish, wish Mother was here."

When they docked at Calais—which did not look very different from England—the loudspeaker blared: "Passengers for train thirty-two." "That's us," said Hugh appearing beside her. He had their tickets, two pieces of pink paper in a folder. "Train thirty-two, and *all* passengers for Paris, turn *right* at the bottom of the gangway," said the loudspeaker. "For these passengers, passports and customs will be on the train." "Which is where they may find us," said Hugh. He only said it to frighten Caddie and thrill himself. It had the desired effect.

Then there were the porters, terrifyingly big men in blue blouses and black caps, pushing through the crowd, shouting in French. On the quayside French notices hung all along the big shed: *"Douane," "Passeports ici," "Calais départ 7.40";* but in the train the notices were in four languages:

"Do not lean out of the window."
"Ne pas se pencher en dehors."
"Pericoloso sporgersi."
"Nicht hinauslehnen."

"We shall have to say *'Pericoloso sporgersi,'* " Caddie whispered to Hugh, "and *'Vietato fumare.'* " That was exciting, but as the evening came the journey had taken on a strange loneliness.

Outside the carriage windows the light grew blue. The little lonely French farms made Caddie think of Topaz, so that for a moment she forgot she was looking at France and not at England but *crépuscule,* which Hugh told her was the French for twilight, seemed to suit the dusk that was creeping across the fields, such wide fields; they made the villages seem far apart; now and again there was a solitary spire, a château. Even in the carriage it was *crépuscule,* then a man in the corner took out his travelling radio and a raucous French voice shattered the quiet.

There was a scene in the dining car which even now made her hot to remember. A man had come down the corridor ringing a little bell. Caddie had known at once what it was, "By instinct," said Hugh, "dinner," and they had followed the other passengers down the long train, past couchettes where whole families had seemed to be encamped, and luxurious *wagons-lits,* but when Hugh saw the dining car he had stopped short, looking at the white ornamented ceiling, red carpet, red plush chairs, the white tablecloths, white-coated waiters and, "It's terribly expensive," he had whispered.

Caddie was too hungry to care. "Ask how much it is."

"I can't. You can see it's too expensive," but the head waiter had already come and motioned them to a table, whisked their napkins to their laps, handed them the menu, and vanished to the next people.

"Présenté par le chef de Brigade Atlas," they read in gold letters. The rest was equally impressive: *"Potage cressonière."*

"Suprème de colinelino Éloise . . ." but they got no further. *"Prix fixe,"* read Hugh. *"18 N.F."*

"What does that mean?"

"It means we don't have any dinner."

"But . . . oh *Hugh!*"

"Eighteen new francs, eighteen hundred old. More than thirty shillings each."

"Thirty shillings for *dinner?*"

"Yes. Come on. I haven't got it."

"But . . ."

"I haven't got it. We haven't that much French money."

"Couldn't you ask if we could just have *one* thing? Even soup."

"You have to have the whole dinner."

Caddie was desperate. "Couldn't you say we are children?"

The look Hugh gave her was annihilating. He got up, threw down his napkin, and rushed past the head waiter from the car. Scarlet in the face, staggering against tables as the train rocked, Caddie followed him.

They ate the refreshment-room sandwiches from the net bag. On the ship Caddie had laid it on the rail and the bread was sodden.

Of the night Caddie remembered chiefly the long way through Paris from one station to the other; there had been glimpses of streets, some wide with trees, once one with *pavé* brightly lit; high houses with lighted windows, empty stations. It was like a train journey in a film. In an eternity of slow bumping motion and whining sounds, they sat silent in their corners, lights and shadows brushing their faces. Caddie fell half asleep and woke to grinding stop. Everyone in the carriage was standing up. It was the Gare de Lyon and the middle of the night. "How shall we know which train?" she had asked in a panic.

"It's that one," said Hugh, nodding opposite.

"Are you *sure*?"

"People are going into it, but we can walk up to the front and see its number."

"Its number? What's its number?"

"Five-nineteen."

"How do you know?"

"It's on our tickets." Hugh was being patient. "Come on. Then we can walk down and find the right coach."

Once again, Hugh's resource had filled Caddie with awe. He looked almost a little boy, red-eyed, his hair on end, dirt on his cheek, his shirt collar crumpled, but he knew what to do and the train opposite was five-nineteen.

It was in the early hours that regrets had begun. We shouldn't have come, thought Hugh. It was stupid. Typical Caddie! He looked at his sister on the seat opposite and almost hated her. Caddie, in those uneasy wakings, had thought it would have been better even to be in the flat. "It was silly, silly," the wheels seemed to hammer in her head. "Silly. We shall never get there."

Once she woke startled. "Hugh! Hugh!"

"Go to sleep," growled Hugh, but Caddie only slept in snatches. A French girl in their carriage had stayed out in the corridor all night talking, a girl in trousers. So Philippa was right; they do travel in trousers. A woman at Dôle was sitting on a bench, a pile of luggage beside her. What was she doing there at three in the morning? They woke to a dawn of eerie daylight and snow, with the train standing still. They were at Vallorbe, which Hugh said was the frontier. "Frontier of Italy?" Caddie had asked hopefully.

"No, you clot. Switzerland."

"But we did have breakfast in Switzerland," Caddie told Rob and Fanny. She thought well of that country ever afterwards.

This time the dining car had not looked as expensive; it had wooden and leather chairs, the tables laid with blue plates, each with a cup and saucer on it, the cups as big as

Darrell's bumper. A man came round with a basket of rolls calling: *"Deux pour chaque personne. Deux."*

"Only two," Hugh cautioned Caddie. Coffee and milk were poured into each cup and for each person, too, there was a miniature saucer of jam, two curls of butter. It was not much but it was good, and the whole world seemed curiously lighted. "They won't turn us back now. We have gone too far," said Hugh. They sat side by side, breaking the crisp rolls—people were dipping theirs *into* the coffee, Caddie saw with astonishment—and drinking the good coffee and they felt almost happy, but the breakfast was inordinately expensive, three francs fifty for a cup of coffee and two little rolls.

"And jam and butter," said Caddie.

"A lick of butter, a spoon of jam. Nearly five shillings!" Hugh had meant boldly to order another breakfast each, "but I haven't fourteen Swiss francs," he said.

The French girl left them at Brig and now people got in and out for short distances; only Hugh and Caddie had seemed to be travelling on and on. Their pink papers had been punched so many times that they were soiled and flimsy. The country people were friendly, but their cigarettes smelled, "Awful," said Caddie. "Pestilential," said Hugh. All the same, when a man offered him one he smoked it right through with aplomb. "I often smoke at school."

The smell clung to him. Neither of them could wash because the water did not run in the lavatories.

At the Italian frontier Domodossola, "What a name!" there were passports and customs but this time even Caddie was quite fearless, and, "We're in Italy. In Italy," she chanted as the train went on, but now tiredness was beginning to catch up with them, and the morning became a jumble. The journey seemed to be a pilgrimage of lakes; one of them was as Caddie had imagined Italy: houses, ochre-walled, dark-tiled; two islands in the middle of the water, flowers; magnolias, and what Caddie thought were roses until Hugh told her they were camellia bushes, growing as high as trees. "Is it Garda?"

"No, we haven't got to Milan yet. It's Maggiore," and then, almost suddenly, they were in Milan under a domed roof like a hangar, crowds on the platform, shoutings, hissing of steam.

It was now that Hugh failed to change the ten-thousand-lire note. On the platform were trolleys, "Selling lovely things," said Caddie. "And the man wouldn't take our note. He told us to go to the ticket office, to get change. The ticket office when the train might have gone any second, and we were *starving*."

Milan, Brescia. All the hot white afternoon, the train bumped over a flat cultivated plain, by low mountains; in the distance were others, not low but high and hazy blue, disappearing into cloud. They saw what must have been a monastery on a hill, its cloisters arched; oxen were ploughing in orchards of blossom, there were little villages, then, "Tidy yourself," said Hugh. "We're nearly there."

In the gravelled Desenzano station courtyard edged with begonias, a blue bus had been standing, the bus Fanny had so often heard passing the villa. Beside it a yellow notice board was written in large letters. Hugh and Caddie spelled out the names: "Salo, Gardone, Limone, Riva."

"Not Malcesine?" asked Caddie, stretched with anxiety.

"This goes the other way round the lake," but Hugh's quick eyes had seen another board laid down on top of others. "Sirmione. Garda. Malcesine. Riva." "That's the one we want," he said.

"But when does it go?"

"It's the next board, so it must be the next bus. They won't change ten thousand lire either. I had better take out note to the ticket office."

It seemed an hour to Caddie but in about twenty minutes a second bus rolled up and sure enough, the board went up. "Sirmione. Garda. Malcesine."

They got in. It looked more like a coach than a bus, with its armchair seats in red leather, each with a picture let into its back, its silvered racks and carpeted gangway.

The conductor came round. "Malcesine," said Hugh and held up two fingers. He pronounced it Mal-see-ziny with an accent on the "mal."

"That Teutonic bang," said Rob. "Mal-see-ziny," and the conductor did not understand. In the end Hugh had to show his map. "Ah, aah! Malcesine!" said the man as if it were spelt "Malchesinay," all the syllables even. Everyone in the bus laughed and Hugh, who never blushed, went red to the back of his ears.

It was a long way. They both went uneasily to sleep. There were fleeting impressions of houses and harbours, of roses climbing up trees. "Can that, too, really be true?" Of swinging away into the mountains, away from the lake, of stopping and going. People jostled and pushed into the bus; Caddie was surprised at the black pinafores of the school children, even big girls; Hugh winced at the guttural German of the tourists, his head was hurting. Only once did they wake right up; when an English woman who had come nearly all the way from Desenzano with them ate the pork pie and offered Hugh, who was sitting on the outside, a piece. "I thought she was going to give you one," he told Caddie. "Or I shouldn't have bolted it like that."

"You were starving too," said Caddie feelingly.

At last, "Malcesine. Malcesine," the conductor called out. They got up, but their legs were so stiff that they almost fell; the bus was not as comfortable as it had looked. Hugh lifted down the grips, Caddie brought the coats and bag, and they were left standing on a dusty road bordered with shops. "You got out at *Malcesine,*" said Fanny. "My poor darlings! Why the bus goes past our gate. The villa is two kilometres from there."

"I know," said Hugh. "We know, because we walked."

"What I don't understand," said Fanny when it was all told out, "what I don't understand is where you got the money. You had a few French francs, some Swiss ones, and the notes. You say you put your school money in the desk for compensation, I think that was very honest of you, but you had to pay your fares and in English money. They must have been nearly twenty pounds."

"Sixteen pounds, fifteen shillings, and sixpence," said Caddie.

"Where did you get it?"

There was a silence. Hugh looked at his feet. Caddie sank lower and lower in her chair until her face was hidden. At last, "Caddie sold Topaz," said Hugh.

"Sold Topaz!" It was a cry from Fanny.

"He had to be sold," said Hugh. "She couldn't keep him in the flat."

The last time he had said that had been in the flat itself. Caddie had been surprised at Hugh's indifference to the money part of their going. Twenty-three pounds, single by air, which was forty-six pounds for the two of them; ten pounds four shillings, for Hugh by cheap train, half for herself, at the very least fifteen pounds six shillings, and it mysteriously came to more than that. "Where shall we get so much?" she had asked innocently, never dreaming of what was coming, until, "I know where," said Hugh.

He was so clever in planning every detail that there had been no escape. "Dear Mr. Ringells," Caddie had written in the script that St. Anne's enforced. "My father says you would like to buy my pony, Topaz . . ."

"I can't Hugh. I can't write it."

". . . for twenty-five pounds," dictated Hugh, and he said, "You must—it must be in your writing, because Topaz is yours."

"As we have to live in London now we think it would be wise . . ." There were big blots on the page, but Hugh let it go; perfectionist though he was, even Hugh did not make Caddie write it twice. "My brother and I will come down and see you on Friday, about twelve o'clock. My father has asked me to write this letter."

"Sign it," said Hugh. "Yours sincerely, Candida Clavering."

"Yours sincerely, Candida Clavering," wrote Caddie and Hugh dictated: "N.B. Would you be able to pay me

in cash as I want to buy a tennis racquet and a bicycle."
But Caddie would not write that final treachery. Hugh
had to copy her script and write it himself.

He had everything planned: "We will tell Gwyneth I'm
taking you down to Whitcross to say good-bye to Topaz before school," which was true, except the "before school."
It was so reasonable that Gwyneth even gave them the
money for their tickets.

Topaz was in a stall. Mr. Ringells had brought him in,
"So your sister can see him," he told Hugh, and he said,
"Nice little pony." Nice little pony!

"His legs are muddy," Caddie whispered to Hugh.

"They were muddy at Stebbings," but there was no de-
nying Topaz was not the shining little pony he had been
under her care. His coat was rough, his ears dusty. "I
didn't leave a speck of dust on him." His feet were filled
with caked mud and dung. "He will get thrush," she said
severely to Mr. Ringells. He had water and hay and was
quite plump, but, "Do you ever give him carrots?" Her
eyes searched Mr. Ringells' face as if they would rake out
of him what kind of man he was. "Apples or sugar?"

"He gets plenty of petting from the children. Never you
fear," said Mr. Ringells, but Caddie did fear. "He will be
a riding-school pony, not anybody's own," she said.

She spoke once in the train on the way back. "He's used
to being loved. What will he *think?*" and Hugh gave her a
piece of advice. "For people, it's much better never to
think what animals must be thinking." Then he did something that Caddie had only known him do once before; he
put his arm round her and squeezed her. Long ago, on the

day he went to that first school, suddenly turning from the car, he had run back and given Caddie a violent wordless hug. The small far-away Caddie had been filled with love and wonder. In the Whitcross train she felt nothing at all.

Now, on the villa terrace, it was Fanny who was weeping. She had jumped up. "Caddie, we must get Topaz back, make Mr. Ringells sell him back to us. Rob and I will have a house soon and probably in the country. We will buy Topaz back, wherever he is, and keep him for you. I promise," but the figure bowed in the chair at the end of the table never moved and Rob stopped Fanny. "I should leave her alone just now."

"But you don't know what this means, Rob."

"I can guess."

"Hugh, how could you? How could you?"

"What do you mean, how could I?" Hugh's head came up. He looked fierce. "It wasn't I who made Caddie sell Topaz," he said. "It was you."

"Precisely," said Rob before Fanny could cry out. They were getting into a tangle of emotions and he made the words brisk. "All the same, we mustn't promise what we can't do. By the time we find a house, Caddie may be too big for a pony and . . ." but Fanny could not bear the way Caddie sat silently bowed in the chair.

She broke away from Rob, and went to Caddie, kneeling down by her. "Perhaps we can't buy Topaz back," she said. "But I shall never forget, never, what you have done to get to me. To sell Topaz." Fanny's voice was broken. "And that long long journey." She held out her hand to

Hugh. "Oh my darlings, if you knew what it means . . . that you ran away to me."

Hugh was silent but Caddie raised an indignant face. "We *didn't* run away to you," said Caddie. "We came to fetch you."

VII

The silence that greeted Caddie's words was like a challenge: nobody answered her, nobody commented; Fanny got up and went back to her chair. Rob's face was expressionless but presently he asked, "Your father should be back today?"

"He was supposed to come last night."

"Then he should have had my telegram."

Fanny turned in sudden alarm. "Rob, what did you say in it?"

"That I was putting Hugh and Caddie on the plane at Milan this evening."

"*This* evening? No, Rob."

"Yes. There's a plane that leaves Milan at six-twenty-five. It's not that we don't want you," he said to Hugh and Caddie. "Of course we do and we hope you will come back, but, you see, it has to be with permission."

"Rob!" It was a wail. "After all that?"

"After all that, I'm afraid."

"When it was so brave and enterprising."

"It was enterprising." Hugh was glad that Rob dismissed the bravery. "Enterprising, but wrong, legally and morally, and we mustn't encourage it."

"Hugh looks ill, Rob. Not fit to travel."

"One more night won't hurt him. It's a short flight." At Fanny's unhappy face he softened. "We made a bargain, dear."

"I didn't make a bargain."

"You did when you let the divorce go through." And he said more gently, "We must leave at three-thirty. You must have them ready."

"I can't."

"You must."

"I can't."

"Then I must. Caddie, you had better get that dress ironed again and are your shoes clean? If not, Hugh can . . ." but Hugh had got up, his hands clasped to his stomach. He gave a moan, took two or three uncertain steps, then rushed to the balustrade and began to retch. Before Fanny could reach him, he was violently sick, "All down the roses," said Caddie.

"Are you sure he's not malingering?"

Darrell's far-away voice on the telephone was curtly hostile—naturally, thought Rob. That the children should run away too must have been a cruel cut. Rob could imagine the chagrin was worst over Hugh; even though he was at odds with Darrell, males should stand together. Run to his mother! Darrell, of course, did not know the reason.

"I don't think he could malinger as seriously as this," said Rob. "He has food pois—" but he was interrupted.

"I am always suspicious of Hugh."

Rob was suspicious too, but, "The doctor says . . ." he began.

"He can twist his mother round his little finger, I warn you. She is foolish about that boy. Wrap him up and send him back all the same."

"He can't travel."

"They look after you very well on these planes; Caddie is with him and I can meet them."

"He can't travel," said Rob more loudly.

"Why not?" and Rob almost shouted. "He's being sick. He has diarrhoea and fever."

"Are you sure?"

"You ought to be here," said Rob.

The whole Fiorita had been turned upside down. Rob and Fanny had got Hugh upstairs, Celestina and Giulietta running after with basins and towels, exclamations and confused orders, while Caddie waited, pale with fright, on the stairs. It was like convulsions; Hugh's light body seemed torn apart with retching, then doubled up with the spasms of diarrhoea. Fanny had been calm and efficient, and as fierce as a tiger, thought Rob. Giulietta had been told peremptorily to be quiet, Celestina to help hold Hugh, Rob to go over to the hotel and telephone the doctor—they used the Hotel Lydia for local calls.

"Doctor Isella is coming. He will be here in a few minutes."

"Doctor Isella?" and Fanny, to whom Italy had become all that was good, turned unexpectedly insular. "Isn't there an English doctor? Or at least an American?"

"Italian doctors are among the best in the world," said Rob but he could see she did not believe him.

"I can't even speak to him."

"I can." Under her calmness, Rob could feel the tension and remorse. "Hugh will be all right, dear." It was odd that it was his comforting that brought an edge of hysteria into her competence. "It will be my fault, my fault if he isn't."

"Nonsense," said Rob. "It was his fault for eating that piece of pie. Caddie didn't."

"Italian food, I suppose," Darrell had said on the telephone.

"It was English actually," Rob had said smoothly. "An English woman on the bus gave him a piece of pork pie. At least we think it must have been that. It was the only thing he ate that Caddie didn't."

Fanny had been icily furious over Darrell's remarks. "Malingering! How dare he say that. He has never been fair to Hugh, never. How could he put on sickness like this, a high temperature?"

"Not high, darling. Only a hundred and two."

"Only! That is high for food poisoning. Doctor Isella . . ." and she accused Rob. "You take Darrell's part because he's a man."

"I don't. Hugh's a sick boy."

"Then how could he put it on?"

Rob did not know, nor did Caddie, yet she, like her father, was not sure. It was Hugh's luck, of course, but how did he attract the luck? Caddie privately thought he could do anything. As Gwyneth said, "Hugh always has the last word."

By lunchtime Doctor Isella had stopped the sickness; his

injections, charcoal pills, potions of weak tea were beginning to wash away the effects of the pie. "Short and sharp,"
said Doctor Isella, who did speak English. Hugh was weak,
still fevered, full of headache, hollow-eyed, tender-
skinned, and filthy-tongued but it was over. When Caddie
tiptoed into the room—he had been moved into the big
bedroom—she had seen his eye peeping out from under
the compress on his forehead and the eye had a glint, au-
thentically Hugh.

"Hullo, Hugh."

"Hullo." It was a croak.

"You're better?"

"Not dead yet," and he whispered. "At least it's put paid
to them pushing us off back."

"You are very, very clever," said Caddie earnestly.

"Clever!" Fanny's voice came from behind her. "What
is clever about an attack of poisoning? What *is* all this?
You make Hugh sound diabolical."

"What is diab—"

"Devilish," said Hugh and winked. The wink heartened
Caddie, who was very much dismayed. She could not know
the chaos in Fanny; the contrition and guilt over their
journey, over the selling of Topaz, Hugh's illness, the
feeling that Rob was criticizing her, and a subtle dislike of
herself for feeling an echo of what Rob had said, to her,
"Children are always welcome." "At *any time?*" Rob had
said and though Fanny would not admit it, Hugh and Caddie were an interruption. Caddie could not know this, it
only seemed to her that Fanny was too angry, "Too angry
for what I said," and she mumbled, "I only meant . . ."

"Yes, what did you mean?"

"I meant, Rob—Mr. Quillet—said we had to go and now we can stay here."

"Not you," said Fanny. "You are going back to London."

"Caddie can come back," Darrell had said.

"Alone?" Rob had asked. "Wouldn't that be rather dismal?"

"Dismal?" The word was barked down the telephone.

"Yes," said Rob. "She's unhappy as it is." After a hesitation he added, "You know she sold her pony, Topaz, to get here."

That produced a pause; then, "I wondered how they got the money." The implication seemed to sink in. "The devil they did! What business . . ." which made Rob ask, out of sheer mischief, "Wasn't it her pony? I thought she won it," and Darrell had said, more curtly than ever, "She must come back. She's missing school."

Fanny's anger could not last when she saw Caddie's stricken face. "I'm sorry, darling, but Father insists on it—he can, you know. Rob is taking you to Milan in half an hour."

In the car Caddie sat as far away from Rob as she could get and kept her face turned away to the window.

Fanny had mistaken her frozen silence for fright. "You will be quite all right. Rob will speak to the air hostess and Father will be waiting for you at London airport." Rob seemed to understand the silence, and respect it; he did not try and beguile her with talk as most adults would have done, but drove in a silence as deep as her own.

For Caddie the silence was partly shock. Until Rob had

issued his edict on the terrace, it had not occurred to her that they could be returned. Indeed, and childishly as she saw now, she had expected Fanny to decide straight away to come back to England with them. Expected? Took it for granted was nearer, as if the sight of them, or at any rate of Hugh, would have been enough. Now she was beginning to see that it could not happen without a fight and one in which they might not win—even if I could have started fighting, thought Caddie in despair.

"I'm here," Hugh would have said. "Don't you trust me?" but Caddie, unwillingly, did not; if Hugh grew to like Rob, and she had to concede that would be easy, he might go over, thought Caddie.

She stole a glance at Rob as he drove, looking ahead. His eyes were hidden by dark glasses so that he looked masked and he was all alien to Caddie: the darkness of his sallow skin, his head with the hair growing so far back that he was almost bald in front—I never knew someone bald could be attractive. People's faces, Philippa said, were divided into horses, birds, and puddings. Rob's, with its leanness and curved nostrils, was unmistakably a horse, which perhaps was why, in spite of herself, he appealed to Caddie. She looked at his wrists coming out from the silk shirtcuff, strong brown wrists with a down of black hair; at his hands on the wheel. They did not have the big knuckles, the thick skin she, Darrell's daughter, had always associated with a man, yet they were a man's hands for all their fineness, big, strong-looking, with, on the left one, a little finger ring with a dull green carved stone. She would have liked to ask what the carving was but she would not speak to Rob. There was no doubt that he was a stronger enemy than they had dreamed and it seemed she had really sold Topaz for nothing. A tear rolled out of Caddie's eye and slid down her nose but, with her face turned away to the window, she thought Rob did not see.

He did not need to see. Disquiet had been growing in him ever since the bravado of that first hour when he had taken Fanny away to San Vigilio, disquiet and a misery against which he had to tighten his mind; and he thought firmly, even if I am guilty I will not be made to feel guilty by a little girl. There was, though, nothing he could do to make either of them feel better and he drove on in silence.

All round them the brightness of the Venetian spring unrolled; neither of them saw it. Rob did not comment when they swung onto the *autostrada* and he paid at the gate, and Caddie said nothing when the speedometer needle moved up to eighty-five, ninety, a hundred kilometres. They by-passed towns and suburbs, came through a large factory town and then to the suburbs of Milan itself. Rob said then, "We're nearly at the airport. Just think! Two hours from the take-off, you will be in London." To Caddie this was only another proof of the way adults could blot one's efforts out. Two hours! To reduce that aeon of uncomfortable, dirty, hungry, and frightening travel to that! "Then it will be all over," said Rob. He meant it to be comforting but Caddie said nothing at all.

"And you will come back and stay with us, perhaps in the summer holidays."

"Thank you," said Caddie, "but that will be too late."

"Too late?"

"Mother will have married you by then."

After that, at the airport too, they sat far away from one another.

The little temporary airport was crowded and Rob was suddenly resentful. The crowds, the stark white light, the rasping loudspeaker voices, the ashtray stands with their stale whiffs of smoke, the bins of dirtied cardboard cups, the scattered cellophane wrappings and newspapers on the floor, were hideous. Tired children staggered and cried, mothers scolded in voices like amplified hens, thought Rob; men argued, older children played and shouted. It seemed a day-nightmare and—I should have been at the Fiorita, he thought, with the peace of a day's work done: Fanny waiting for me alone on the terrace: a look at our star, a walk perhaps in the garden, a drink, dinner, and here, because of this plain little lump of a girl . . . His voice was terse as he tried to be kind to Caddie. She knew he was trying to be kind and she was even terser.

"Would you like some coffee? Lemonade, before your flight?"

"No thank you."

"A sandwich? An ice would be better—it's fearsomely hot. An ice?"

"No thank you."

"A magazine? Or wouldn't you like a book?" There was a small kiosk and he said, "Look. That little silver model is Milan cathedral. You could take that home to show where you have been? An Italian peasant doll? One of those souvenirs?"

Caddie did not even answer. The brown eyes flicked a glance at his tactlessness and went back to their fixed look. Rob had seen that look before, on a famine child in India, doomed hopelessness; but that's exaggerated, he thought angrily. Caddie is neither hopeless nor doomed. She is going back to a father who wants her, and to an excellent school, but Caddie still did not take that look off her face.

"Listen," he wanted to say. "This all seems dreadful now but it will be all right," or "When you are older you will understand." Even, "Forgive me. You see I love your mother," but in the face of that look they were easy phrases, empty comfort. And why shouldn't she hate me, poor little toad, thought Rob. He ended by saying nothing but sat looking at his hands, turning them over, examining the fingers while Caddie, at the other end of the bench, looked at her feet in her brown walking shoes that were nearly as flat and large as her sandals.

"British European Airways announce the departure of Flight 507 for London. Will passengers please . . ." "This is for you," said Rob. "Come along," and, picking up the grip Fanny had packed, he led the way to the customs barrier. "This is Candida Clavering, travelling to London," she heard him begin to the girl in her pale blue suit and cocked cap. "She has her passport, tickets, and five pounds in English money," and to Caddie, "You just follow the blue lights. Here's your grip. Good-bye."

"Good-bye," and, "I should have left then," said Rob to Fanny later. "Not stayed to watch her out of sight."

The corridor from the barrier to the customs and waiting rooms was long. Other passengers walked with Caddie, around her and past her, almost brushing over her: Italian businessmen in heavy suits, black hats, with opulent pigskin brief cases: women in high heels that tapped briskly, their arms laden with coats, handbags, bucket bags, magazines. Two walked each side of Caddie as if she were not there, one bumping her with a bandbox.

Carrying her raincoat, the grip swinging, she looked small and unprotected in the skimpy green checked frock, green blazer, extinguishing hat. Why can't they send her to a school where the uniform isn't so ugly? thought Rob irritably. The irritation was no good, already his heart was betraying him; the back of her arms looked so young, and unexpectedly thin, "Like a lamb's bones," he told Fanny.

One of the women, turning to speak to a man, brushed Caddie in the face with the coat she carried—and didn't apologize, thought Rob, which made him unreasonably hot with indignation. Can't they see she's only a child, and travelling alone? But Caddie was too old, and too young, to arouse any interest and she only turned her head away and went on, though Rob saw that even her buttocks shrank from the women and once again Rob was reminded of a small bullock, but this time driven down the ramp. He seemed to have a whole menagerie of animals for Caddie. It was her helplessness, he thought irritably.

At the far end of the corridor, passengers had to show their passports and tickets. That seemed to startle Caddie. She put the grip down between her feet—in case it should be stolen? thought Rob—and began to search through her wallet. The ticket and passport were not there. "In your blazer pocket," Rob wanted to shout but he was too far away. The air hostess was standing, not looking at Caddie but over her head to where two other passengers were fumbling with their papers, her hand held out; it was automatic, Rob knew, but it looked relentless and he could see Caddie was getting in a panic. She began to search through the raincoat pockets, holding it out. The other passengers began to chafe, a man pushed past her, "And suddenly," Rob told Fanny afterwards, "I couldn't stand it any longer. I ran back to the desk. I had signed for her as her stepfather," he told Fanny.

"Stepfather!" Fanny sounded as if that were a shock. "But . . . you are not really that."

"I suppose that's what we have to call me," said Rob. "They thought I was mad, of course, but they spoke over the loudspeaker and Caddie was fished out and given back to me."

She had been stunned by being made to go, now she was shocked. "But . . . they will be very angry with you," she said.

"I expect they will," said Rob. "I'm a fool."

Fanny later was to probe. "But why?" she asked bewildered. "Why?"

"God knows," said Rob.

That answer would have satisfied Caddie. This sudden intervention was in Greek-god style. The face she turned to Rob when he announced they were going back to the Villa Fiorita was still white but transformed, luminous, eyes shining. Rob did not flatter himself it was happiness; it was only relief. He hoped that the sudden hollow feeling in himself was only hunger and, walking away from the airport to the car park, he said, "Caddie, shall we sink our differences, just for an hour, and have dinner together?"

"You took her to the Continentale? *Caddie!*"
"Why not?"

"In those dreadful clothes?"

"The clothes didn't matter and the dining room there is good."

"But what a waste."

"I was there too," said Rob, "and it wasn't a waste. She enjoyed it." He corrected himself. "*We* enjoyed it."

Caddie had not been in such a hotel before. Coming from the foyer, with its rows of desk clerks—they bowed to Rob as if they knew him—and into the immense marble-pillared lounge she had felt as if she had walked into a palace and, shaken out of herself, she was still as trans-formed as in that miracle moment at the airport; like the princess in the fairy tale who shook off the frog, thought Rob. He liked the way she sat upright on the banquette in their corner, while the brown eyes that were so like Fanny's took in the room with its white arches, pale walls, great baskets of flowers. The next table had been made ready for a party with small vases of pale pink tulips, "One for every person!" said Caddie, and in its centre a minia-ture fountain bubbled pale pink water. "A fountain on a table!" she said. She looked a little askance at the knives, forks, and glasses arranged in front of her, the size and starchiness of the napkin the waiter unfurled and laid across her knees, but her manners were so naturally polite and modest—"Like yours," Rob told Fanny. "You did very well with her there"—that there was none of the gaucheness of every day. "Yes, Caddie can rise to an occa-sion," said Fanny. Looking across the table, Rob had seen, for the first time, some promise of beauty in this ugly duckling; it was in the shape of her face, a peach bloom that had come up under the freckles, and those will fade, he thought. Her hair, under the shaded lights, had points of gold in its ginger which looked a deep red brown, and her eyes, tonight, were astonishing; but Rob was too hungry to look for long at Caddie and they ate, "Extraordinary things," as she told Hugh afterwards. "There were artichoke hearts with brains"—"Ugh!" said Hugh—"a mixed grill of fish with squids, tiny octopus, and prawns and mussels, veal cooked in wine."

"At ten o'clock at night!" said Fanny.

"It was ten o'clock," said Rob. "Remember I had to arrange a message to Darrell at London Airport. I tried to telephone him but couldn't. That took two hours. Caddie wanted to go to the ladies' room, that seemed perpetual," said Rob unfairly. "Then we had to drive to Milan."

"But still, a full-scale dinner at ten."

"This is *Italy*," said Rob patiently. "In Rome we never dine before half past ten."

Dinner had just ended when something happened to Caddie that she, child of Fanny and Darrell, had not experienced before: she was forgotten. A man came into the restaurant, an Italian, she thought, looking at his small, thick-set body, his hair that was cut in a crew cut, thick and brown, his eyes black as berries in a sunburned face. They searched the room as he stood for a moment in the entrance, then lit up as he caught sight of Rob. "Rob! They told me you were here."

"Aldo!" Rob had jumped up.

"This is wonderful! Wonderful!" Then they sat down. "I have been sending you telegrams all afternoon. Renato says there is no telephone at that tiresome villa."

"None, thank God," said Rob.

"But that's *impossible.*"

Rob smiled. "I don't want even you, Aldo, ringing up." As Aldo looked at Rob, the bright eyes were very friendly. "You are happy, Rob?"

"Happier than I could have imagined," and Aldo stretched out a hand and squeezed Rob's arm. Then, for a brief moment, Rob did remember Caddie.

"Caddie, this is Prince Brancati." Did Rob say *prince?* As a well-trained child, she had stood up; now she wondered if she ought to curtsy, but the prince shook hands with her and that was the last time they remembered her—"For hours," said Caddie.

Prince Brancati was, Fanny told her afterwards, one of the many strange and floating people attached to Rob's work. She had already learned that every picture seemed to have them. What were they? Producers? Associate producers? "I don't know but it's something to do with the money part," said Fanny vaguely, "which is probably why they seem to have a say on the casting and scripts."

"But Prince Aldo"—Caddie could not remember Brancati—"said he hadn't any money." It was one of the things he said. "I have no money, Rob," and he spread his hands out like that.

"He knows the people who have, and he has big estates and a castle," said Fanny.

Now he bestowed a fleeting smile on Caddie and turned back to Rob. "'Tonight is *Rigoletto* and I heard today, only today at four o'clock, that Renata Scotto, the Gilda, is ill. They have flown the little Letti up from Rome. Bianca

Letti. You remember my telling you? She is ver-y ver-y pretty." He tapped Rob's arm to emphasize this. "Beautiful, besides the voice. She is singing Gilda. Gilda! tonight. It's a unique chance." He looked at his watch. "We could be in time for the third act. Guido will let us in, but we must go at once. Rob, I tell you . . ." and he lapsed into Italian; a stream of it went from him to Rob, from Rob to him, over Caddie's head. If they must go, why don't they? she thought, but no, the waiter brought more coffee, brandies, a cigar for the prince and still they sat on talking, talking.

Caddie feared she was growing sleepy and put her elbows on the table, stretching her eyes open with her fingers, but her eyes still seemed to have an annoying way of curling up at the corners.

She suddenly and unexpectedly gave an enormous yawn. Made awake by shame, she glanced at Rob to see if he had seen but he and Prince Aldo were still talking, cigarette and cigar smoke curling between them, Rob's fingers flicking away the ash as if he were excited.

She was forced to intrude. She was growing more and more uncomfortable, trying not to wriggle on her chair. At last, "Mr. Quillet—Rob," she said desperately.

"Rob."

"Rob, *please* Rob . . . Rob, I must . . ." and the prince broke off. "Rob, she is asking you . . ."

"Rob, is there a ladies' room here?" She said it far too loudly and blushed but the waiter had understood and was motioning her to follow him across the floor.

"Wait." Rob fished in his pocket and brought out a note. "Give this to the signorina."

"But . . . Mother gave me some pennies."

"Give the signorina this," and he turned back to the prince. He was right. She did not need the pennies and the ladies' room was not at all like the airport. It was as full of grandeur and marble as the lounge; even the cubicles were pale glossy pink and there were marble basins, hot water, immaculate small towels, a signorina in black with starched lace cuffs. Washed and feeling very much better, Caddie returned. She had been afraid they would go without her, but no, they were still talking.

At last the bill was brought, a pile of the outsize Italian notes put on the plate, and they stood up. The kind waiter brought her things. She had not time to pick them up properly; if he had not whisked her past the table to the door, she was sure she would have been left behind. The men had gone, still talking, and she, with her coat and grip trailing, ran after them through the marble lounge and hall, past all the people, out into the noisy Milanese night. The street was full of traffic, the pavements swarming, trams clanking past, as Caddie hurried after Rob and the prince, dodging people or bumping into them, coming up short at a traffic light where a man flung out an arm to stop her, then running to catch up with them, but they had not far to walk before they turned into a big cream-coloured portico hung with theatre bills.

There had been only one night between this and the journey, only two anxious and exhausting days, and now Caddie was so dogged with tiredness and filled with good food, that the night began to behave like a dream, in which things came nearer and then went away, swelled up into distinctness and faded, with curious blanks in between. She remembered standing in a lit space, thick carpeting under her feet, an impression of mahogany, brass, marble, crystal, while the prince and Rob talked with a tall man in evening dress whose name seemed to be Guido. Do all Italian men's names end in *o*? asked Caddie's tired brain—Aldo, Renato, Giacomino, Mario? Women in *a*? Celestina, Giulietta, and now this Bianca of whom they were all talking. Or was she a woman? A coloratura, they said; it sounded to Caddie like a cockatoo.

Then they were in a wide corridor, cream-walled with countless little cream doors lettered in gold. They were led by another man in black, wearing a heavy silver chain round his neck. "Four and twenty white mice, with chains around their necks" . . . but this was a man, not a mouse. Was it true? thought Caddie, or was she dreaming?

The man opened one of the doors, someone whispered, *"Silenzio. Fate silenzio.* Absolute quiet," and she was steered into what at first seemed darkness, a red darkness and a din of sound. She felt hardness, covered in velvet against her hands, that was the rim of a box; velvet against her legs, and found a chair into which she sank, though first she had almost sat on the floor. Then before her opened a width of light, so violently lighted that her eyes could not take it in, yet below the light, they caught what seemed to be hundreds of movements. After a moment she saw they were movements of arms working, hands holding the bows of violins, cellos, violincellos, basses, fingers working on them and on wind instruments, a hand poised over drums, hands lifting gleams of brass that were trumpets, hands held still on harpstrings where a harp frame caught the light. It was a huge orchestra pit and, "You were in La Scala," Fanny told her afterwards.

"What is La Scala?"

"The most famous opera house in the world," but the ignorant Caddie did not really know what opera was. "A play, stupid," said Hugh. "When all the words, or most of the words, are sung."

"Why?" asked Caddie and she could have said, "We didn't go to a play. We went to look at Bianca Letti and hear her sing." That much Caddie had fathomed. Rob was looking at Bianca Letti, hearing her, for the part of Berengaria, in something called *Saladin*. "Just look at her, Rob. That is all," Prince Aldo had pleaded. "Just look at her."

At first Caddie was deafened. They were almost on top of the orchestra and, too, she was blinded by the light. They were so close to the stage that when her eyes did grow accustomed, she could see the cracks in the paint of the scenery, the lines of the floorboards, the crease in the Duke's top boots, powder on his slashed sleeves, the make-up on the singers' faces, particularly white as flour on the hunchback's. Guido told her he was Rigoletto though who and what Rigoletto was she did not know. While Prince Aldo and Rob whispered together, Guido did pay some attention to Caddie. "Enrico Rufini is singing Rigoletto," he whispered, which added to the confusion.

On the stage was what seemed to be a hut, brightly lit, and a great stone bridge outside a wall with cypresses; Caddie recognized those from the villa garden. Inside the hut was a young man, "The Duke," whispered Guido, and a woman in red and yellow striped skirts, a red shawl over a white blouse, red beads, a fall of dark hair. "The Maddalena," Guido whispered again and Prince Aldo turned his head and said, quite loudly, "She is nothing." Outside the hut, the hunchback in a long cape swung and lumbered about the stage and with him was a girl, young, with a golden plait that hung over the shoulder of her long grey cloak. Its hood made a frame for a small face, and Caddie could see it was indeed very, very pretty. When it lifted, there was a flash from a pair of great dark eyes. "That is Gilda, Bianca Letti."

Caddie was aware now of a sea of heads below her, the auditorium, and of honeycombed tiers of boxes like the one they were in, rising up to the roof with gleams of deep rose, deep red. "On gala nights," Guido told her in his soft whisper, "it is all carnations. On the front of every box is a wreath, carnations everywhere, but then it is not opera," said Guido, "it is a dress parade." His whisper had carried and, "Ssh! *Basta!*" someone hissed from the box next door.

The orchestra seemed to take a breath and as a rocket soars up and bursts into a rain of coloured stars, it burst into music, gay, pronounced, and the fat young man in the thigh boots and doublet, the Duke, began to sing.

At the end, the clapping burst too, but Caddie, her hands between her knees, her face fixedly turned to the stage waited as if she were mesmerized, waited through the recitative until, once again, there was that breath. Then the four began to sing together, Gilda and Rigoletto outside the hut, the Duke and Maddalena in. "The quartet, *Bella figlia dell'amore,*" said Guido.

"What is *dell'amore?*" Caddie's whisper was too loud and, "Ssh! *Basta,*" came even more fiercely. She shrank with shame but Rob, as if he had suddenly remembered her, put his hand for a moment on her knee. "Listen to Gilda's notes," he said.

Listen to Gilda. Caddie could not understand a word of what they sang, nor did she know what the opera was about, except that the hunchback and Gilda seemed in terrible distress but as she listened to those four voices, it was as if a skin parted in her mind, something tight and stretched in which she had been sealed and against which her unhappiness had boiled and seethed. For days she had been too small a Caddie for all that was in her. "I have grown too big for me," she could have said. Now she escaped, let out on the sound of that music, sound that she could not have believed. Oddly enough, it was to do with Topaz. What could a little pony in England have to do with singing in Milan? Yet, mysteriously, she seemed to be stroking Topaz's neck again; his mole warmness had vibrated and flowed under her hand, as this singing vibrated and flowed through her so that she seemed to be stroking, not a pony but life itself.

Up and up went Gilda's voice and Caddie seemed to be going with it as if she were one of Celestina's birds let out of its cage. Then Rigoletto's and the Duke's blended with Gilda's, Maddalena's came up in such an orgy of sound that Caddie was lost, yet still she knew it was there; the bigness could not be split up, not into an individual girl and her pony, into a man's or woman's voice. The pony was more important than the girl, the song than the singers. Caddie sensed that—and how few people sense it—but it and they were one. It was all a oneness and—everything is everything, thought Caddie certainly, on the tide of that singing.

It was only a few minutes, a glimpse. Afterwards it was as if, for a moment, she had laid her hand on truth, tried to grasp it and her hand was empty—but not quite empty, because she knew now it was there. The quartet ended, there was a thunder of clapping, and Caddie was once again a small alien girl who had somehow got into this box. Nor did she catch another glimpse again, in the rest of the singing.

She was interested in the stage storm, in the way the cypresses really bent and shook but the washing on the roof did not shake enough, she thought critically but slowly emotion, dinner, and tiredness overcame her, the tide of sound on the stage seemed to sink away and she must have gone to sleep. She woke with clapping ringing in her ears, clapping and shouting. The lights had gone on and the singers were bowing in front of a vast velvet curtain, carnations were being thrown down—forever afterwards, carnations, for Caddie, meant Milan—some hit the singers' heads, the front of the stage was strewn, but she could not stay to look. The men were leaving the box. She was just in time to stumble out after Rob, Prince Aldo, and Guido. Blinking in the brilliance of the corridor she asked, "Rob, are we going home?"

"Going round," said Rob. She had not time to ask, "Going round what?" because they were already walking away, one of them each side of Rob, talking, gesticulating. "We shall be quicker," Guido was saying, "to go outside and in at the stage door." Once more they were out on the street, threading through a café of little tables half hidden by trees in tubs, while the crowd milled round the Scala entrance. Then they turned down a side street into a paved courtyard where cars were waiting; Guido spoke to a man in a grey uniform and led them up a flight of stone stairs, Caddie's legs aching as she tried to keep up, through a great many doors and rooms until, "We're on the stage!" cried Caddie.

It seemed to her eyes enormous. A gang of men in overalls was working and great expanses of scenery were being wheeled into position, others were going down through the floor—again was she dreaming or was it real? But again too she could not stay to look; as it was she had to scamper over the bare boards to catch the others but, I have been on a stage, a stage, thought Caddie. Even Philippa had never done that.

They climbed another staircase, went through more doors until they came to a pair of heavy swing ones and here they stepped into quiet, a small rich corridor, with a dark red carpet—and two dear little chandeliers, thought Caddie. She was wide awake now. The corridor was lined with mahogany doors at one of which Guido knocked. It was opened a crack, Guido had a whispered conversation, the door was opened wide, and they all went in.

It was a box of a dressing room, mahogany again, with a sofa covered in old gold velvet and gold velvet chairs to match. Down one side was a long open wardrobe filled with dresses; a woman in a white overall was hanging up the doublet and cape of lavender velvet that Gilda had just worn. There were other dresses, a shelf of crowns, a cap of pearls, from which hung a plait of gold hair; Gilda's plait, then, did not belong to Bianca Letti. The room was full. "Who were all those people?" Caddie asked Rob afterwards. "Bianca's mother and grandmother," said Rob, "and every relation she has living in Milan." The grandmother sat in state in a chair. One of the men was eating a roll split with sausage and a little boy was playing with a carnation, perhaps one of those that had fallen on Gilda's head. He was not more than three or four years old, and, "It must have been nearly midnight," Caddie told Fanny. Then, from an inner room, Gilda or Bianca came out, not dressed but wearing a short little dressing gown of white nylon with blue roses, her face covered in cold cream.

That astonished Caddie. Even Philippa would not have come out in front of strangers like that, but the cold cream did not disguise Bianca's beauty, "And for a prima donna to be beautiful is extremely rare," Rob was to tell Caddie. Bianca was also shy—but Rob talked to her in a soothing, gentle voice. Caddie noticed how the other men, the whole room, became silent, from respect, she thought, and presently Bianca sat down with Rob and began to talk too, but all the while Rob's eyes were examining and watching her just like the judges with a pony at a show, thought Caddie.

The powder in the air made Caddie sneeze, her eyes were stinging from tiredness, but it did not seem as if the night were over yet. The voices were in full spate. There was a suitcase in the corner. She sat down on it to wait.

Next morning Celestina, going out to hang her bird-cages in the magnolia tree, heard voices raised high in argument: Signor Quillet and the Signora. "It was only an argument," said Fanny. She insisted it was not a real quarrel but it began to sound like a quarrel. *"È rientrato alle tre!* At three o'clock!" said Celestina to Mario who, on his way to clean the Mercedes, paused to listen too.

"Three o'clock. *L'ho redito,* I heard him," said Mario.

"English ladies no allow that," said Celestina.

"E chi sposerebbe una Inglese!" said Mario, but Celestina and Mario were not just. Fanny had not even reproached Rob—not about that.

It was when Giulietta brought their coffee, up to their room, "The Signor was so late," Fanny had said and, *"Un altro piatto e una tazza,"* she said in her halting Italian, "Another cup and plate. For Hugh, *per il Signorino."*

"È per la piccola Signorina?" asked Giulietta. "Mees Caddie."

Fanny stared. "The little Signorina is in England. *Inghilterra."*

"Non è in Inghilterra, è a letto . . . in beds," said Giulietta with a great effort.

"In bed?" asked Fanny incredulously.

"Sì, sì," and Rob woke up and explained and Fanny had exploded into something like wrath.

"But three o'clock in the morning, Rob, when a child was with you!"

"I had her with me," said Rob, "and it didn't hurt her.

She slept part of the time. Of course she had had some wine."

"You gave her *wine?*"

"This is Italy, where we don't keep our children under glass."

He sat up and saw her angry face. "What *is* the matter? You're not a puritan, Fan." He looked at her more closely. "My darling goose, you're jealous."

"Jealous of Caddie? Don't be ridiculous," but Fanny was jealous, humiliatingly, violently jealous. Those hours of waiting for Rob had frightened her. The villa without him, even with Hugh there, had been desolate and there had been practical difficulties too. She had not known what to do about Prince Brancati's telegram, and Celestina had gone on keeping dinner hot.

At eleven o'clock Fanny had sent Mario over to the Hotel Lydia to telephone the airport. Mario came back; Flight 507 had left on time. Then Fanny had had to sit calmly while Celestina told her of the terrible accidents there had been on the *autostrada* and on the lake road. "Italian driver *all* bad," declared Celestina comfortingly. "Signor Quillet drive much fast, too fast." She told graphically how a bus had pushed a car over the road edge. "Here, by Malcesine. Three people kill." She held up three fingers. "All deaded." Fanny sat through it but after Celestina had gone she paced the floor, until the villa itself seemed to check her. Its châtelaines, it seemed to suggest, should not gossip with servants. Madame Menghini, for instance, would have kept Celestina in her place, nor would she have paced. "You cannot have it all ways," Fanny told herself. If Darrell had said he would be back at eleven, he would have been; that reliability was not in Rob. Well, you love his quicksilver quality, thought Fanny. He has probably met someone, or something has turned up to do with work, man's business. "Keep to a woman's," Fanny told herself and made herself go upstairs, have a bath, give her hair a good brushing, look in on Hugh, then find a book and go to bed. "Then if anything has happened, you will be fit to deal with it. If it hasn't, this is where Rob will want to find you." "Never be tiresome." Fanny felt that could have been Madame Menghini's motto.

Fanny was not tiresome—then. In fact she had been asleep when Rob came in beside her. "I'm sorry, Fan."

"Did you meet someone? Tell me . . ." she murmured half asleep.

"In the morning." He kissed her. "Sleep now," and she had gone back to sleep never dreaming . . .

"But it was you who insisted that Caddie and Hugh must go at once," she said bewildered.

"I changed my mind. People do." Rob was sitting up in bed. "Give me some coffee."

"But what made you?" Fanny still asked. "What made you change?"

"Caddie." He leaned over and patted her hand. "She is so like you."

"Like me?" Fanny was touched, then she could not help the jealousy coming again. "Nonsense. Except for her hair and eyes, Caddie is Darrell all over again."

"No one is anyone all over again," said Rob. "There are always contradictions," and yet Caddie seemed to him almost pure Fanny. She had that same slightly clumsy gaucheness that to him always seemed young and vulnerable, something innocent. Fanny, for all the airs she put on over her children, would never grow out of that. "She has your smile," Rob could have said only he would not, that shy flickering smile that had charmed him across Margot's dinner table; to see it repeated on a child's face made his heart turn over with tenderness, but Fanny was in no mood now for tenderness and when they came to Hugh a quarrel began. "I didn't see," said Rob, "why Caddie shouldn't go back with Hugh this evening or tomorrow."

Fanny sat up in her chair. "Hugh can't go back today or tomorrow."

"Fanny, he must. You say he has no fever now. It's over."

"It may be over but he's weak, and Darrell would send him straight back to school."

"And if he did, would that be wrong?"

"It would be for Hugh. Hugh has always been delicate. He hasn't any stamina."

Darrell's "I warn you, Fanny is foolish about that boy" echoed in Rob's ear but he tried to argue gently. "Schools have matrons, trained nurses to look after the boys. Doctor Isella said . . ."

"Doctor Isella doesn't know," said Fanny, "and after all, you don't know, Rob, because you never went to one, how tough an English public school can be. Strode is one of the toughest. I always think that's why Darrell chose it."

"Hugh seems to be a bone of contention, doesn't he?" said Rob. "Please give me some more coffee," but Fanny was holding her hands together in distress.

"Don't make me send him back until he's well. Not for

a few days." Again there was a note almost of hysteria in her voice.

"Fanny, you are not going to make me a scene?" and Fanny recovered herself. "Not if you let me do what I want," she said and took his cup.

"That's honest, anyhow." Rob was feeling too contented to argue. He watched the steam going up from his filled cup, a curl of fragrant steam catching the light. Reflections of the lake rippled gently along the walls, the sun shone on Fanny's hair, her clear skin. He was, too, full of *Saladin* and of Bianca Letti. She would make a ravishing Berengaria—if we can get her. She would have to be released but Aldo has influence—this had given him a new impetus. He wanted to get up and work, not stay here arguing, and, "I suppose a few days won't make any difference," he said. "We can tell Darrell that Doctor Isella . . ."

"Darrell won't believe an Italian doctor."

At that Rob's temper flared. "God! You middle-class English!"

Fanny's tautness broke to match it. "Darrell's not middle-class, by *any* means. Lady Candida . . ."

"Damn Lady Candida," and Rob said, "His behaviour *is* middle class; stuffy, conventional, prejudiced, and ignorant."

"Like mine, I suppose?" They were facing each other over the coffee tray.

"Exactly like yours," said Rob, "when it touches your children."

"Thank you. Stuffy, conventional, prejudiced, and ignorant." She got up, turned her back on him and went to the window. After a moment, Rob got up too. She heard him light a cigarette.

"Fan." No one could say that as Rob said it and, as he touched her, Fanny began to quiver. "Fan, are we going to quarrel over a clutter of children?"

"Only two children," she said with a half-sob.

"They seem like a clutter. Well, let's treat them like that. Just a clutter, under our feet. Of course they can stay until you think Hugh is well."

"What about Darrell?"

"He can have another telegram," but it was Darrell who sent the telegram, a cable from Peru: "Unavoidably delayed." "I told you, he was always being delayed," said Fanny. "Unavoidably delayed stop am unwilling Gwyneth take responsibility despatch Hugh Caddie school and prefer deal with them myself stop please keep them until twenty-sixth Clavering."

"The twenty-sixth," said Fanny. "That's over a fortnight." Her face was shining. "Oh Rob! You agree, don't you?"

"I have to agree," said Rob, then he gave a half-rueful smile. "There's only one thing for me to do."

"What is that?"

"Send for Pia," said Rob.

VIII

"P IA? Who is Pia?" asked Caddie.

"Rob's little girl."

"I didn't know he had a little girl." Fanny thought she had not known it either. She knew of Pia, of course, but it had not really dawned on her, perhaps not really on Rob. He was oddly silent about his affairs while I . . . I have been making a clamour, thought Fanny, as she had thought when she had touched the split olive tree, still making a clamour; she had been selfish, so absorbed in her own children that she had forgotten the existence of his. How could I? she thought ashamed.

"Pia is ten, about two years younger than you," she told Caddie now. "Her mother, Lucia, died when she was born."

"Her mother died? Oh! Then Rob didn't put her away."

"Caddie! What an expression."

"That's what the Bible says."

It was only, Fanny told herself, that those words had caught Caddie's attention; she meant nothing deeper than that, but all the same Fanny seemed to glimpse something formidable in Caddie. "Nonsense. She's only half aware of what goes on," she told herself but Rob did not seem to think so. "That child's an infant Hannibal," he said.

"Why Hannibal?" Fanny smiled.

"Hannibal took a solemn oath he would never be at peace with the Romans. I'm the Romans," said Rob. "He crossed the Alps; they had never been crossed by an army before. I don't remember hearing of a child fighting a divorce."

"Rob, don't be absurd. Caddie's not fighting, not consciously. Hugh perhaps but . . ."

"Caddie is fighting," said Rob, "and she's a good fighter. In fact I'm not sure she isn't the general, and her arguments are like elephants. They squash you flat."

It had been his own fault. He had introduced it, the thing they had been careful not to talk of all through that dinner at the Continentale, until warmed by the wine, the good food, the intimate atmosphere of the restaurant, he had been moved to try and talk of himself and Fanny, in a way he had thought a child would understand. Perhaps, too, *Saladin* was pervading his mind. "If this were a tournament—and life is a tournament" he had said. "If your father and I were knights, well, we fought and I won Fanny. If I won her, shouldn't I be able to enjoy her?" but Caddie had no use for knights, she lived strictly in the present. "I won Topaz, and I wasn't able to enjoy him," she said.

Her face had gone back to the sullen heaviness he had known before and she laid down her knife and fork. It had taken Rob ten minutes and all the blandishments of the waiter, the display on the trolley to get her to eat again. She had *torta di mandorle*. She had never tasted anything as delectable, but forever afterwards *torta di mandorle* tasted, to Caddie, of treason.

"She will sleep it off," Rob had said, but Caddie's broken night stayed broken. With the first dawn she had appeared at Hugh's bedside. "Hugh. Oh, Hugh! Wake up."

He had struggled out of sleep, his first deep sleep without fever or dreams. "Wha—what is it?" At last he took in the fact of Caddie's being there. "Then you . . . then you didn't go?"

"Rob took me off the plane. He took me out to dinner and Hugh, I *liked* it."

Hugh stared at her in disgust. "Can't you forget for *one* minute?" he demanded. "Go back to bed."

Caddie was altogether a torment to him—on top of all the other torments, thought Hugh.

She had been led to go into Fanny's bedroom and find a Bible, to look up that verse about putting your wife away, thought Caddie, and when she was there had been struck once again by the bedhead. Covered in a silver brocade with a pattern of pink and turquoise flowers, it had a gilded frame that was carved and fluted, and from which hung a necklace, a gold chain with green stones. "Emeralds?" Caddie had asked awed. "Emerald paste," said Fanny, who was in the room. The necklace ended in a cross and, "A cross," said Caddie. "That's a funny thing to have hanging over your bed."

To Caddie the cross had no deep significance. It was just another of the unexpected objects of which the villa had so many: Japanese combs, snuffboxes, chips of Roman pavement, jewelled daggers, and, "A funny thing," she said quite naturally, "to have over your bed." Nor did she put the emphasis on the "your" that Fanny's sensitivity heard, but Fanny rounded on her with quite extraordinary sharpness. "What are you doing here? This is my room and you don't come in unless you are asked. Now go and don't come back."

All the same Caddie did come back—she still meant to look up that bit in the Bible—and she noticed the necklace and cross were gone.

She found the passage in St. Matthew; they had had it at school in the Sermon on the Mount. When she had pored over it she went in to Hugh. "What's fornication?" she asked in unadorned Caddie fashion. His reaction was startling. "Get out of my room," shouted Hugh.

A month ago he would have told her with his accustomed lordliness but now it was as if Caddie had touched him where he had been flayed.

"I must blink facts," it was as if Hugh had been saying to himself. "If I don't, I cannot bear them."

It was Fanny who quite innocently would not let him blink them; in fact she seemed to Hugh to rub his nose in them; she was, for instance, always in and out of his room. "I must take your temperature."

"I haven't got a temperature."

"We must make sure," and, helpless, he had to watch her while she put the thermometer in his mouth and waited, standing by the window, humming a little tune.

At Stebbings she had not gone around in her dressing-gown half the morning like this, lingering, smiling, looking at the lake, touching the cowslips on his dressing-table. There, when her hair was down, she had worn it in a plait down her back, not in a loose tail over one shoulder so that it flowed, its tendrils framing her face. He took the thermometer out of his mouth and said with hostility, "You are different."

"Hugh, put that back," but she knew she was different.

All those days as she had lain, in the long chair on the terrace, the sun had baked her, gently because it was still spring, though an Italian spring. It had browned her arms and legs, and brought a dewy flush on her cheeks, as if I had new sap in me, thought Fanny. Rob, though he had grown heavier, could not brown any more, his sallowness was sun-accustomed, but she had changed every day, "Like a brown rose opening," said Rob.

"A rose again?" Fanny teased him.

"Yes, a rose," said Rob. "One day we will endow a rose and call it Fanny Quillet."

Fanny had caught up with Rob at last. She was filled with "well-being," she could have said. It was from the quiet and sun, the loosening of the strain; she had wound up the long thread of anguish, worry, and excitement into a secret ball and put it away. The change was from idleness after years of hard work, yes, hard work, thought Fanny; Stebbings was a big house and I only had Gwyneth a few hours a day, the whole garden with Prentice only three days a week. It was from the beauty, she thought; the lake in this May weather was so blue it might have been painted; the wisteria was full out, the roses twining up the cypresses; every puff of wind brought a different scent. It was from Celestina's cooking, her pastas and risottos, the fresh cheese, fruit, wine. I have never had wine with every meal, thought Fanny. It was from the care, she thought. At

Stebbings, she had not had time to spend ten minutes brushing her hair, to have it washed every week at the hairdresser's, *Luigi, Parrucchierre,* to have her nails done, to cream and massage her face, have her clothes pressed by Giulietta before each wearing. It was all these but most of all, it was in Rob's love-making. "What would you say, my scornful little son," she wanted to say to Hugh now, "if you knew I had just been kissed from my heels to my head?" But Hugh knew more than that. Hectically he knew everything, and he groaned. He took the thermometer out again and said, "Where did you get that dressing-gown?"

"At Fortnum's. I paid thirty guineas for it. Put that thermometer back." Fanny seemed driven to try and be provocative, as if Hugh were a man too.

"I oughtn't to have bought it," she said almost automatically, but she did not look in the least repentant; she looked radiant, thought Hugh.

He scowled but Fanny was impervious that morning, even to him. She was sealed away, into what may be a secret, she could have said, a happy secret. It was in her step, the curve of her cheek, the way she could not help breaking into a smile.

After the reconciliation with Rob—and it was almost worth quarrelling for that—Fanny, brushing her hair, had happened to pick up her diary and idly look at its markings. She had lost track of the days, and weeks, thought Fanny startled. Weeks. She was two weeks overdue. Two weeks and two days, and she laid down her brush in the stillness of all women in the moment of first suspicion. But it can't be, she thought, I am too old. It's eleven years since Caddie. It's just this new life . . . but a wild hope insisted: I am always regular, most healthy people are. Sixteen days is a long time.

She had said nothing to Rob—it's far too early yet, give it another month and then I must see Doctor Isella—but every moment since, everywhere she went, she felt as if she were holding some precious excitement, holy and secret.

Hugh lay flat in the bed and could have ground the thermometer between his teeth as he looked at her.

When she bent to take it out he could not help noticing the swell of her breasts, the warm white of her neck, that neck Rob had touched, thought Hugh. He shut his eyes, but it was no use shutting them; he could see Rob's hand, petting her, thought Hugh in fury. Even when he refused to look at her, she seemed to spill scent, a fragrance he did not remember.

"When did you start using scent?" he growled.

"In London," said Fanny lightly. "Don't you like it?"

"It makes me feel sick. Go away."

"But darling, I must make your bed."

"I can make it myself." He meant his voice to be gruff but it squeaked an octave higher which made him furious.

"Don't be silly. I must make you comfortable." But he had lifted his head, his eyes glaring banefully under locks of hair that hung down over his face where he had been screwing his head into the pillow. He looks savage, she thought.

"Can't I have *anything* private?"

To be private, at this moment, was all he asked, but even his thoughts were no longer private.

Raymond of the photographs at school was only a year

older than Hugh, but, if one could believe him, years older in experience. Hugh had covered his own ignorance by refusing to subscribe to Raymond's talk. "Obscene little chap, isn't he?" he said, which earned him some admiration, but Raymond was not stupid; he was only in a class below his age because he was untidy and did not choose to work, and his descriptions were vivid. Up to now, Hugh had simply looped round them in his mind; he acknowledged them but would not let Raymond throw him off balance. Now, set off by Rob and Fanny, Raymond seemed to have entered into Hugh, to be in full control. "I didn't know what it would be like seeing her with him," he could have moaned.

His imagination seemed to have become independent, as now and again his body dismayingly became: My . . . parts, thought Hugh shrinking. They behaved in an unwarrantable fashion. I can't go out among people any more, he thought in panic.

"No fever," said Fanny briskly. "Get up while I make your bed."

"In my thin pyjamas!" Never! Never! Never! thought Hugh.

"Hugh, don't be absurd. I'm your mother."

"That's why. That's why," he could have cried in agony.

Ostensibly he was better; the fever and pain had gone but a bad taste was in his mouth and, as often after food poisoning, his skin and head felt tender; they hurt if they were touched but a worse hurt was in him; he saw his mind as black, spongy, soaking up "Even what isn't there," he could have cried. Over and over again he saw Rob's hand on Fanny's neck. Why that should have made such an impression on him he did not know. Over and over again, too, he told himself "There was nothing to it." It was no more than affection, but that was not true. Hugh was quick now, alive to Rob and Fanny. That ordinary simple gesture of loving might have been fire for what had come out of it; it had seared Hugh's brain and mind. Phrases he had never noticed seemed like signposts now, words that made Raymond snigger. In *Hamlet,* the last school play—McIndoe, the English master, believed in unexpurgated versions—"Paddling in her neck," Raymond had said with glee. "Paddling in her neck for a pair of reechy kisses." What was reechy? Hugh did not know but he had that hot shiver again.

What made it worse was that he was beginning to have a liking and respect for Rob. Hugh, as well as Caddie, had thought of grown people as shades, uninteresting, middle-aged—anyone from twenty-five to fifty for Hugh was middle-aged. After that they were simply old, out-used; Mr. McIndoe, at school, perhaps was different, he had sense, but Rob was more than different. He made Hugh feel, for the first time, not inferior but ill-equipped; as if there were, after all, some sense in growing older, working, learning; that he, Hugh, was not completed. But I used to be complete, he thought, and he saw himself, Hugh Clavering, all of one piece, light, sure, agile, quicker than anyone else he knew. Now he was in pieces. Rob, too, made him pity Darrell. Darrell, his father, was pitiable and Hugh resented that; he was ashamed, too, of what he thought of as Darrell's feebleness. If Rob had talked to Hugh of tournaments, he would have understood. "Father couldn't keep her." Somewhere in Hugh was a feeling that a woman should be subjugated, even if you had to beat her, and now, because of circumstances, Darrell was letting them stay with the enemy. Grown people were strangely puny, strangely blind. "For a fortnight, more. Isn't that lovely," said Fanny.

"I can't stay." Hugh pressed himself down in the bed; if he kept himself flat his voice might not betray him.

"Don't be silly, darling. After that journey!"

"I should never have come."

"But you did come." Fanny was calm, reasonable and, "Shock her. Shock her. Shock her," cried Raymond in Hugh. "Say filthy things, boy's language that she doesn't know exists." Fanny instead of going away, came nearer, sat down on the bed. "This is going to be the rest of my life, Hugh. Can't you accept it?"

He was drowning, suffocating. "I must go back."

"You will when Father gets home."

"God! Can't I go by myself?"

"You must do as he says."

"I won't. I can't."

"You must." Fanny kept her voice crisp to hide her hurt. "To begin with you haven't any money."

"I shall walk. Walk and hitchhike," but he knew he would not. Once . . . but now he was in pieces.

"Hugh." He opened his eyes and looked at her, a witheringly scornful look. It broke through her shell. Abruptly she got up and went away.

"We have two weeks," said Caddie. "More than two weeks." At Fanny's order she had brought Hugh the tea that Doctor Isella had said was still to be drunk, tea and charcoal pills every four hours for three days. Hugh was up but looked unwell, his skin was livid and he had dark marks under his eyes and on his lids. He was, too, in an evil temper.

He would not touch Rob's Lapsang Souchong. "Filthy taste." Celestina had said that she had tea and produced with pride a very old tin; "Queen Mary's tea." "Tea *della Regina Mary. La Regina Mary. Eccellente!*" said Celestina.

"Queen Mary's been dead for years," said Caddie doubtfully and sure enough, Fanny said the tea was musty, and Caddie had gone with Giulietta to the *alimentari* to buy more. The alimentari, kept by Celestina's cousin, was one of the new shops opened in every village along the lake road, each with a stand of fresh oranges and lemons outside and hanging bundles of the straw-covered Chianti bottles, "If it is Chianti," said Rob. "Chianti or Bardolino. Spivs borrow those famous names to sell cheap made-up wines that are mostly powder. There is a proverb in Italy now," said Rob. " 'You can also make wine with grapes.' " It took Caddie a long while to puzzle that out.

The only tea the alimentari had was in the tea bags that Caddie had seen in Switzerland. "I wonder what Gwyneth would say to them," she said, and to there being no kettle in the villa; the tea each time took a long while to make in Celestina's little pan, and then Hugh said it was abominable, but, "Take it to him," Fanny said, "and see that he drinks it."

"He won't drink it for me," said Caddie. Fanny still would not take it. "You have been foul to Mother, haven't you?" Caddie asked, and Hugh nodded. "Good," said Caddie. "She will mind that."

Everything seemed to be playing into their hands; they had been reprieved by this extra fortnight; Hugh was evidently being as unkind as only he could be, where Caddie had been afraid he would be renegade; Pia was coming, "And that's too many children in this villa," said Caddie.

"If it's bad weather, we shan't be able to get away from one another," said Fanny.

"No," said Caddie with satisfaction.

"Oh dear! I hope Pia's nice."

"I hope she's horrid," said Caddie silently, all the same it was a little alarming. Pia, Fanny told them, lived with her grandmother in Rome, in fact she had been brought up by her grandmother, "And by her grandmother's mother, who is still alive," said Rob, "and by great-aunts, great-uncles, aunts and uncles, and dozens of cousins." It sounded almost like Celestina's family.

"Can Pia speak English?" asked Caddie in alarm.

"Of course. I have brought her up too, a bit, and she has an English governess."

"There's no room in the villa for an English governess."

There was, in fact, very little room. Hugh had been moved back into Rob's dressing room and in the north bedroom the small daybed, carved in walnut with a tapestry cover, was made up for Pia, though Celestina was mystified as to why this new child and Caddie could not sleep together in the big bed. Caddie was dismayed enough as it was. "I can't sleep with Pia. I don't know her."

"It *is* a little hard," Fanny said to Rob. "One mustn't expect them to like one another straight away."

"Being with people you don't like is part of growing up," said Rob.

"Does Pia *have* to come?" asked Caddie.

"Rob had you, so I have to have her." That was too ungracious to say though it was the truth—but not the whole truth. "I want her to come," said Fanny. "When you love someone, you want to love the people they love."

"But will you be able to?" asked Caddie.

That was the rub. No one, thought Fanny, is as foreign as a foreign child. To her, Italian children still looked much alike, small-boned, alabaster-skinned, dark-haired, dark-eyed; if the boys' eyes could be called meltingly brown, the girls' eyes seemed to be bright, even a little beady as if already they had a feminine calculation—and they have, thought Fanny. Gianna, Celestina's niece from the trattoria, had it and all of them, even two-year-olds, the tiny girl at the telephone café for instance, had a feminine elegance. Will Pia look like that? Be like that? thought Fanny.

Rob's complete confidence made it worse. "Suppose she doesn't like me?"

"She won't be able to help it. She has never had a mother, remember. This will be wonderful for her."

Fanny had gone with Rob when he telephoned to Rome. The grandmother's voice had come, high, eloquent, and indignant, thought Fanny, through the booth door into the café. It was a swelling flood of words and when Rob came out and ordered himself a coffee and cognac, he rubbed his ear. "Nonna's voice doesn't grow any softer."

"I heard it," said Fanny, and suddenly she asked, "Is Pia a Catholic?"

"Naturally. Lucia was."

"Then, what does she, Nonna, what do all of them, think about me?"

"I haven't asked them," said Rob. "You are not their business. You are mine."

"If Pia is their business, I am," and Fanny said, "I'm surprised they let her come."

"She happens to be my child."

"I meant—before we are married."

"That shows how little you understand," said Rob and he said very gently, "To them, Fanny, we shan't be married even when we are. We can't be married while Darrell is alive."

"But we shall be married, legally." Fanny was defiant.

"Legality is man's law," said Rob. "To them, marriage is a sacrament."

"And to me," Fanny could have cried out. "I want our marriage to be a sacrament."

"It can't be that," said Rob. "Except to us. Isn't that enough for you? It is for me," but Fanny could not get the sound of Nonna's voice out of her head. "Why go tormenting yourself over a pack of people you will never meet?" said Rob.

I shall meet them in Pia, thought Fanny.

Rob fetched Pia from Milan. She was coming, Fanny told them, on the *rapido di lusso*, "which couldn't have been more different from our travelling," said Caddie. It was the most luxurious train in Europe, Fanny told them, with only a few passengers, large salons in each coach, a dining car, a kitchen as good as the best hotel's, a guide, and a hostess, "Which is why Pia is travelling on it," explained Fanny. In charge of the hostess or not, it seemed to make Pia important, far removed from themselves. Caddie washed carefully, gave her hair a good brush, put on clean socks, all she had in the way of clean clothes, but as soon as she saw Pia she knew that it would be wiser not to try and compete.

Fanny had thought Hugh slim and graceful until she saw Pia, who had the immediate effect of making the English three of them seem large and lumpish. She was an exquisitely made little girl, having at present the long legs of a fawn, made longer by dark stockings—"Only they are not stockings, they are tights," Caddie reported later. "Lots of children wear those in Italy and Germany," said Fanny. Pia had an erect carriage, Fanny had never seen such a straight back, a poised head, small hands with slim wrists, little feet. She had too the waxen paleness of some Italian city children—not enough air, rich food, late hours, thought Fanny—the skin almost transparently fine. Fanny had been prepared for all these but not for the beauty of Pia's face. "She's like Nonna," said Rob, "who was a beauty, *is* a beauty, even now. Both far more so than Lucia. Perhaps that's what binds them together." It was an old beauty; one could trace in it the face of generations, perfect in proportion, the forehead more wide than high, level brows, a small goat nose, a mouth with teeth so even and pearly that they might have been first teeth. Fanny had searched Pia's face for some sign of Rob, as every woman must, she thought, when she looks at the child of the man she loves, if it's not her child. One day perhaps, thought Fanny and, for a moment, that hope thrilled through her with added life. "I'm too old," she told herself as she told herself twenty times a day. "It's almost twelve years since Caddie. All the same it's sixteen days late, no, seventeen, now," and very kindly she put her hand on Pia's shoulder. "Hullo, Pia. I'm so glad to meet you." Caddie thought Fanny meant to kiss Pia, but Pia made a small curtsy and held out a gloved hand.

Caddie was struck by the curtsy and yet it looked obedient, drilled. I suppose manners do cover up your feelings, thought Caddie. It had never struck her that was one reason for them. Pia had not chosen to come as Caddie and Hugh had, and Caddie was reminded once again of Hugh's "Posted about like parcels." Pia perhaps had been on the point of going back to school; Rob said she went as a weekly boarder to a convent, "One of the Sacred Heart's." "What's a Sacred Heart?" Caddie had asked. Pia had probably been happily sunk in her own affairs when she was suddenly "demanded," and put on the *rapido di lusso* and dumped down in the middle of them all here in the villa.

Hugh had thought Pia would be too young to be of much interest, "Another Caddie," he had said, lordly, and going purely by age; but, to his surprise, he found he was taking in every inch of her, or every centimetre, he thought with a smile that was new to Hugh, the smile of a boy looking with a little interest at a girl. He took in her clothes: Pia wore a loose belted coat hanging from her shoulders, a pleated skirt, a jersey, ordinary clothes for a girl but immaculately fresh. "You had sat up all night in those dirty carriages," said Fanny who, in her uncanny way, had fathomed what he was thinking. "Pia would have looked rumpled then," and Caddie voiced Hugh's thought, "I don't believe she would." Pia had white gloves, a handbag in scarlet—the jersey had a small white cambric collar embroidered in red—and an upturned hat of brushed white felt with a red ribbon streamer. When Caddie saw that hat she went straight upstairs, took her school panama, and squashed it down behind the chest of drawers. Giulietta carried up the luggage—no servant at the villa ever allowed anyone to carry anything—a big and small case in scarlet leather—and Rob had the book Pia had been reading in the train, *Murder for Ten Dollars,* but she also had a comic. Caddie would not have been allowed to read either.

"Caddie, will you show Pia her room?" Why did grown people put something as a question when it was meant as a command? Suppose I said "No," thought Caddie, but of course she could not say "No" and she led the way upstairs, through the brocaded door, on which Pia did not bestow a glance, and into the north bedroom. "I'm afraid you have to sleep with me," she said indicating the daybed. "I hope you don't mind."

"At school you have to sleep with all sorts of people," said Pia. Perhaps she did not mean it to be as rude as it sounded, but then she spoke English very well.

"If you would rather have the big bed . . ." Pia shrugged. That nonchalant shrug was the most silencing thing Caddie had experienced and she sat stonily on her own bed and watched while Pia unpacked piles of her small personal linen and two or three dresses folded into her case on hangers. She shook them out, and, "Shall I hang them up for you?" asked Caddie who could not be stony for long.

Pia allowed Caddie to do that, and take shoes out of white linen bags and arrange them in the bottom of the cupboard: espadrilles, a white suede pair with buckles, short rubber boots with buttons, no school sandals. "Don't they wear sandals at your school?" Caddie longed to ask but did not wish to draw attention to her own. There was a white ivory brush and comb, a manicure case, handkerchiefs, more white gloves. Whoever had packed Pia had taken great trouble. A thick prayer book in black was wrapped in tissue paper. Pia put it by her bed. "That's not a proper prayer book," said Caddie looking at it.

"It's a missal."

"What's a missal?"

Really! Pia's eyebrows seemed to say but she answered, "It's for Mass."

"And that string of beads?" Caddie knew it was ill-bred to ask questions but she could not help it.

"My rosary."

"A rosary! Oh tell me how you say it. I have always wondered."

"You wouldn't understand."

"I would," but Pia put the rosary away.

Caddie transferred her gaze to a photograph in a heart-shaped frame that Pia put, too, by her bed.

"Who's that?"

"My friend." It was said firmly and Caddie blushed. She had not meant to be inquisitive, only friendly as to a new girl at school. "Remember," Fanny had said, "if it's difficult for you it's far more difficult for Pia."

"I don't see why," said Caddie.

"There are two of you and I'm your mother."

"Rob's her father."

Caddie thought she had been right; Pia gave no sign of finding anything in the least difficult. Then the bell rang from downstairs. "I expect that's for dinner, *cena,*" said Caddie; she had been learning Italian words from Giulietta.

As they were going down, "Caddie?" said Pia. "That is not a name. That is golf, for carrying the clubs."

"My name is Candida, after my grandmother."

"Your grandmother?" A queer spasm crossed Pia's face; it made her, for a moment, look as ugly as a monkey.

"Pia . . ."

"We have to go down," said Pia coldly.

IX

<< ——————————————————————— >>

"THEY DON'T mean to do it," said Fanny. "It happens."

"It has happened ever since they came," said Rob, but Fanny shook her head. There had always been pricks: Renato's awkwardness over her name for instance; the scene about the ring, and for her, always, the sight of other children. She had not been able to bear it when the trattoria children came to play in the garden, filling it with the sound of running feet and high voices, just as she had not been able to look at the toddling procession from the *Asilo* and had to shut her ears to the gabbles of delight from the babies feeding the church pigeons. These were expected pricks, but now every small awkwardness was magnified: "Mr. Quillet." Hugh and Caddie had punctiliously called Rob that until Fanny stopped them, "Call him Rob," but neither of them did except when they talked of him to one another. The awkwardness of what Pia was to call Fanny was worse. "I hope one day she will say 'mother' like the others," said Rob but Fanny shook her head. "We can only hope for that." Pia's manners shrank from saying "Fanny." She said "You" and to Hugh and Caddie, "Your mother."

"Though you say 'Mozzer,' " said Caddie.

"After all, you're half English, half spaghetti," said Hugh at which Pia flew into a rage.

"You are not to say that. It's vulgar. I am English-Italian."

"Treat them as a clutter of children under one's feet."
"One has to be careful everywhere one steps," said Fanny.

Fanny and Pia were thrown much together. Rob was trying to work and Hugh, now he was better, seemed to shut himself out of the house. He had struck up a friendship with Mario. Fanny knew they smoked together, "And they drink wine," said Fanny disturbed. "I wish you would speak to Mario, Rob."

"I can't do that," said Rob, "and I think it's mostly fishing and boats." It was. Hugh helped Mario with the boats; Mario had lent him a rod, let him help to run the outboard motor, and, best of all, was teaching him to sail.

Sitting on the end of the jetty, on the warm boards with his legs hanging down, watching the shallows where the water eddied and moved with that timeless lap, lap, Hugh could get rid of Raymond. He was himself again. Each time he dropped his hook in with its gobbet of bait, small fish darted from all sides. "You would think they would have more sense, but they haven't." The sun made a warm spot between his shoulders, and shone on his head until he slipped into a daze dream in which he could forget Fanny, Rob, Caddie, and Topaz. Now and then Mario would come and pull up the line with a brown hand seamed with oil or tar, examine the bait, grunt, and put it back again or change it. *"Non abboccaranno mai.* You won't get a bite." Now and again he would teach Hugh to cast. *"Così,"* he would say showing him how to throw the line far out into the lake and Hugh would take the rod from him and throw.

"*Gentilmente, non in modo brusco. Così,*" said Mario, and would show Hugh how to wind in his line gently, without jerking. Caddie hung around but Pia would not come down to the boathouse; fishing, Pia's look said, was for boatmen and boys. Left alone in the house she was often, rather against both their wills, with Fanny.

"Leave her to herself," suggested Rob.

"Poor little soul," said Fanny. "It's fearfully dull for her." There was nothing to amuse any child in the villa and Pia had brought nothing to do. "Well, none of us did," said Caddie.

She had discovered plenty of things of interest. The water snakes for instance. They were pale, small snakes, chequered over with a pattern of light brown, and had pointed heads in which their eyes glittered like specks of jewels. Rob said they were not poisonous and Caddie liked to catch them as they lay coiled on a rock, half drugged by the sun; they were quick to disappear, but sometimes she could catch one, tickle it into drowsiness, let it slide over her hand. "*Sweet* little snakes," she crooned but Pia, when Caddie tried to show them to her, shuddered. Caddie watched the lizards, especially a pair of large ones, entrancingly emerald green, that at first she had thought were salamanders. Celestina's birds, hopping, endlessly hopping from perch to bar to perch in those tiny cages, were always a pain, but there were a pair of hoopoes nesting in the garden; the swallows had nests high under the eaves and there were wagtails, dipping and running. Down at the boathouse a tabby cat was almost ready to have kittens; "You can feel them," said Caddie, and Mario had a dog, Cesare, the dog of *"Attenti al cane"* on the gate but though he was kept almost always on the chain he would never have hurt anyone and Caddie had made friends with him and took him for runs. She was too shy to try and talk to the trattoria children, Gianna and Beppino, but she liked to watch them play. None of these things interested Pia at all. There were no games to play, "Not even ping-pong," said Pia. The wind was still too cold for them to bathe; only a few intrepid German tourists went in from the hotel jetty for a hasty splash. Pia went out with Fanny; she liked the Mercedes and Fanny's driving and even paid Fanny a staid little compliment, "You drive very well, better than my aunts."

She was completely biddable. With Hugh and Caddie she submitted to Fanny's morning and good-night kiss, though submitted is the right word, thought Fanny. She went where she was told, but she would not answer when Fanny tried to draw her out. When Fanny said, "You must teach us about Italy," Pia looked back at her without answering.

Pia's least beauty was her eyes. They were small, black, almond-shaped, and as hard as almond shells with a kernel of light Fanny shrank from exploring. When Pia wished, she could make them as blank and opaque—as lozenges, thought Fanny exasperated, as when, for instance, Fanny asked her help in a fruit shop or restaurant. "What is lasagne, Pia?"

"Pasta," said Pia.

"I know that. What kind of pasta?"

Shrug and blankness.

"I never know what she is thinking," Fanny complained.

"You won't know," said Rob.

Compared to Pia, my children are open books, thought Fanny, perhaps a shade virtuously, and, "I have always thought that the fault of nuns as teachers, is that they train the children in duplicity," she told Rob.

"If that's what you call self-control," said Rob. "If you live in a community, or even with other people, it's as well to keep your feelings to yourself. At least Pia is never a bother."

"Meaning that Hugh and Caddie are?"

"Hugh is. You have to admit that, Fanny. Isn't he bothering you a good deal just now? And I resent that," said Rob.

He was oddly disturbed himself. The villa was perfectly quiet but he could not work. He would leave his cell and go out on the loggia and stand, moodily looking down. Fanny was often on the terrace below, as she used to be, thought Rob; still within reach, but not lying peacefully in the long chair but sitting, mending perhaps, her head bent over Hugh's green shirt, his pyjamas. Quite often, Rob had to admit, it was his own shirt, his socks but he did not want her to be busy, just quiescent, thought Rob. Not doing; being.

Sometimes the children's voices came up to him as they came to Fanny. If Mario turned Hugh out of the boathouse, and Mario could grow surly, Hugh sat for preference on the kitchen-terrace wall with Giacomino. Caddie liked that back terrace too. "I can understand. It's comfortable there," said Rob. He himself often went in and drank a glass of wine with Giacomino and Celestina, or would sit there an hour, teasing Giulietta.

Everything round the kitchen was shabby, well used, unpretentious; washing hung on a line, there was a block for splitting wood, a heap of empty bottles lay in a corner, there was a tank with fish swimming in it; they were trout from the lake caught by Mario and keeping fresh until Celestina came with her net; Caddie always tried not to look at them. Hugh, oddly enough, did not disdain big sweaty Celestina with her loud voice and smell of garlic. Like most Italians she was good-natured with children, and to her Hugh, Caddie, and Pia were just children, complicated or uncomplicated. Hugh liked Giacomino, who, without stirring his indolent finger, so obviously had his women in full control, but he avoided looking at or being near Giulietta. She was too noisily gay and friendly for Hugh just now—and too physical. Her black skirt was short; when she ran upstairs they could see her strong brown knees; her hips seemed almost to speak as she walked or swept, bent, dusted; she wore a brassière that made her breasts stand out in points under her black jersey. Hugh's eyes seemed to stray of themselves to those points and his ears thrummed, which was strange. Caddie noticed that even in this friendly homely part of the house he was bitingly bad-tempered.

She and Giulietta exchanged English-Italian. *"Pollo arrosto."* "Roast cheeken." *"Patate."* "Po-tay-to." *"Pane."* "Brread." *"Pesce di lago."* "Feesh from ze lake."

"Do you ever think of anything but food?" Hugh said.

"It's such lovely food."

"Lovely! Italian food is ghastly. All pasta and cheese and tomato."

"It isn't," said Caddie and her indignant tones carried right up to the loggia. "Think of the pork we had at lunch. Think of those little spring chickens fried with parsley and chips. Think of all the asparagus." It was the asparagus season. Celestina gave it to them almost every day. "With melted butter and Parmesan cheese," said Caddie. "Lovely, heavenly asparagus."

Hugh's sneer came up to the loggia too, and out to the terrace. "Asparagus. That's highly suitable." Erotic foods were one of Raymond's specialties. Curry, asparagus.

"Why is it suitable?"

"It's an aphrodisiac."

"What's a . . ." but Fanny had not waited to hear any more. Rob saw her get up and go indoors. He met her at the top of the stairs. "I heard him," said Rob laughing but she was biting her lip to stop tears. "A boy of fourteen ought not to say things like that." There was a sharper edge to it. "Ought not to *have* to say things like that."

Pia would not hobnob with the servants. Now and again she would walk down through the garden and onto the jetty to watch Hugh fish; she seemed to like him the best of the Claverings—or disliked him least. Hugh immediately knew she was there and, contrary to the effect of most females upon him, he fished a little better, but if he came up to the kitchen terrace or went into Mario's little room in the boathouse, she would retreat to the drawing room where she would sit, her skirt carefully smoothed under her, reading one of the detective novels that Fanny did not think the right reading for ten years old.

Caddie, Pia dismissed. Caddie knew this but could not help finding Pia intriguing: her life in Rome, the school nuns, the grandmother who was a beauty—and *loved*, thought Caddie—the clan of uncles, aunts, cousins, the religion. She pestered Pia with questions. As Fanny had changed with the villa, so Caddie was changed too; widened, altered, though she had a feeling that often she could not interpret what Pia said. For instance, Pia told her of guardian angels. "We each have an angel of our own, at least I have."

"If you have, I have," said Caddie.

"I'm not sure about Protestants," said Pia.

"Protestant angels are just as good as Catholic ones," said Caddie stoutly but she did not tell Pia that she had already allotted her own and Hugh's; they would each have one of the golden winged ones over the drawing-room fireplace.

Only once did Pia come alive, when Fanny took her with Hugh and Caddie to Riva to buy new clothes. They had only the suit and dress they had come in, with a pair of pyjamas each, some socks, and handkerchiefs. Hugh, having been in bed, had had his shirt washed, his suit pressed. "But he can't wear that good suit fishing or sailing," said Fanny, and Caddie's state was pitiable. "Even for ten days they must have something," she told Rob.

In the dress shop, Pia's eyes, the whole of her face, lit up and she took charge of Caddie. For half an hour they were even friendly. Though Riva was a small town, its clothes had elegance, as all Italian clothes have, Fanny was beginning to think, though the village girls seemed to have a depressing uniform, thin dark nylon raincoats, flat pointed shoes, and head scarves. In this shop, Pia willingly spoke for Fanny, changed Caddie in and out of clothes in a way Fanny would hardly have had the face to do; she discarded, studied, her face so earnest that Fanny wanted to smile.

Hugh looked at this odd small girl with even more respect and the very feminine Pia sensed that; just as Hugh had fished a little better for her presence on the jetty, so she became more charming, a little more decisive, in the shop. "Not red, of course," Pia told Caddie. "Not even red-brown. It will bring out your freckles, and you should never, never, wear bright blue. It takes all the colour from your face. That green is too lime-coloured. You will get tired of it." She waved it away. "That amber colour is nice, very fashionable, but not for you. Now this," and her voice grew caressing, as she picked up a jerkin in fine suede, caramel-coloured with jersey sleeves. "This will last you forever."

"Until she grows out of it," said Fanny.

"There are turnings," said Pia, in reproof. "And feel the quality."

"Yes, but that's too expensive. Caddie only needs it until she gets back."

"She can wear it in the holidays."

"It's too warm for now."

"It's only spring. The wind is still cold and, look, this matches it," a pleated skirt like Pia's own, caramel too and barred with pale blue.

"The pleats will come out."

"Oh no," Pia assured her. "Not if she hangs it up properly, and I will show her how to pack it, rolled in a silk stocking. See how it suits her." Pia was right. The colour brought out the gleams in Caddie's hair, a pink that had not been suspected in her cheeks. "Please let her have it. *Please*." Pia's eyes were so pleading that Fanny had to give in. "You look nice, really nice," Pia said to Caddie, with what would have been unflattering surprise if she had not been so disarming. She looked as pleased and proud as if the skirt and jerkin had been for her, a flushed and eager little girl.

Then, looking at him from under her lashes, she found a shirt for Hugh, dark blue woven like Rob's that he secretly admired; two shirts, a jersey, two pairs of shorts. She found vests and briefs. "You must be careful with Italian cotton," she told Fanny. "It shrinks," and, "Don't you want anything for yourself?" she asked and her eyes surveyed Fanny; she was palpably longing to re-dress her. They were suddenly united, a happy family group, "Until the money," Fanny might have said.

As she put down the notes, Hugh wheeled round. "Who is paying for these clothes?"

All that Hugh threatened to say hung in the air: "That man is not to pay for our clothes. I won't wear them if he is. I won't have him paying for us." There were white patches round Hugh's nostrils, Caddie was looking distressed, while Pia had instantly walked away and stood in the doorway, her back turned to them, humming a little tune. "Who is paying for them?"

"I am," said Fanny.

"Whose money is it?"

"Mine," but Hugh was not to be put off.

"Where did you get it from?"

"From—Father," said Fanny reluctantly.

"*Father?*" It was such a surprising answer that it took Hugh's whole argument away—and the money was, in a way, from Darrell, thought Fanny miserably.

"Your husband has been magnanimous, to say the least of it," Mr. McCrae had said, and he told Fanny that Darrell could have legitimately and reasonably sued Rob for enticement. "In Mr. Quillet's position the enticement was very real," said Mr. McCrae, looking away from Fanny.

"That had nothing to do with it. Nothing at all," Fanny had wanted to cry, but it was no use saying such things to Mr. McCrae, who had gone on to point out that Darrell had lost the services and enjoyment of his wife; all the same, he would not sue, nor ask for damages, on condition that Rob settled an appropriate, "And equivalent," said Mr. McCrae, sum on her, Fanny. "In your own right, absolutely."

"But I couldn't. I *could not*," Fanny had cried, almost choked with shame and misery, but not only Darrell, Rob had insisted. "It's right," said Rob. "Anything may happen at any time in the film world. Besides being magnanimous, it's sound."

It was like Darrell, honourable and protective, and it stabbed Fanny as nothing else had done.

Aunt Isabel's annuity had died with her but there would be something when the house and furniture were sold and there had been a few hundred pounds of her savings for Fanny. She had spent much of this on keeping herself since she left Stebbings, on paying Mr. McCrae, on those days in London and her air passage to Milan and on clothes, that dressing-gown for instance, but now, besides

Aunt Isabel's, who would so much have disapproved, Fanny, who had never had a penny of her own, had this settlement money, a private bank account, stocks and shares, dividends, business letters and, "Really, Hugh," she was able to say haughtily as she paid, "will you *please* not interfere so continually in grown people's affairs?"

Riva looked sunny and peaceful when they went outside. All along the harbours, under the willows, the boatmen were getting ready for the season, painting the hulls of their boats, picking out the names, *Delfina, Maria Cristina*. On a big fishing boat, the figurehead was being painted in blue and gold. Pia and Caddie stopped to watch but Hugh walked on alone, kicking the stones, his hands in his pockets. He did not whistle; Fanny had not heard him once whistle at the villa. She was still trembling from that ugly little scene. All round them, too, were German tourists. I like Germans, thought Fanny, but these! There were massive women in heavy tweed coats and pygmy felt hats perched on their heads; their husbands were even heavier. They were in all the gift shops, and in the cafés where they ate huge quantities of chocolate cake with whipped cream, or apricot pastry or ices. The air was filled with their gutturals and Fanny longed to get home, but she hurried to catch up with Hugh. "Hughie."

The eyes he turned on her were angry. He was still in his black mood. "I suppose he pays the villa bills."

"Naturally. He rents the villa," and she said, "I think you have to consent to be Rob's guests." It was, she knew, sometimes ignominious to be a child and she spoke gently. "His guests."

"Guests are invited."

"His not-guests then. Rob doesn't think about money. He and I are ready to have you at any time," she said. "You are my son, but you are *our* family now." Hugh snorted. "Even so, for the next few years I shan't have much of you," said Fanny. "Hugh, can't we try to . . ." she could not say "enjoy," "try not to spoil this little time?" but Hugh hunched his shoulders and walked away to the car.

All Fanny's efforts seemed to fall to the ground. "We mustn't waste this time in Italy," she would say. "You may never be here again."

"Not if I can help it," said Hugh.

"But you can't—*not* like Italy." Silence. "Under certain circumstances we cannot like it," the silence seemed to say, but Fanny still tried. "We must go to Verona. That's where Romeo and Juliet lived."

"I thought Romeo and Juliet weren't real people," said Caddie without a flicker of interest.

"It's all Shakespeare country." Fanny was trying to sound enthusiastic. Why, wondered Rob, must mothers be so determined to improve their children? "Mantua, Padua, Verona. They are all in the plays."

"We know that," said Hugh.

"You are silly if you don't see Verona," said Rob. He was nettled by Hugh's ungraciousness in the face of Fanny's sweetness. "The old streets are beautiful. Old yellow houses, grilled windows . . ." Hugh yawned.

All the same, for Fanny's sake, Rob still tried to interest him. "There is an arena, like the Colosseum. If you learn Latin . . ."

"I'm on the modern side," said Hugh.

Fanny tried a bait for Pia. "They say the Verona shops are exceptional."

"They are provincial," said Pia, as if that put them outside the pale.

"There is a famous Madonna in the market place. Wouldn't you like to see her?"

"We have famous Madonnas in Rome," said Pia.

Even Caddie was adamant. Fanny showed her a book about Mantua, one of Madame Menghini's. "Look, Caddie. In the Ducal Palace, the palace of the Gonzagas, there is a whole room of horses, life-size horses painted on the walls. Wouldn't you like to see it?"

"No thank you," said Caddie. "I don't like looking at horses." The unspoken "now" seemed to ring in the air.

"They say at this time of year, we should drive through miles of peach blossom." Fanny still tried to be beguiling. "There is Cremona where they make the violins. You would see oxen ploughing."

"We saw them from the train."

"If they don't want to go, let them stay at home," said Rob.

"This isn't our home, thank you," said Hugh.

"Who would have believed Hugh could be so abominable," Fanny said to Rob. "He was always sweet to me."

"That, of course, is why."

"I didn't know a child could be so bitter."

"You didn't always treat him as a child and now this is hard on him."

"I try and make it up to him, in love and attention."

"Far too much attention," said Rob wearily, "I think

that's a mistake. Children are children and they should learn to keep their places."

Even when they kept their place, they made themselves felt. Meals were an agony. "Pia watches everything I do, Caddie watches everything you do," said Fanny. "Hugh looks at his plate and says nothing."

"Can't they eat alone?"

"It makes twice as much work for Giulietta and Celestina who have a lot of us to cope with as it is. Besides, it looks as if we were running away from them," said Fanny.

Rob tried to enliven one dinner by talking about the script he was struggling with—which is difficult enough for him, without this, thought Fanny in remorse. Almost every day, telegrams came from Renato, the Prince, or the mysterious Herz, and they usually summoned Rob to the telephone; half-hour marathons, Rob named these calls. "It would be simpler to move to Malcesine or Milan," said Fanny.

"I won't be bullied," said Rob. He was amazingly patient and though he sometimes swore, more often he laughed. "They want Saladin to fall in love with Berengaria," he told them at dinner.

"But he didn't," said Caddie who had just read *Ivanhoe* and *The Talisman*.

"I know he didn't, but Renato and Mr. Herz and Prince Brancati want him to, and they say it's their film. They think it would be much more interesting, for Bianca Letti —if we can get her."

Then Hugh did speak. "Italians have no business to monkey about with English history," he said into his plate.

"Anyway," Rob went on, ignoring Hugh, "I'm trying to

build Richard up so that it will be as much his story, but I'm afraid, unless we can find someone very strong, he hasn't a chance against Saladin."

"But Richard was Cœur de Lion," said Fanny. "Surely, that's romantic enough."

"It's always the enemy who steals the thunder," said Rob. "The villain. Not that Saladin was a villain, just the enemy."

"I always liked Satan much the best in *Paradise Lost*," said Fanny.

"You could play Saladin," said Caddie suddenly to Rob.

"Or Satan?" He was laughing but Pia slid her hand into his and looked at Caddie and Hugh as if she could have stabbed them.

When Pia came, Caddie saw a father as she had not imagined a father could be. "You upset all our ideas," Fanny told him. It was clear that Rob and Pia loved one another, deeply, almost jealously, but with her he was completely natural. He was patient when he felt patient; one day he would let her climb all over him, drag him about the garden, steer the Mercedes or the motorboat, interrupt; but the next, if he were feeling impatient, he would shout at her, order her out of the room and not allow her to put her nose into the study.

"But Pia never knows where she is," Fanny protested.

"She does," said Rob. "She knows she has to study me and find out what mood I'm in. That will teach her to deal with other people."

"You must hurt her feelings," but Rob shrugged.

"Children are *people*," Fanny insisted.

"Not yet," said Rob. "One day we hope they will be."

He was the same with servants. "You must be considerate," Fanny had always taught, but if Rob wanted coffee at midnight, he would ring for it. "But poor Celestina," Fanny would say.

"Why poor? She's perfectly happy," and, oddly, Celestina was, "But I couldn't do it," said Fanny. "She would object. Why?"

"You are a nice woman, darling, so every servant and child who comes near you takes advantage of you. You spoil them and when I say 'spoil,' I mean it." He was serious.

"How spoil them?" asked Fanny.

"You make them less than they are. Children should be free to grow up," said Rob.

Pia, thought Caddie, was left remarkably free, almost as if she were grown up. "What time do you go to bed?" Caddie had asked her the first day. Pia seemed surprised.

"What *time?*"

"I have to go at nine."

"But, suppose you are not tired?"

"I still have to go." That plainly seemed to Pia idiotic. "I wish Rob were my father"—Caddie almost said it.

It was hard to resist him. At four o'clock, stale with work or if he had to make one of those calls, he came down and yodelled, "I want a child." Pia came running, all her dignity forgotten, and Caddie, almost against her will, followed. Rob took them up the mountain road, "Though it's wicked for the Mercedes," up behind Monte Baldo to pick wild flowers; cowslips, narcissi, lilies of the valley, "Fields of them," said Caddie.

She had not imagined they grew wild. He took them,

too, into Malcesine, or right down the lake to Sirmione, or up to Torbole, and Riva. Fanny was strict about eating between meals, but Rob took Pia and Caddie to see Rita in the waterfront café and gave them *cassata,* ice-cream cake filled with nuts and crystallized fruit, or else chocolate cake and cream, "like the Germans." They were all amazed at Pia's capacity; a slice of cake in Italy seemed to mean a whole quarter of the cake, rich with icing, heavy with cream; even Caddie was defeated after half a piece, but Pia finished it in a few minutes and licked the last crumb from her elegant fingers.

Rob let them taste everything, even when Fanny came. "What's that?" Caddie had asked of the pale pink slices of mortadella, and Rob put some into a roll with butter and gave it to her. "You won't like that. It's garlic," said Fanny.

"She might, if you don't tell her she won't." This edge seemed to come into their voices whenever they spoke of the children. "They seem to set us at one another," said Fanny, when she and Rob were alone.

"Isn't that because we are tender? These are just pin-pricks, Fan. Don't take any notice of them," but she could not help it and sometimes it flared into a real quarrel. On the evening of the shopping expedition, for instance, Fanny was in the drawing room with the children, waiting for Rob, who was working late. With Pia in mind, she had put on one of her new dresses, of heavy silk, honey-coloured. Pia stole up and felt its stuff between her fingers: *"Seta pura,"* she said and, "That colour is good for you," but, *"Another* new dress?" said Caddie and Hugh gave it a cold stare.

When Rob came down he was tired, but satisfied and exultant. "Got it. Got it at last," he said. "Got the scene with Saladin and Richard. It's right. Balanced, thank God," and on his way to the drinks tray, "That's a lovely dress," he said to Fanny, bent down, put his cheek against hers and kissed her. It was only a light kiss but three pairs of eyes noted it, Caddie and Pia openly but Fanny saw Hugh curl down in his chair, bend over his book too close to see it, while a deep blush spread up his neck to his ears.

"Rob." Fanny, brushing her hair that night, stopped to look uncertainly at him in the mirror, as he lay on the bed, smoking. "Rob, do you mind if I ask you something?"

He answered, as she had answered once to Anthea and Margot, "It depends what it is."

"I think it might be wiser . . ."

"Wiser to do what?" Rob stretched. He was tired.

"Wiser not to kiss me—or touch me," said Fanny with a rush, "in front of the children."

"Why on earth not?"

"It—embarrasses them . . ."

"Does it now?" said Rob and Fanny knew there would be trouble.

"Yes." She had to go on. "Especially Hugh. When you kissed me this evening . . ."

"So that was it!" For a moment Rob had to compel himself to be silent. He had come down to find them all waiting for him, as a family should wait for the father, he thought. All the faces had been turned to him, the little girls' silken heads, Fanny in the midst of them in her honey-coloured dress. The firelight, the beautiful room, the—the welcome, thought Rob now, and he had thought it was a welcome, had filled him with content and a possessive pride. Caddie and Hugh were not his, of course, but through Fanny he had almost a lien on them, and Pia was taken out of that rarefied atmosphere of her Nonna's that had worried him for so long. She has a real mother now, thought Rob and in that kiss for Fanny was a kiss for them all, if they had only known it. For Rob the disappointment was curiously bitter and his voice was curt as he said, "So I'm to condition my feelings to Hugh?"

"It doesn't alter *our* feelings."

"This kind of thing may alter them considerably."

"Oh, Rob. Don't be hurt."

"Why shouldn't I be hurt? Has it *ever* occurred to you, Fanny, for one minute, that in all this business, someone else than these precious children has feelings?"

"Occurred to me! I feel as if I'm being pulled in half."

"You will be, if you play the children's game. I warn you, Fanny. . . ." He had got up and was walking about. "As for Hugh. Has it also ever occurred to you that he is trespassing?"

"Trespassing?"

"Yes, trespassing. Children are secondary, Fanny. They are meant to be that. The man and the woman are first. First. Get that into your head. You are out of focus."

"I am?"

"Yes. The mother-and-child relationship isn't as important as you, and dozens of other women, I expect, make it. Hugh will grow out of you, beyond you, and you will lose him; should lose him. What Hugh needs is to fall in love himself."

"At *fourteen*?"

"Age doesn't matter, and nothing else will distract him. Don't you see?" said Rob. "This has forced him physically without the balance of loving. That's what makes boys, and men too, turn into—not monsters, gluttons. Something goes wrong in them. If Hugh could only love someone tenderly. Tenderness is the cure. Let's hope it will come sometime. Meanwhile he will probably have two or three bad years. Don't make them worse, by turning life into a hothouse for him."

"It's you who do that, when you kiss me."

"I do, do I?" and they were back where they had started, quarrelling.

X

"FISHING's no good," said Caddie.

As a matter of fact, it was the only thing that was any good, that and sailing.

The *Fortuna* belonged to Renato, a little sailing boat of the international twelve-foot class. "The cream of dinghy racing," said Hugh. Renato had said Hugh could use her, but, "She's not a beginner's boat," Rob warned him. "You would have been better with a ten-foot-six," but Hugh loved the *Fortuna*.

Almost every afternoon, when the south wind sprang up, Mario and Hugh would take her out, and it was infinitely soothing. The lake, it seemed, was a world of men; the campers' small inflatable boats chugged out from the shore but almost always there were only men in them, browning their naked chests and backs; perhaps they wanted to get away from women too, thought Hugh. If they took a woman with them, or children, it was as appendages. The speedboats were driven by men, real men, fishermen from the harbour. If they wore yachting caps trimmed with gold, the caps were refreshingly dirty, and they dealt with their cargoes of tourists as they would have dealt with a catch of fry or trout. All along the shore in the evenings men fished to catch the evening rise, never a woman among them. Mario, now and again with Giacomino or more often with a man from the village, would put out in his old boat, which was really a rowing boat; its motor was broken more often than not. They came along the shallows, one man standing at the oars, the other paying out the two-foot narrow nets, fine and weighted with corks, to catch the fry of small fish near the shore. Later, they would go far out on the lake, using this same small silver catch as bait, setting large nets to catch the deep-water trout. It was a man's world. Mario, taciturn bachelor, even resisted Celestina and no woman trespassed in the boathouse, "Thank God," said Hugh.

"Take me sailing," Caddie would beg.

"No bloody fear," Hugh could have said, but he only told Caddie, "It's not for girls."

"Piffle-paffle. Lots of girls sail."

"Yes, but I'm not good yet and you don't swim very well."

"Mario's there."

"He doesn't like women," but Caddie was like a limpet. "Look," said Hugh, driven. "I promise you, if I ever take anyone, you will be the first," and Caddie had to be content with that.

Hugh fished every morning, borrowing Mario's bicycle to go into Riva to buy bait. "What is it?" Fanny asked, looking at the gruesome mess. "Meat maggots?" She recoiled and went away. Even the bait frightens them off, thought Hugh contented. Fishing all morning, helping Mario to deal with the temperamental outboard motor or sailing the beautiful little *Fortuna* in the afternoon, made the villa possible for Hugh, even likeable. This and, he had to confess, sometimes Pia; but the feeling for Pia was only budding and he liked best to be on the jetty, in the boathouse, out on the lake where no human antics disturbed him—there they dwindled to antics but, "We came here to fight," said Caddie. "Six whole days have gone and we have done nothing. *You* do nothing," she said accusingly.

"What can I do?"

"Something." Caddie's face was desperate. "Can't you worry them, Hugh?"

"No," said Hugh.

"You used to worry Father, beautifully. And we must . . ." but Hugh only dropped his hook in again with a plop that spread ripples and absorbed his whole attention. "You won't even think," said Caddie.

"How do you know what I'm thinking, you silly little clot? Leave me *alone!*" said Hugh like a savage. Caddie's sigh came from her depths. Hugh was more difficult in Italy than he had been even in London.

She tried to enlist Pia. "Pia, do you want your father to marry Mother?"

"Certainly not," said Pia.

"Why not? You have to live with your grandmother." Caddie could not imagine a worse fate. "Wouldn't you like to have a father *and* a mother?"

"Not your mother," said Pia, with unflattering promptness.

"Why not?" asked Caddie bristling.

"She is not *elegante.*"

"What's not *elegante?*"

"Not chic."

"What is chic?" Caddie pronounced it "chick."

"Don't you know *anything*?" asked Pia again.

"I think Mother is chic," said Caddie loyally.

"You can't tell because you are not chic yourself," said Pia, which was true.

The more she saw of Pia, the more hopelessly clumsy and childish Caddie felt. Pia was so well arranged. Her side of the room was always neat. On her bedside table was the current detective novel, with her missal, that she read every night, the photograph of the friend, whose name Caddie was not permitted to know, and a vase of flowers put there by Pia. Her habits were orderly too; she would get up while Caddie was still half asleep, banded like a mummy in the bedclothes, though Pia dressed under her nightgown, which Fanny would have said was a flaw. Another was that Pia did not wash very much; she did none of the stripping Darrell insisted on, the rubdown with a towel, face plunge into cold water—Hugh skimped it but Caddie still faithfully carried it out—but even Pia's socks were put on exactly; she had discarded the long tights. Her skirt and jerseys were taken down from their hangers; Caddie had seen her bestow a pitying glance on the way she, Caddie, slung her dress or skirt over a chair when she took it off, often leaving her jersey with the sleeves inside out. Pia had even hung them up for Caddie. Her own clothes were always without the smallest crease.

She brushed her short hair for a long time, standing at the window, her small face inscrutable. The window was another of their differences; Pia liked to sleep with her windows closed, the shutters down. Caddie wanted them wide open. Fanny supported her. "In this balmy air, and the lapping of the waves makes a lovely sleepy sound," she said, trying to beguile Pia, but Pia only looked at her with those lozenge eyes. "In the night, the wind blows off the mountains. The *tramontana* gets up."

"I still think you must have the window open." Pia retaliated by winding a small white shawl round her head and writing a long letter to her grandmother.

When Pia was dressed and brushed, she would kneel down and say her prayers. From delicacy or shyness, Caddie always pretended she was asleep but from under her lids she would look at Pia's hands, placed together like one of the angels in a holy picture, and wonder what it felt like to be so certain God would listen. "Pia," she asked one day, "do you pray it won't happen?"

Pia did not need to ask what "it" was.

"I pray for my father."

"Not for my mother?"

"No."

"Isn't there," asked Caddie, *"anything* we can do?"

Pia shrugged, yet it was she who found the weapon. It was the day Caddie had failed to stir Hugh. "I have noticed," said Pia thoughtfully, "that grown-ups are upset, if children will not eat. Suppose we try and eat very, very little? Though that," she said with a darting look at Caddie, "will be difficult for you," but Caddie had already gone a large step further. "Suppose we eat nothing at all. Let's go on hunger strike," said Caddie.

"Children do go on strike," she argued with Hugh, who thought it a stupid idea. Soon after, she brought him a newspaper. CHOIR BOYS ON STRIKE AGAINST VICAR. "They wouldn't sing because they weren't allowed to bring books in to read in church," said Caddie, "and it says some school children went on strike too. They sat down and wouldn't get up because a boy was expelled."

"Yes, but going without food," said Hugh. "It would be futile. You could never keep it up."

"I can if Pia can."

"You know how greedy you are."

Caddie was not only greedy, she was hungry. All of them were except Hugh in this lake and mountain air. Celestina, too, was a superb cook. Caddie gave a great sigh. Certainly, when you actually came to it, a hunger strike was a daunting thought but it was also dramatic. "A real sacrifice," said Pia as if that were extremely commendable. "We can start now with lunch."

Lunch, that day, was to be gnocchi alla Romana. Caddie had seen it being got ready the night before; she could also smell it cooking. No one, here in Italy, had comfortable elevenses, so that they had had nothing since breakfast, and that had been only coffee and rolls. "Four rolls, two apples, and a banana," said Hugh of Caddie.

"Yes, but that was hours ago," and, "Let's start after lunch," Caddie suggested to Pia. "We can eat so much that tonight we won't mind."

"I shall never mind," said Pia and, "You see,' said Hugh to Caddie. "You will never do it."

"We shall start with lunch," said Caddie.

Pia shook her head; Giulietta passed on to Caddie, and Caddie shook her head. Giulietta, holding the dish, looked inquiringly at Fanny.

"No gnocchi?"

"No thank you."

"No thank you."

"But I thought you liked it?"

"We do, but not today."

"Are you not feeling well?"

"Quite well, thank you."

"Thank you."

"Very well, Giulietta. Put it down."

"Posala sulla tavola," said Rob and Giulietta, as was the custom at lunch, put the beautiful cheese-smelling dish, so invitingly browned on the top, down on the table. It happened also to be beside Caddie—"Right under my nose," as she said afterwards. Her stomach immediately gave a loud gurgle. "You *are* hungry," said Fanny. "Don't be silly. Have some gnocchi."

"No, thank you."

Perhaps they are sick of cheese, thought Fanny. She was remembering what she had heard Hugh say—but that was just anti-ism, she thought and Hugh was eating a little. "Have some salad and rolls and butter," she said to Caddie and Pia.

"No thank you."

"You mean you are not eating anything at all?"

"No thank you."

"Then would you like to go?" Thankfully Pia and Caddie escaped. "I almost couldn't," Caddie told Pia, who said kindly, "Gnocchi alla Romana is a very good dish."

It was a long afternoon. They both felt yawningly empty. "Who would have thought one meal would have made so much difference," but, "It's going to be meal after meal," said Pia. Fanny, who had to go to the post for Rob, took them into Malcesine and down to the harbour where, to Rita's amazement, they refused cake or an ice, even orange juice or a coffee. "Are you both ill?" asked Fanny again.

"We just don't want any." Fanny could understand Pia, that waxen pallor might mean an erratic stomach, but Caddie? She looked perfectly well, if a little pale. "Perhaps you both need a good dose," said Fanny at which they relapsed into giggles.

"Is it a joke?"

"Certainly not." Yet each time they refused, they looked at one another, and Caddie had adopted Pia's trick of making her eyes blank. For the first time since the day in Riva, she and Pia seemed drawn together. "You must expect," Pia warned, "that when they do understand, they will be angry."

Fanny began to understand at dinner.

Dinner was asparagus soup: slices of roast pork, tender as Celestina knew how to make them, in a gravy of young carrots and parsley: a puree of potatoes and after it, artichokes to be eaten leaf by leaf, dipped into bowls of vinaigrette. Then cheese—bel paese that Caddie loved—ripe pears, and Rob always gave them wine in their Perrier water. The soup was left untasted; Giulietta again looked questioningly before she took the plates away, Caddie and Pia had not as much as picked up their spoons. They shook their heads to the dish of pork, though Caddie felt almost faint, to the potatoes, the artichokes. "I see," said Fanny. "You are going to eat nothing at all."

"No thank you."

"What is this? A hunger strike?"

They looked at their plates.

"Hugh, what is this?"

But Hugh said, "They are idiots, that's all."

"You had better go," Fanny said to Caddie and Pia, but Rob was more cunning. "No, don't let them go. Let them sit here and watch us eat."

"Saint Sebastian was shot with arrows," said Pia. "Look," and she showed Caddie a picture of a young man naked, his face serene and upturned though he was bound to a post and, as a pincushion is stuck full of pins, his body was stuck with arrows, each with a trail of bright crimson blood.

"Ugh!" said Caddie.

"He smiled," said Pia. Pia's eyes had plenty of expression now, they were lit and dreamy, almost ecstatic. "Saint Agatha had her breasts cut off," she said. "You can see paintings of her with them on a plate, and of Saint Lucy with her eyes. They were pulled out." She meant gouged and made the appropriate gesture with her two small thumbs. Caddie thought Pia enjoyed telling about these things and she was not sure they were an inspiration. Saint Agatha or not, both Pia and Caddie had headaches and they felt curiously sick, "And it's only the second day." They had not been able to sleep. "Of course not," Fanny had said. She had heard them moving about and had come in—then she had not been able to sleep either. "You are too empty to sleep, you silly little girls." She had gone down to the kitchen and, fathoming the difficulties of Celestina's cooker, a battered Calor-gas one with four rings standing on top of an old range, she had brought up two tumblers of hot milk and a plate of biscuits. "Drink this and stop this nonsense."

"If we had one biscuit each, would they notice?" asked Caddie.

"She probably counted," said Pia. "You see, she *is* getting upset."

Pia counted the biscuits herself, as if she doesn't trust me, thought Caddie. After Pia did that, nothing could have made Caddie take even a sip of milk, though she lay awake trying not to smell the steam, and in the morning Giulietta found the tumblers, the plate of biscuits untouched beside their beds.

"The martyrs were brave," said Pia. "They suffered terrible things." Could they, thought Caddie, have been more terrible than the aching emptiness of one's inside? The continual resistance of temptation? For lunch on that second day there was risotto, rice cooked until the good chicken liquid was absorbed right into it, risotto, followed by crisp eel fritters.

The first time they had these, Caddie had not known they were eel, or Fanny and Hugh either, but the fritters were so delicious that when they did know they didn't care, and now, "I'm sure they are having the nicest things on purpose," said Caddie.

"Naturally," said Pia. "My father is clever." "Your mother may be a simpleton," was implied, "but he is very clever."

He was. He did not argue with them, he simply took as long as possible over every meal with Caddie and Pia pinned in their chairs. "Have some more, Fanny." "Pia, pass those peas to Hugh." "Beautiful coffee this morning,

Fanny." "Such fresh rolls." "Nice crisp lettuce." Pia and Caddie gazed stonily over his head, but it was torture.

The strangest part was Hugh. He, who had condemned Italian food, had picked at it, now ate as never before. "Does he *want* to be unkind?" asked Caddie of Pia, who shrugged. Hugh did want to be unkind, a hard little lust of cruelty was in him; the more he ate, the more impatient he was of Caddie, the more he hated Fanny.

Fanny herself, even more than Caddie, was hurt and displeased. "I thought he would have been more loyal," but no one, it seemed, was loyal. That second day she had a registered parcel from Paris, a box, labelled *Fragile,* and heavy. "Philippa!" she said, looking at it in amazement.

"Flip?" said Caddie. How far apart the family had grown; she had not thought of Philippa for weeks—days, corrected Caddie. Was it only a matter of days since she and Hugh had seen Philippa off to Paris?

"Flip." Fanny sounded both tearful and excited. "She hasn't written to me since . . ." She saw Caddie's and Pia's curious eyes and took the box away up to Rob's study.

Inside, when she had unpacked them from the shavings, were revealed two ornamental cups and saucers, lettered in scrolled gilt: *"Toi"* and *"Moi."* "Oh, poor darling!" said Fanny defensively.

"Wait a moment," said Rob, picking them up. "Philippa has a better eye than you. These are not the tourist things you think. Early Victorian," he said, looking at the markings. "She must have paid a great deal for them, particularly in Paris," but Fanny was devouring the letter that was with them.

"Oh Rob! She says they are a wedding present!"

"Well? Isn't that nice of her?"

"Philippa shouldn't give us a wedding present—a wedding present to her own mother! It seems all wrong and she asks if she can come to us this summer. She says she is longing to meet you."

"Well? Isn't that good?"

"She was Darrell's especial one," said Fanny slowly. "He was counting on her."

"Does that exclude you?" but Fanny only said, "Darrell will mind—terribly."

"Do I have to agonize over Darrell now?" said Rob. For the first time he was impatient. Then, "I'm sorry, Fan," he said. "It's all these alarms and upsettings. I married you, not your family," but Fanny, sitting by the table, had to say, "I am my family."

XI

<<———————————————————>>

R o b l a i d a trap for Pia and Caddie. He came out
of his study at four o'clock and gave his call, "I want a
child," and, without thinking, Pia and Caddie came running. "I'm going into Malcesine. Come along and we will
buy an ice."

"What do we do," asked Caddie in the car, "when he
orders ices?"

"Let him order and then not eat them. That will make
him crossest," said Pia.

They had not had a warmer, thirstier afternoon, a drive
that met more dust and, in all she had met in Italy, Caddie
liked best the orange ices they made in Garda, whole oranges filled with water ice, tasting of the fresh juice. Now
she and Pia sat on the wicker chairs with the ices on the
table in front of them and did not taste a morsel. "Not
good?" asked Rita.

"*Grazie sono buoni, molto buoni.* Very good," said Pia
and she and Caddie left them.

"I have a good mind to make you walk home," said Rob.

At dinner that second day, asparagus, veal cutlets with
lemon and fresh peas, apricot tart, Fanny could hardly get
her own mouthfuls down, nor did Rob eat much. "I told

you," said Pia afterwards. "Nothing upsets them more."

"Dear, this is a children's game," said Rob when he and Fanny were alone.

"Then children's games can be extraordinarily cruel." Fanny's eyes were filling. "That they should feel they need to do it. That's what hurts."

Rob swore. "I begin to think there's only one way to deal with children and animals: to treat them totally without imagination. You must ignore them, Fanny. They will never be able to hold out."

"They must be getting food from *somewhere*," he said, after breakfast was refused the third day.

"Where?"

"In the trattoria?"

"They don't go there and Celestina would know. Nothing happens in the villa that she doesn't see or know."

"Besides they haven't any money," said Rob. "Pia gave me hers for safe-keeping and you haven't given Caddie any. Though, of course, there's Hugh."

"Hugh doesn't approve," said Fanny, "but I will ask Celestina."

"No," Celestina said. The trattoria had sold nothing to any of the children. They had had, Celestina was sure, no food from anywhere. *Non un boccone.*

Almost none. Towards noon on the second day, wandering down to the boathouse, Caddie had come upon two rolls, a few olives, put down on a half-sheet of newspaper. It was one of the fishermen's lunches, for beside it was a bundle of nets. She looked over the water and could see two men working in the motorboat where the outboard motor kept spluttering out. They were too busy and exasperated to look shorewards. In each of the rolls was a wedge of salami. It was too much. She took a quick look round and ate them.

The worst part was confessing to Pia. "We might as well give up," said Pia.

"Oh no! Nobody saw. Not even Celestina. I let Cesare off the chain and they will think it was him," but it was hard work persuading Pia not to end the strike—Caddie had a suspicion that Pia made it more difficult. In the end she was mollified but no more.

Celestina tried leaving a plate near them, not when they were together, when they were alone, which was far more subtle: an omelette sizzling gold, ham sliced on a bed of lettuce, a meringue with cream. "I no tell," Celestina would say and disappear, leaving them to temptation. "Exactly what the devils did to Saint Anthony," said Pia.

"What devils?"

"Devils in the form of women," said Pia, her eyes lit with interest.

"Celestina isn't a devil. She's kind. Perhaps she really wouldn't tell," said Caddie wistfully.

"She would. She would go straight and tell." Caddie knew Pia was right and the plates were left, not one mouthful touched, not a bite. *"Neppure una bricciola,"* Celestina would tell Fanny in a kind of triumph.

At first Celestina had felt slighted. *"Due ore per fare le lasagne,"* which Pia told Caddie meant "Two hours to make that pasta." Every ribbon of it was homemade and to have it sent away was hard, but by the third day Celestina had changed to admiration. "It like the Hindus," she told Rob. "Tara Singh. That Sikh man on radio. And Gandhi. Very holy mans," said Celestina.

The village was not far behind Celestina. The story of the saintly children had spread: not to eat when one had the chance! That seemed superhuman, akin to saintly madness. Still in the village memory were the hard years after the war and, for all the tourist prosperity, the springing up of bars, ristorantes, hotels, camping sites and their canteens, there were still families living in tumbledown hovels, even in caves; still children who spent the whole day minding a single goose or goat; still women without a coat in winter. Food prices had risen so that every gramme was precious, most of all meat. These children, the stories ran, could even resist meat.

Fanny could feel that her own popularity had declined. Celestina no longer came in to chat with her or called out a greeting when she saw her in the garden. Fresh flowers were not put on her dressing table. Giulietta's big smile had disappeared and Giacomino looked the other way. Even the old milkwoman no longer nodded and gabbled her incomprehensible dialect—and Fanny had grown to like the old milkwoman. The couple in the alimentari handed out soap flakes and face tissues without a word. Fanny began to be looked at askance as far as Malcesine; people stared at her, gathered together in knots and whispered. "She really is getting upset," said Caddie to Pia, and they begged Hugh, "Won't you join in? If *you* didn't eat, she would mind most of all."

Anyone would have thought that now, by this third day, Hugh's scorn would have given way to respect, which would have done more than anything to stiffen Caddie, but no, he was even more deeply taciturn. "If you joined in now she might give in. She might come back."

"I'm not sure I want her back."

"*Not—want—her?*" If the villa roof had fallen on Caddie, she could not have been more astounded. "But . . . that's what we came for."

"I know. It was idiotic. Look, Diddie." Once again Hugh called her by that baby name, and this time it alarmed her. "Look. It's done, the divorce I mean, and nothing can ever be the same."

"Why not?"

"She's not the same. I'm not the same, or you, or Father. Even if she came back it's gone—forever. Can't you see that?"

"No," said Caddie. "It's got to be the same," but Hugh escaped her. Mario had said he could take the *Fortuna* out alone, though he must keep in sight. "*Non allontanarti,*" said Mario.

"I suppose he is all right," said Fanny watching the white sail swing as Hugh brought the *Fortuna* up into the wind.

"Mario has taught him very thoroughly," Rob reassured her, "and the lake is like a mill pond today."

"It can change very quickly. They all tell you that."

"Hugh can swim, can't he?" said Rob.

"Of course," and Caddie chimed in, "He got his bronze medal for life-saving."

"To see all the lights and the reflections," said Fanny.

"They are bribing us," hissed Pia and sure enough when they were ready to go, "You can come if you like," said Rob carelessly.

"Can we?" In spite of Pia, Caddie could not help falling into this trap too. "Oh, can we?"

"Yes, if you will both eat some dinner," and Fanny said, "It will be such fun. Come." It was said beguilingly.

"You think you can bribe us with a boat," said Pia but Caddie thought they could have—easily. She did not know what gave her the power to resist and it was heartbreaking to see them sweep away, the great wave with its sparkling wash behind them.

"My Uncle Bertrand has a better boat than that," said Pia. "I go in it often." Sometimes Caddie hated Pia.

"Niente cena; ne carne, ne verdura, e neppure il dolce, niente!" said Celestina, still with that tinge of triumph. "No supper; not meat or vegetables or pudding!" said Rob and Celestina whispered to him, *"Il signorino non è rientrato."*

Fanny's quick ear had heard it. "Did she say Hugh hasn't come back?" From the jetty they had walked up through the peaceful moonlit garden to find Celestina waiting for them. "Hugh? Not come back? Oh Rob!"

"Not yet," said Rob. He spoke calmly to calm her, but his face looked suddenly weary. "Damn all children! Damn them!" said Rob violently.

"Don't, Rob, something has happened." Fanny's eyes were terrified.

"We should have heard." Rob was still dogged in that.

"There are not many English boys staying on the lake."

"Then I think he has run away. He said he would."

"Ha preso la bicicletta di Mario senza chiedergliela," Celestina poured out Italian and Rob translated for Fanny. "He has taken Mario's bicycle without asking. Mario has been up as far as Tempesta. At the alimentari they saw Hugh riding towards Riva."

"Presto. Presto," said Celestina, imitating someone riding furiously on a bicycle. *"Schnell! Schnell!"*

"He can't have gone far," said Rob. "He hasn't much money and that bicycle is old and heavy. Very well," he said with a sigh and took the keys of the car out of his pocket. "Fanny, you go to bed."

"Bed? When Hugh . . ."

"Yes," said Rob. "I don't think he is in any danger. I will go and look for him."

"How will you know where to look?"

"If he is running away, he will be heading towards the Brenner. I will find him and bring him back, and that will be easier without you."

"Why?" asked Fanny indignantly.

"You may not have noticed that Hugh has been getting himself into a state."

"I notice everything about Hugh, and I thought he was settling down."

"It would seem he wasn't, or else something has precipitated this, and I have a feeling this will be best handled by a man."

"But you won't . . ."

"I will be gentle," said Rob. "Fanny, you have had enough. You must go to bed. Promise me," and in Riva,

driving along the quays, Rob saw a thin lonely figure leaning on the harbour wall. Beside it was propped an old
bicycle.

"Rob, how old should you be, when you could be expected . . ." Hugh picked at the wickerwork on the bar
table. Rob had taken him to the Marbella Club. "A night
club?" Fanny said doubtfully next morning.

"It was the only place I could find open where there
was food."

"I thought Italian hotels served dinner up to any hour."

"It's too early in the season," said Rob, "and it must
have been nearly midnight. We didn't get back from
Sirmione until eleven. We were lucky to find the Marbella."

Rob had watched Hugh ravenously eat a plate of soup,
some chicken; now some colour had come into his face; he
turned his glass of wine round and round in his fingers,
while Rob, opposite, sipped a brandy and waited. "How
old when you could be expected . . ." The words seemed
to have hooks from which Hugh could not free them. "Be
expected to have— I mean make lo— I mean . . . expected to sleep with . . ." His eyes lifted to Rob in a
tense pleading.

"You mean go to bed with a woman."

"How old should a man be?"

"There's no should about it," said Rob. "It depends on
the person, but usually, I should say, seventeen, eighteen,
nineteen."

Some of the tenseness went out of Hugh. Well, even
seventeen is three years away, thought Rob.

"Would you say . . . fourteen is too young?"

"I should say it was a bit precocious."

"A woman wouldn't expect it?" The question was so nervous that Hugh's voice went down at least an octave.

"If she did she must be, shall we say, sex-hungry?"

"Oh!" Hugh visibly recoiled. Then he buried his face in his hands and said, "I can never go back to the villa. Never."

"Suppose," said Rob with extreme gentleness, "suppose you try and tell me what happened."

Taking the *Fortuna*'s sails down Hugh had slipped, "I was up to my waist in the water and had to go into my room to change. I was going back to the boathouse, but Giulietta . . ."

That was evidently the fatal name. He could not go on. Rob, trying not to move a muscle of his face, said, "Giulietta?"

"Giulietta was cleaning the stairs." It came out in jerks.

"Cleaning? In the afternoon?" said Rob, trying to keep the level normal.

"Yes. I don't know why. Perhaps she hadn't had time before, or hadn't done them properly. She was sweeping," and in such a way that Hugh had stopped to look. It seemed quite pointless; Giulietta was sprinkling each marble step with sawdust and then sweeping the sawdust up. "That's an age-old way of keeping the dust from flying," said Rob. "Go on." She had been too absorbed and used to Hugh to stop or look, but he had stood on the top step watching.

Giulietta had been below him, her strong back bent

double; as she turned to brush the corners, her hips in the tight black skirt rippled like some splendid animal's quarters; her black hair fell forward over her face to show her neck, and, "I suppose I am possessed by necks," said Hugh. Giulietta's neck was brown pink, healthy as an apple, crossed by a gold chain that, like the sawdust, was a little damp. He could see a drop of sweat on it.

Giulietta was probably the only person who had really welcomed his and Caddie's coming to the villa; she was interested and friendly in spite of the extra work. It was she who taught them to say, *"Grazie," "Tante grazie,"* and answered, *"Prego,"* with the smile that showed her perfect white teeth. It was Giulietta who joked with Rob, never ready when she flung open the glass door for dinner calling, *"A tavola,"* or, if she were more sedate, *"Il pranzo è pronto."* Now for Hugh she was a different person. He looked down at the drop of sweat on the gold chain and he knew how her neck would feel, warm, damp, a little sticky, but a woman's living flesh. "Go on. Those girls expect it," Raymond would have said, but it was not Raymond who made Hugh put out his hand. It was Hugh. He bent and wiped the drop off with his finger.

"Giulietta," he whispered, and his hand did what Rob's hand had done with Fanny, played on her neck. With Hugh's slight fingers it could not have been called "paddling" but it was unmistakably a caress. It was only for a second; Giulietta straightened in a flash. She was taller than Hugh but he was a step above her and he could see that her dark eyes were sparkling, whether in anger or pleasure he could not tell. "Go on. Don't be a little boy," Raymond seemed to say. "Go on," and once again, "Those girls expect it," but now they were face to face, Hugh had no idea what Giulietta would do. Her face looked large, her eyes, seen so close, were not black but brown with a yellow tinge, her nose was high and her mouth alarming. Her breath, like Celestina's, smelled of wine and garlic— "Well, it was not long after lunch." Hugh was terrified. His breath seemed to stop. He wished the stairs would open and swallow him up but, "Don't be a little boy," that voice persisted. He put out his hand again and tremulously touched one of those points of Giulietta's, under her jersey; they were not hard as they looked, but soft, and springy, thought Hugh, surprised.

That odd hot shiver seemed to come up the back of his legs, into his stomach. He gave the swelling a squeeze. Giulietta laughed; her deep laugh; she seemed not to care if it sounded through the villa. Her arm came round Hugh's neck, pulled his head forward and she kissed him squarely on the lips, a long kiss that bruised them and was unexpectedly wet and warm. He felt her tongue and started as if he had been burned but she would not let him escape. At last, *"Così,"* said Giulietta, as one would say, "That's what you asked for." *"Questo è quanto hai chiesto."* "Now you have had it—and more than you expected," and she picked up her brush and went back to the sawdust and the stairs.

"Was that all?" Rob asked cautiously.

"All?"

Somehow Hugh had got himself down the stairs and out of the house. He fled to the garage, where he stood childishly wiping his lips with the back of his hand. Then he took Mario's bicycle and pedalled furiously towards Riva, and on the wrong side of the road until a motorist stopped him and, shouting angry Italian, pointed him onto the right. "And then I got to Riva," said Hugh.

"You have been here ever since?"

"I think so."

Hugh took a sip of his wine and shuddered at the taste; Rob could see the shudder go down his spine, then he turned to Rob again. "Should I have stayed?" he asked in anguish. "Should I? Is that what I should have done next? Raymond, a boy at school told me . . . But, as a matter of fact," said Hugh, in a burst of confidence, "I don't believe I *could* do it . . . yet." He looked at Rob with haggard eyes. "But suppose she wants me to? Suppose she . . . liked what happened?"

"The question is," said Rob, "did you like it?"

"No." The poor voice cracked and went down, cutting the word in half.

"Then you don't go on," said Rob. "Don't forget, men are the prime movers. It's for you to choose. So many of us," said Rob, "let other people choose; especially we let women. If you do that, you will never be a man. A man chooses—and abides by his choice," said Rob, his jaw obstinate.

"You chose Mother," said Hugh.

"The first time I saw her," said Rob.

"But what shall I do when I see her?"

"Your mother?" Rob was teasing, perhaps in relief but, "Giulietta," said Hugh, still in anguish. "What *can* I do?"

"Nothing."

"But . . . suppose she expects something to happen?"

"If she does, and I am sure she doesn't, she will soon

give up expecting. It may be awkward for you when you see her at first, I grant you that. It may even be painful." Rob did not look at Hugh, for which Hugh was grateful because he had blushed. "But it's the only way and always kinder in the end, to make your intentions clear; and I don't think, as a matter of fact, you need to be kind to Giulietta. She is engaged to a very nice young man, Carlo Lucchini in the village."

"Engaged?" The misery lifted from Hugh's face. "Oh, thank you, Rob. Thank you."

"He's back," Rob reported to Fanny, "and safe in bed. He will sleep, if you leave him alone."

"But where . . ." Fanny had started up in bed.

"I will tell you in the morning. Now I'm tired, and sick to death of children. Let me sleep."

XII

"SHE MUST have led him on," said Fanny, sitting on the edge of the bed.

"I gather not." Rob was still in bed, oddly tired—and sticky, thought Rob.

The weather had been growing steadily warmer, more balmy, but this Monday, the fourth day of the strike, promised to be hot, too hot for May, and not blue but lowering. Rob did not want to argue with Fanny, he did not want to work. I feel thoroughly out of sorts, thought Rob.

"I thought she was a nice girl."

"She is a nice girl. Hugh was lucky." Rob stretched and sat up.

"Lucky!"

"Yes. She frightened him off, in fact frightened him almost to death. I had hard work persuading him it was safe to come back."

"You're laughing." Fanny lifted accusing eyes.

"Not really," said Rob. "But perhaps we should laugh. Try and laugh a little too."

"I can't laugh," said Fanny. She had had an almost white night; now her head ached; in fact she felt a physical unwellness that had nothing to do with the worries in her mind, though it made them sharper, and she said, "It's our fault. You said we had made him grow up too quickly. At fourteen! With a servant girl!"

"It has happened thousands of times," said Rob. "Thousands, all down the ages, everywhere. The only pity is that you had to know of it. He did that by running away, the little fool."

"But what are we to do with him?"

"Leave him to Giulietta."

"To *Giulietta*? After this?"

"Yes."

"We should send her away."

"She's not our maid. She's Madame Menghini's. Look, Fanny, Giulietta is a sensible girl. She is engaged and she has plenty of brothers and cousins. I think you will find she knows very well how to deal with a little boy who has ideas, if he has any now, which I doubt."

"Don't." Fanny put her hands over her face, but Rob leant forward and pulled them away.

"Where's your sense? Don't be a tragedy queen."

"It isn't only Hugh."

"I know it isn't."

"What is in these children, Rob? I'm frightened."

"Frightened? By children?"

And Fanny said again, "I feel as if I'm being pulled in half."

"I think," said Rob, putting back the bedclothes and getting up, "the time has come for a showdown."

"Rob wants to see you in his study."

They stood in front of him, as he sat at his kitchen table.

"You know why I have sent for you?"

"Yes." It barely escaped Hugh's lips.

"You, Hugh," said Rob, "are not, I think, in this but I want you to hear," and he turned to Caddie and Pia. "As far as I am concerned," said Rob, "you can starve yourselves. I don't care."

Hugh looked at him with respect. Caddie caught that look and Rob's answering one; it was a kind of comradeship, a truce.

"I don't care," said Rob, "but I am not, repeat not, going to have your mother worried like this."

"She is not my mother," said Pia.

"Fanny—worried like this."

"How are you going to help it?" asked Pia in a silken voice.

"You will see," said Rob. "It is now three and a half days since you started this nonsense." For nonsense it seemed to be having a remarkable effect, and for all his not caring Rob looked ravaged. "If you don't eat your lunch, there will be trouble. Now go."

They went.

"He can't make us eat," said Pia. "We can shut our lips tight."

"They forcibly feed you in prison," said Caddie. "Will they do that to us?"

"They wouldn't have the things here," said Pia. "They need tubes."

"Tubes!" cried Caddie in horror.

"They put them down you and feed you through them."

"But what could they put down tubes?"

"Soup," said Pia, and Caddie was very nearly sick.

It was a miserable morning, for everyone, and a heavy hot day. "Thunder. *Tuoni. Donner,*" said Celestina. Fanny looked white and strained and she had red eyes as if she were tired out or had been crying. Hugh tried to keep out of the way in the boathouse but the outboard motor had broken again and Mario was in a temper. He curtly ordered Hugh to remove himself and, Giulietta has told him, thought Hugh.

That made Hugh quail. I never knew I was such a coward. In fact he dared not be alone. He did not want to give Fanny the chance of asking questions—as it was she followed him with her unhappy eyes every time he moved. In the end he attached himself to Pia.

More and more he was taking to being with Pia. She seemed to be the only person who did not exacerbate him. Her bony little body was still straight up and down, whereas even the familiar Caddie had two swellings on her chest that he could not help seeing when she wore the gingham dress which was too tight. He liked, too, Pia's detached coolness, and she had the great attraction of not wanting to talk. She preferred to read. At the moment it was *Deal Twice for Death,* but as she read she had the habit of absent-mindedly singing a maddening high-pitched nasal song.

"Don't do that, Pia."

"Do what?"

"Sing."

But she did not know she did it and unconsciously began again. This morning it made Fanny want to put her fingers in her ears and it penetrated to the study upstairs.

Caddie found a water snake asleep in the cypress hedge

by the stone table. It was so fast asleep, its head on one of its loose coils, that it did not hear her on the gravel, "And usually they try and flick out of sight at once," she told Fanny. "You have to be clever to catch one." Unfortunately, Celestina, coming out on the terrace, saw it too.

"*Non velenoso. Nicht schlimm,*" she yelled encouragingly to Caddie; but she ran and got a broomstick and killed the snake with the handle. If it was not poisonous why did she want to kill it? It seemed so insensately cruel that Caddie, in her foodless state, burst out crying like a baby; Rob heard her upstairs and shouted, "Stop that bloody din."

He was too worried that morning to be kind. Fanny's face haunted him and he could not concentrate. Besides he had reached a stage on *Saladin* when he needed a typist, a secretary. "And nobody seems to speak English, let alone type it, round this confounded lake," he said. He could have asked Renato to send a secretary out from Milan, but, "How can we import a secretary here when every available inch is taken up by children?"

"She can stay over at the hotel, the Lydia," said Fanny, "and work on the dining-room table. We can eat on the terrace."

"In this heat? Middle day? Anyway, I can't work. The house is pervaded by children, and *need* they be so abominably noisy?"

"Rob, be fair. They are not usually noisy."

"They are today. Caddie bellowing on the terrace and Pia singing like a hypnotizing dervish."

"I know. It goes right through one's head."

"Then why don't you stop her?"

"Because she is Pia. I have to be careful."

"Do we have to be so bloody delicate with one another's children?"

"I think so," said Fanny wearily. Her headache was worse; she had a backache as well, a dragging pain that made her thin-skinned, and she snapped out, "You know nothing at all about children."

"I do. I have been a child."

Hugh, bored with Pia's impersonality, began to fiddle with the knobs of the old radio and a wave of violent jazz swept through the house. "Stop it! Stop it! Stop it!" shouted Rob.

Over everything else lay the dread of what he would do at lunch.

"Do you think they will send for Doctor Isella?" asked Caddie.

"No, but they may beat us," said Pia.

In Pia's missal she had a picture of Saint Agnes with her lamb. "She was *killed*," said Pia, "and she wasn't much older than we are."

Lunch began with tagliatelle alla Bolognese, fine strings of pasta in tomato sauce, with minced meat. Giulietta, as usual, handed it as they sat round the table. Fanny took some; Hugh, sitting next to her, helped himself, keeping his eyes down. Caddie shook her head. Rob took his and Giulietta came to Pia. Pia, her hair brushed, her hands and face washed, her napkin unfolded on her knee, sat quietly though she was breathing in strange little snorts down her nose. Caddie felt cold with apprehension. Giulietta held the dish. Pia shook her head. Giulietta was taking it away when, *"Un momento, Giulietta,"* said Rob. He reached across Pia and helped her himself. "Give some to Signorina Caddie."

"*Servo la signorina?*" asked Giulietta startled.

"*Sì.*"

"*Permesso,*" said Giulietta to Caddie and put some on her plate. Rob sprinkled cheese for them both and, "Eat it," he said.

Nobody moved. Pia and Caddie looked straight in front of them.

"I said eat it," said Rob. He took a spoon, chopped some of the tagliatelle and held it to Pia's mouth. Pia kept her lips shut and breathed through her nose. "Eat it." With his other hand Rob gave Pia a sharp slap on the back of her head. It sent her forward against the spoon with such a jerk that she opened her mouth. The spoon went in. As Rob took it away, he too was breathing hard. "Now swallow."

Pia looked at him with her small black eyes and spat out the tagliatelle. As with everything she did, the spit was direct and it landed on the tablecloth in a stain of tomato and gravy. Caddie gave a little hiss of terror, and Rob lost his temper.

He jerked Pia out of her chair and, in a second, she was face downwards across his knee. He turned up her skirt, showing her little rump outlined in snowy-white briefs edged with lace. "You asked for it; you shall have it," said Rob and, before all their eyes, he gave her a good spanking.

Hugh and Caddie sat too shocked to speak; Fanny was white to the lips, only Giulietta watched with amusement in her eyes as if this were entirely natural. At last the sound of slaps ceased and Rob lifted Pia off that powerful knee.

"Now, are you going to eat it?" But Pia, her face contorted so that once again she looked like that ugly monkey, had made for the stairs. On the third step she paused and loosed a flood of invective at Rob. It was Italian so that Fanny, Hugh, and Caddie could not understand, but they heard Giulietta give a gasp.

"*Vigliacco, cattivo, ti odio.*"

"*No! No! Santo Cielo,*" cried Giulietta in horror and ran up to silence Pia but Pia shook her off.

"*Mostro, non ti posso vedere.*" Her face was curiously patched as if the slaps had landed there, her cambric blouse was pulled sideways, her hair ruffled, but there was not a tear. "*Cattivo, vigliacco.*" Then she turned to Fanny. "*Anche te, strega.*"

"*Taci, taci, vergognati,*" screamed Giulietta again.

Suddenly Pia remembered, thought Caddie, remembered she was Pia. She put her blouse straight, shook out her skirt and smoothed her hair. Then she drew herself up, and spoke to Rob in English with immeasurable scorn. "I will ask God to forgive you," she said, opened the brocade door and went upstairs.

"Caddie, do you want the same?"

Caddie stared at Rob, her eyes as full of horror as if she were trapped.

"Then eat your lunch, or in spite of your mother, you will be spanked as well."

"Caddie, eat it. You must."

With her eyes on Rob, Caddie picked up her fork, lifted a piece of tagliatelle. It had grown cold and felt slimy.

The memory of the mangled snake came back. Caddie made a loud retching noise and was sick.

"Nessuno ha toccato cibo," reported Giulietta in the kitchen. "This time nobody ate a thing."

"God above!" Rob had shouted, standing up and sending his chair back with a push that knocked it over. "Do your children perpetually have to vomit?"

"That's not fair." Fanny sprang up too. "They are not used to seeing people hit."

"Hit! I didn't hit Pia. I gave her a spanking where she needed it."

"You used force."

"Of course. What else could I use?"

"It's never fair."

"Fair! This isn't a case of being fair. It's discipline."

"Discipline shouldn't humiliate."

"I see," said Rob at white heat. "You think I oughtn't to have beaten Pia. That I should allow anything these little rats choose to do."

"They are not little rats. They are people. People." And Fanny said, "We have never beaten Hugh or Caddie."

That "we" seemed to ring out and, "I didn't mean . . ." Fanny sat down suddenly among the litter of plates and dishes and put her hand across her eyes.

"If they had been beaten," said Rob, and now he was quiet, "they probably would not be here. They would be obedient. Come," he said. "We can't lunch here now. Let's get out and clear the air. I will take you to San Vigilio."

"I couldn't eat any lunch."

"We will have a drink then. Come."

"Caddie . . ."

"Hugh, take Caddie upstairs, then get Celestina. She will look after her," but Giulietta had already brought a pail and cloth and was mopping Caddie up.

"Poverina, povera anima innocente." Celestina followed and guided Caddie upstairs. Fanny got up, hesitated, then went after Rob; Hugh, finding himself alone with Giulietta, jumped up as if he had been scalded and ran down to the jetty. When Giulietta had cleaned the floor she began to clear away the untouched tagliatelle.

XIII

PIA HAD changed from her skirt and blouse into a cherry-coloured linen dress banded with white. Now elegant again, she was sitting on her bed, her eyes shut, her lips moving. The eyes flew open when she heard Caddie come in from the bathroom. Celestina had told Caddie to lie down.

"Did they make you eat?"

"I was sick," and Caddie felt bound to say, "I think you are brave, Pia, much braver than I am, especially when you are so empty. I . . . I . . ." "Perpetually howling," Hugh said of Caddie these days. The tears were brimming now and she hastily changed the subject; "Are you asking God to forgive Rob?"

"Yes, and you might help," said Pia. "Ask Him to send your mother back to England."

"I have asked and asked," said Caddie. "And He doesn't take the slightest notice. I wish I was a Catholic," she said.

"I wish your mother was."

"Why?"

"*Catholic* mothers don't go marrying other people's fathers when their husbands are alive."

"Don't they?" Caddie digested this. "What happens if they fall in love?"

This disconcerted Pia. She could not deny that Catholic mothers fell in love—one had only to go to the opera, the theatre, watch television. "They fall in love," she said, "but they don't go upsetting everything."

"You mean if Mother were a Catholic, she wouldn't have done this?"

"Certainly not," said Pia. "It would be a sin."

If Caddie had not felt as sick and weak, her head aching, her legs feeling as if they were made of wet paper, she would not have been as naïve. She had, too, always been impressed by Pia's certainty.

For instance, on Sunday, there had been no question, as with the Claverings, as to whether Pia should or should not go to church. At a quarter to ten she had appeared in her white hat with the scarlet streamer, her coat, gloves, neat white socks, and buckled shoes, carrying her purse and missal and Rob had broken off his work to drive her to Mass in Malcesine, waiting in a café until it was over. "Won't you come in?" asked Pia as if she wanted him to, but Rob only smiled and said, "I'm a heathen; besides I want a coffee. Celestina will go with you." Celestina, Giulietta, and the trattoria children had driven in with them.

"Can I come?" Caddie had asked.

"Ask your mother," said Rob.

"If you want to," Fanny had said. "But you won't understand."

Yet, in a mysterious way, Caddie had understood. True, the Mass was for the greater part incomprehensible; a

mixture of Italian and Latin, which latter, Pia had explained to her, was the language of the Church; but Caddie
had been struck by the way not only Pia, all the children,
knew what to do. She had copied Pia's genuflexions and
knelt down, stood, sat as she did, though Celestina's hard
hand had impelled her to kneel each time the bells rang.
Caddie had an impression of candles shining, the smell of
incense, smoke, of chanting, mystery, and great solemnity,
yet everyone seemed quite at home. Towards the end, Celestina and Pia had gone up with a crowd of other people
to the altar; it was a big crowd: old peasant women in
black, old men, young men—all the men sat together on
one side of the church, the women on the other—there
were dressed-up young women, mothers with babies, boys
and girls.

"Where did you all go?" asked Caddie afterwards.

"Up to the rail for communion."

"Do *you* have communion?"

"Of course. I am *ten*," said Pia, as if that were middle-
aged. "I made my First Communion when I was eight."

"Like Beppino?"

Beppino, the elder of the two trattoria children, was, Celestina told them, to make his First Communion on the
third Sunday in May. He was to have a new grey suit, and
a white bow with gold fringes tied round his arm.

"Pia, did you have one of those beautiful long white
dresses we saw in Riva?"

"I should hope not," said Pia. "Mine came from Lavori
Artigiani Femminili at the corner of the Via Condotti in
Rome. Every tuck, every little insertion was handmade. I
had a white veil, a circlet of white silk roses." Caddie could

see the roses on Pia's small black head, the long white dress.

"You must have looked like a bride."

"I did. I had thirty presents."

There was no doubt in Caddie's mind that Pia was an expert on religion and she asked trustfully, "How do people become Catholics?"

"If they are not born one, they have to learn," said Pia.

"How do they learn?"

"I suppose they speak to a priest or nun."

Caddie could not imagine herself speaking to a nun, though she knew Pia's teachers were all nuns, but she had seen the priests in Malcesine. There was one of whom Celestina talked reverently, Padre Rossi, the *arciprete,* Celestina called him, which seemed to make him very important, like an archangel, but, all the same, Caddie had made up her mind. She went to Hugh and asked, "Is there any Topaz money left?"

"A little. I have been using some to buy bait. I thought you wouldn't mind."

"I want some," said Caddie.

"How much?" asked Hugh reluctantly. "I want to buy a rod. How much do you need?"

"Enough for the bus into Malcesine."

"Why don't you walk?"

"I don't think I could," said Caddie. "I feel queer." Reluctantly he gave her a hundred-lire note. "Bring me the change if there is any." She must have looked white, because he asked, "Are you going alone?"

"Yes," said Caddie quickly. She had a strong feeling that Hugh would not approve.

It was hot, even for early afternoon, the hottest part of the day. The sky looked heavy, white grey; Caddie was still squeamish and the bus smelled of hot rubber, hot oil, dust—and hot people, thought Caddie. She was glad to get off at Malcesine, but here too the white glare lay over the whole town.

Caddie walked along the motor road until she came to the steps that led down to the church piazza where the heat came off the bricks. There were always people round the church and now boys were playing football, women sat on the low balustrade under the trees, gossiping and knitting, while babies played and staggered at their feet.

The women and boys stared at her, making her feel an intruder. She remembered having seen yesterday a side door into the church and she walked past the big front doors trying to whistle, her hands, though Pia would have reproved her, in the pockets of her caramel-coloured jerkin. Fanny had been right; the jerkin was far too hot for Italy and, I'm boiling, thought Caddie, but I couldn't come and see an arciprete in a frock that crumples and is too short and tight. She wished she had a linen dress like Pia's.

At the side of the church, under an arch, was a courtyard with a stair leading up from it to a little house. Was that where Father Rossi lived? She stole through the courtyard to a small door covered in leather and slipped into the church.

She stepped into a merciful coolness and dimness, even that short walk from the bus had made her sweat; in fact, she was feeling so giddy that she had to sit down and lean her head against the polished wood of a pew. I ought to kneel down, she thought, but her knees were too weak.

A Catholic church, Rob had said, was never empty and that seemed to be true. This was a Monday afternoon but candles were burning in front of the side altars of the big church, at least, they looked like altars; they were spread with lace-edged cloths and had vases of flowers. Pia had told her that candles were lit for requests or in thanks; evidently a great many people had been asking or thanking.

The big candles were a hundred lire, the little ones fifty. Caddie wished she could light one, but her hundred-lire note was only enough for the bus.

People were praying. Some of the women had shopping bags or baskets, some were in slippers. An old man was having a comfortable nap. A woman came in carrying, with the utmost care and pride, a pot of arum lilies. In front of the high altar a red lamp burned, and Caddie saw, sitting in the front pew, a man dressed in black and reading a book. She tiptoed to an old woman, a cleaner with a box of spent candle ends and a small whisk broom, tiptoed to her and pointed at the man.

"*Il prete?*" whispered Caddie.

"*Sì, sì, il prete, Padre Rossi, arciprete.*" It would be the arciprete, but the old woman nodded encouragingly, "*Sì, sì,*" and went back to her candle-trays.

Cautiously Caddie drew nearer. She saw a big man, with brushed brown hair, a fresh rosy face, his neck rising rosily from the narrow band of his soutane. He did not look very alarming and he was alone, but could she dare to disturb him when he was praying or reading a holy book?

Then she remembered something that had impressed her yesterday. They had been far too early for the Mass.

Celestina had said it was at ten but it was at half past and while they waited a priest had been there, not the arci-prete but an old man with white hair, kneeling, deep in prayer. A small girl had come in, a handkerchief over her head; the village children all wore handkerchiefs or head scarves, not hats like Pia. She had come walking in with small important steps, had gone straight up to the old priest and tapped him on the shoulder and he had stood up at once and, in his long soutane and black cloak, had gone to the door of what looked rather like a sentry box at the side of the church, but a sentry box hung with purple curtains. The little girl had gone round to the other side and knelt down behind the curtain—Caddie could see her legs.

"What's she doing?" she had whispered to Pia.

"Making her confession."

"She interrupted him."

"Of course. That's what he's there for," said Pia. "If he's a good priest."

Father Rossi, Caddie knew, was a good priest. She had heard Rob and Fanny talk about him. Though he was not old he had been made arciprete and he was a scholar in Latin, Greek, Hebrew. He spoke German, French—many languages, said Celestina—Caddie prayed that he spoke English.

But, if I go and tap him, he will think I want to confess, and what shall I do then? thought Caddie. She longed for Pia. Pia, she knew, would not have hesitated, and if Pia can, I can, thought Caddie.

She tapped so gingerly that at first he did not feel it. She had to give him a small thump. Though she did not know it, this was not a confession time and for a moment he looked displeased. *"Was wollen Sie? Wer seid Sie?"*

He can see I am not Italian, so he thinks I'm German, thought Caddie. They all think English people are German. Perhaps he can't speak any English, and her heart sank.

"English?" asked Caddie, and desperately, "I'm English."

His blue eyes took in her pallid, unhappy face and red eyes and he stood up. He was big, burly, in his soutane, in fact, anyone's idea of a fat priest, but there was more to him than that; a calmness about him, something strong. He looks as if he could tell you things, thought Caddie and now, "English?" he said gently. "I speak a little English." He said "spik" and "leetle" but it was such a relief that, for about the sixth time that day, Caddie began to cry.

This time she could not stop, and at last he took her hand and led her out of the church, bending his knee to the altar—Caddie bent hers too—and then out through the courtyard, empty now, and up the stair. She had guessed right, it led to his house. At the top was a little piazza shaded with oleanders and an olive tree. There were geraniums in tubs, a hen and chickens scratching, a hutch full of rabbits, and a vine making an arbour for a table and chairs.

The front door had two bells, one marked *"Notturno."* Even through her tears Caddie wondered why anyone should want a priest in the night; then he took her into a narrow waiting room with a marble floor, a table covered with oilcloth, some hard chairs, a crucifix, and a painting of the Pope. He made Caddie sit down. *"Subito, subito,"* he said, and disappeared.

It was as quiet and peaceful as it was poor and bare; anything less like the vicarage at Whitcross it would be hard to imagine. Caddie tried to dry her eyes but her handkerchief was a wet ball. At last she gave up, put her head down on the oilcloth table, and sobbed.

"But, my dear little girl, I cannot make your mother a Catholic."

"Can't you?" The tears began to stream again and Father Rossi said hastily, "Drink your coffee."

It was a miniature cup, the sort of coffee, thick and black, that Rob drank while they ate ices. An old woman, "My mother," said Father Rossi, had brought it on a little tray. Caddie found it odd that an arciprete should have a mother. "Did you think he had fallen from the sky?" Hugh said scornfully when she told him of this, but the arciprete's mother was kind. *"Una Inglesina,"* she said softly and touched Caddie's cheek. The kind gesture unfortunately set Caddie off again. The old woman patted her, making clucking noises of concern and hurried out and, "Drink," said Father Rossi. "Drink before you try to talk." The coffee was so strong that it took Caddie's breath away but it stopped the tears.

"Now you can tell me," said Father Rossi, and Caddie began. "I . . . I . . ." but it was difficult to put into words and she said, "Oh, I wish I had brought Pia."

"Pia? That sounds Italian. Who is Pia?" and he said,

"You must speak slowly if you want me to understand. Now tell me."

"I can't," but he was not an arciprete for nothing and slowly, bit by bit, with a gentle question here and there, he drew the whole story out of Caddie. But it was no good.

"My dear little girl, I cannot make your mother a Catholic."

"Why can't you?"

"Only God can do that."

"Then why won't He?"

Father Rossi shook his head. "That is not for us to know. You must pray and I will pray." That did not seem to Caddie a hopeful answer but he got up. "Come, I will put you on your bus and, as soon as you get home, you will ask Celestina—I know her, she is a good woman, Celestina —to give you a strong soup. The little Pia too. This, to starve, is not the way."

"What is the way?" asked Caddie.

"I wish I knew," and he sighed again. The old woman brought him a flat black hat that looked as if it were made of beaver—Caddie had once had a beaver bonnet—and they went out into the sunshine.

They were waiting at the bus stop, the blue arrow on a yellow sign that said *"Fermata,"* when the Mercedes came along the road, Rob and Fanny coming back from lunch. Before she thought, Caddie had waved. Rob braked with a screech of tires and pulled up, just past the stop. Fanny was out of the car in a moment.

"Caddie! Has something happened?" But Father Rossi stepped in front of Caddie.

"Indeed it has happened." The passengers waiting for

the bus all looked; people in the road paused, seeing their padre with the English Signora. "You are Candida's mother?"

Rob had come up. "I'm afraid, Father Rossi, that Caddie has given you a wrong idea," he said.

As Rob knew everyone, he seemed to know the arciprete, but here was one person who did not smile at him.

"Signor, she has given me a singularly clear idea," said Father Rossi.

"We are not Catholics and have no right to bother you."

"Every child has the right to bother me." Father Rossi kept his hand on Caddie's shoulder. In his long soutane he seemed much larger than Rob and his voice rang down the road. A small crowd had begun to gather. This, clearly, was no ordinary conversation.

"Look at this child," said Father Rossi. "See her state."

Fanny's face was flooded with a burning colour.

"See her state, and she tells me there are two of them. Two little girls, starving, to bring you to your senses."

Someone in the knot of people was translating for the others. The petrol girl and two mechanics had come from the garage, people from the shops, some of the tourists had stopped. There were murmurs, of admiration for Caddie, of indignation against Fanny and Rob. Father Rossi heard the murmurs and he sank his voice as he said to Fanny, "You are not a Catholic, Signora, but I would suggest to you that you should go into my church, kneel down there, and think what you are doing."

Fanny took a step back against Rob.

"Kneel down there and think before it is too late," said Father Rossi.

"Caddie, get into the car at once. At once!" said Rob.

She was frightened by the silence. No one spoke. Rob drove so fast that, alone in the back, she was bounced up and down and flung from side to side. Fanny sat with her head bent; Rob looked straight ahead. He drew up at the villa gates but did not turn in.

"I'm going on to Riva," he said to Fanny. "Will you come?"

She shook her head and he leant past her to open the door; before she got out, he put his hand under her chin and turned her face up to look at him. Caddie expected him to say something momentous but all he said was, "I have to telephone Renato and get some money."

Caddie could see that Fanny's lips were shaking but she said nothing and Rob let her go. Then he reached back, opened the door for Caddie, and said, "Get out," as briefly as he had said, "Get in." Caddie understood that she was beyond the family pale. He slammed the door and drove away in a cloud of dust.

Fanny went into the house. In this long afternoon her pain had grown worse and now she knew what it was. She went into the bathroom, came out, passing Caddie on the landing without a word. Caddie heard her opening drawers, moving about the bedroom, but then there was silence. Cautiously she pushed the door. It was open and she looked in. Fanny was lying face downwards across the bed.

In Riva the paths along the harbours were deserted. On this uncommonly hot and heavy afternoon people were sleeping or had gone to the beaches, or taken refuge in the

cafés. Rob left the car and sat down on a bench in the
shade of the willows, but the scene in Malcesine still
danced before his eyes. He could not even smoke but sat,
his elbows on his knees, his head in his hands, staring at
the dust, dust pocked with little stones. He saw Caddie's
face. Fanny's. "Poor little toad," he muttered. "Poor little
toad," though which of them he meant he did not know.
Perhaps he meant himself. Poor toad. Hugh, Caddie, Pia,
piling things one on another; it was too much. When he
thought of the hunger strike his lips twitched, as they
twitched when he thought of Hugh and Giulietta, but behind lay an immense aching. He felt Pia's lightness, her
small bones, under his hand; it had been like beating a
bird—contrary to what he had told Fanny, Pia had never
been beaten—and indignation came up in him. They
should never have been drawn into this, he thought, then
he remembered that it was he who had drawn them in and
he groaned aloud. Hugh and Pia were bad enough, but
when it was Caddie the whole problem suddenly grew
deeper. Caddie, thought Rob, brought you into real truth.
I knew that the first time I saw her on the terrace, that little bungling ignorant girl and—they won the first day
they came, thought Rob.

How long he sat on the bench he did not know. The air
cooled a little, the town woke to life. A sudden puff of
wind sent the willow fronds streaming and blew the dust.
Far off, towards the Brenner, thunder rolled, so distant
that it sounded like far-off drums. Then it was still. It has
not grown much cooler, Rob thought.

At last he sat up, lit a cigarette, and smoked. The tenseness was gone; he was very thoughtful. He lit another,

pitched it away, stood up, and shook his shoulders to settle his coat. Then he walked away to the post office and the
bank.

"Mother." Caddie felt she had stayed at the bedroom
door for an hour. "Mother."

No answer.

"Mother, aren't you feeling well?"

"*Mother!*" It was a wail.

At that Fanny looked up. Something of Caddie's bewil-
derment and remorse reached her. Eleven-twelve is a painful age to be, thought Fanny. Too young to understand, too
old to be unconscious and, "You're not a criminal," said
Fanny. "You needn't look like that," but Fanny could not
spare much pity. Her skin was clammy, there were dark
rings under her eyes and she was full of pain, pain and disappointment. That secret hope was gone. I was late, that
was all. Thank God I didn't say anything to Rob. It was
only that I was nearly three weeks late. "Run away," said
Fanny to Caddie.

"But Mother . . ."

"For goodness' sake, Caddie, leave me *alone*. I must be
alone!" and Fanny got up and ran downstairs into the garden.

Caddie followed and watched.

At Stebbings, when anything upset Fanny, and she had
to try and control herself, if Lady Candida had driven her
beyond bounds, or there was some bad news, or when the
vet had put Bracken, Danny's predecessor, to sleep, Fanny
had had a way of going into the garden, walking up and
down there, under the familiar trees, past all her flowers,

touching them, as if to touch nature steadied her, brought her anger or grief into proportion. She was doing that now. As Caddie watched her, Fanny stood by the wisteria, drawing its tassels across her hand. She explored with her finger the split bark of an olive tree, avoided the magnolia where Celestina's birds were hung, but stopped by a lilac, bent to pinch a spike of rosemary. Yet she seemed not to be able to calm herself; even her shoulders looked hunched as if they had had a blow. She went on walking, touching. Caddie could not bear to watch her any more. What had she precipitated by going to see Father Rossi? At last she wandered miserably down to the boathouse.

The *Fortuna,* her mainsail furled and tied, was in the little harbour, tied up alongside the old rowing boat. There was no sign of Mario, or of Hugh, thought Caddie at first. Then, walking out on the jetty, she stopped. There were voices, children's voices, laughing and talking. They sounded as if they came from the back of the boathouse; and through the wisteria on the boathouse fence, its twisting stems and flowers, Caddie caught sight of something cherry red; Pia's dress.

It was odd for Pia to be in the boathouse. Caddie stepped nearer. She had to step nearer again to believe her own eyes. Behind Mario's room in the boathouse was a small veranda where nets and oars were kept. It had a bench and a table. There, hidden from the villa by the wisteria, the line of nets, Caddie could see Beppino and Gianna and, sitting at the table in that immaculate dress, Pia. On the bench beside her was Hugh and on the table were bottles of orange soda with straws, plates, tubs of ice cream and Pia was, "Eating," breathed Caddie. "Eating!"

In one hand Pia held a roll, split by pink ham, and as Caddie watched she took an enormous bite; in the other was a
cardboard spoon for the ice cream. Hugh was watching
and laughing! Dumb with amazement, Caddie stood there
until the last of the roll disappeared into Pia's mouth and
a tongue, small as a kitten's, came out to flick the last
crumbs inside. She took another roll. Now the plate was
empty and Pia commanded Beppino, *"Va a comperare due
altri panini con prosciutto ed un altro gelato,"* which Caddie knew meant more ham rolls and another ice. She saw
Hugh pull his wallet out of his shorts' pocket and give a
note to Beppino. He was paying Beppino to go and fetch
them. Buying paninos with my money, my Topaz money!
It was the final insult. Caddie tore in at the boathouse
gate, up the veranda steps, and launched herself at Pia.

The table was pushed aside. The plates, bottles, spoons
were on the floor and in a moment Pia was down, Caddie
pummelling her with both fists, banging her head among
the streams of orange soda.

The tumult came into the villa garden, Pia's shrieks and
Beppino's and Gianna's. Their father and mother ran
across the road from the trattoria, and down the back lane,
and the mother added her scolding to the pandemonium
when she saw the broken plates and bottles. Celestina and
Giulietta came running from the villa, Giacomino walked
after them and all the while Hugh, trying to catch Caddie's fists, shouted to her to let Pia go. It was that English,
"Let go, Caddie! Caddie, let her go!" that brought Fanny
running too.

"Caddie! Caddie! Caddie!" shouted Fanny as she ran
past the wisteria fence. Caddie looked up and in that sec-

ond's pause Hugh plucked her away, holding her with her wrists twisted so that she screamed, while the trattoria father picked up Pia.

"Caddie! Have you gone mad?" panted Fanny.

"She was eating," screamed Caddie incoherently. "Eating! I think she has been eating all the time."

"Hush, Caddie. Hush." But Caddie would not hush. She bellowed.

"Hugh! Hugh was helping her . . . helping her eat and they never told me. . . . It was my money . . . my Topaz money."

Hugh had loosed his hold of her wrists and she was rubbing their hurt redness in an anguish of sobs. He stood by, sullen and defiant as always when caught out. Pia, trying to look unmoved, was wiping her dress with a napkin, picking ice cream and bits of ham out of her hair.

A knot of villagers had gathered, amazed by this sudden outbreak of the English. Beppino and Gianna had taken refuge by their mother and all of them, with Celestina and Giulietta, talked in torrents. Only Mario who had come back from the village kept away at the far end of the boat-house beach.

"Helping her eat, with my money."

"Is this true, Hugh?" asked Fanny.

"I helped Pia once or twice," muttered Hugh.

"But . . . how was it Celestina didn't know? If you got things from the trattoria?"

"We didn't get them; Beppino sneaked them out to us. I paid him," said Hugh virtuously.

"With my money. My Topaz money."

"Hush, Caddie. Hugh, you did this, while Pia let us think she was on strike."

"Well, no one but Caddie would be silly enough to strike properly."

"But why didn't you tell me?" broke in Caddie. "Why did you shut me out?"

At that Pia lifted her head. "*You* wouldn't have been able to pretend," she said and, even in her woe, Caddie knew that this was true; but it still seemed to her the depths of treachery for Hugh to do this. Her own brother! Hugh! Caddie thought she had exhausted all her tears when she was with Father Rossi, but now she sobbed as if her heart would break.

"Is anything else going to happen today?" said Fanny. To Hugh she said, "I think you are disgusting. Pia, tell the trattoria people I will pay for the broken plates and the bottles, and tell Celestina I want to speak to her. Now, all of you, come with me." She put her arm round Caddie and took her away.

XIV

"VERY WELL," said Fanny. "Very well."

They were sitting round the dining-room table eating, and drinking tea. Fanny had made the tea herself, while at her orders Celestina lightly boiled eggs and made hot toast. Fanny had buttered the toast, cut it into small pieces and broken the eggs over it. For a moment, it was the old Fanny presiding over the tea or breakfast table at Stebbings. "You must be careful after so long. Eat slowly or you will have a pain."

Ironically, now she could eat, Caddie did not want to. "I shall be sick again," she said, but Fanny coaxed her and slowly it went down, a bit of toast, a lick of egg, though the tea was best of all. It revived her more than Father Rossi's coffee and, though she still felt sodden and salted with tears, her eyes sore, her head stupid, pride began to stiffen her. *I* starved, thought Caddie, really starved, and I was the only one. She was able to sit up, hold her head up with Hugh and Pia.

Then, "Very well," said Fanny. Her face looked as if it were made of paper, with two holes for eyes. "Very well. When you have finished tea, we will go upstairs and pack."

"*What* did you say?" asked Caddie.

"We will go to a hotel for tonight," Fanny went on. "We —you, Hugh, and Caddie and I. We will send a telegram to Gwyneth and tomorrow I will take you back. We can probably get on one of the planes. I expect Rob will take you, Pia, back to Rome."

"Do you mean you will come back and live . . ." Hugh could not go on. It took Caddie to blurt out, "With us and Father?"

"Perhaps—if he will have me."

Caddie did not like the look of this Fanny and, "Are you sure?" she asked, but Pia pounced.

"Do you promise?"

"I promise," said Fanny.

"What will . . . he say?" asked Hugh.

"Rob? He has gone to telephone Milan. I expect about the same thing," said Fanny with a wry smile.

"But you said *nothing* to him," said Caddie.

"Rob and I don't have to say things."

"Then it's my fault," said Caddie.

"You can't say 'fault,' when it was right."

"Was it right?"

"Perfectly right."

Hugh, Caddie, and Pia looked at one another. Had they won the battle? Then why did it feel so flat? As if everything had collapsed? Hugh went to Fanny and put his arm round her, but he went mechanically and, "Please don't touch me," said Fanny in a voice she had never used to Hugh, and he stood helplessly by her chair. It was as if they had been dolls, worked by strings; the strings had suddenly been let go and they were left limp. Pia alone sat erect in her chair. At last she said, "I thought you were going to pack."

"She is going to pack."

All of them jumped. Rob was standing in the doorway. Coming in from the terrace in his rope-soled shoes he had made no sound. How long had he been there? He was an intruder, yet at once the strings were gathered up, were taut and everything began to move.

"She is going to pack." Rob came round to Fanny's chair. Hugh moved out of the way. "Pack, but not to go with you, because *we* are leaving," said Rob.

"Leaving?"

"Yes. Fanny and I."

"Leaving—us?" That was Caddie.

"Leaving you," said Rob. "You fought us; now you can take the consequences." Fanny made a little sound of protest but he silenced her. "You will be quite all right with Celestina until they come for you."

"Come for us?" It seemed that all they could do was to repeat what Rob said.

"I spoke to Nonna on the telephone," he said to Pia. "Miss Benson is coming to fetch you; she will be here tomorrow morning. Hugh and Caddie will have to wait until Friday or Saturday. Colonel Clavering will probably not get here till then."

"Darrell coming here?" Fanny sounded dazed.

"I expect so. He must think nothing of travelling. Anyway he will make his own arrangements. They will be quite all right with Celestina. I have given her money," and to Fanny he said, "Renato has found us a flat in Milan. That's why I was so long; I had to wait until he rang me. It's his cousin's. We will move in there; a service flat with not a single inch of room for children."

"But . . . Mother has promised." Caddie had risen, holding to her chair.

"Promised," said Pia, and to Rob, "You heard her; she promised."

"Under duress, which is a kind of blackmail," said Rob, "something you must not apply. That is what you have been using, all of you. In law, a promise made under duress doesn't bind you, bind anyone. Fanny hasn't promised. I see your strike is over," said Rob, looking at the tea table, and to Pia, "I hear you are a blackleg. Caddie, you have been very brave and I respect you but, you see, children cannot be allowed to dictate, or govern. Someday you will come and visit us again—but when *we* ask you. Have you finished tea, Fanny?"

Fanny did not speak or move; he bent, put his hands under her elbows and, as if she were powerless, lifted her out of her chair and turned her towards the stairs.

"You are kidnapping me," she said with a breathless little laugh.

"I am not," said Rob and let her go. "You are coming, that is all." Then he held out his hand; "Come, dear. Come with me." Fanny put her hand in his and, leaving the children, they went upstairs.

XV

«————————————————————————————»

"*Tortellini*," said Celestina. "*Cannelloni*." She knew Caddie liked cannelloni best. "Feesh. *Pollo arrosto,* roast cheeken. *Patate. Asparagi.*"

Celestina meant to be kind but Caddie was not listening even to this recital of delights; her ears were strained to what was happening upstairs. "They are packing; they are really going." That beat in her head. Giulietta had carried all the cases up. "We are defeated." Caddie had wandered into the kitchen, "To be with someone," she could have said, and she felt cold which was curious because the air, with Celestina's cooker going full blast, was hot and close.

It was growing dark. If she had not been so shocked and numbed, Caddie would have thought it was early to be so dark, the kitchen clock only said seven o'clock; all the same, the darkness seemed fitting—"It soon much rain," said Celestina glancing out of the window—fitting that even the sky should weep on this dreadful evening. Caddie herself had no more tears. She was simply limp, cold, defeated. We had won—her eyelids quivered—won, and then it was taken away. She could hear footsteps going backwards and forwards upstairs; it was evidently a thorough packing.

little girl before that—and she remembered how young other girls going back to St. Anne's had seemed to as she sat in the Victoria Station refreshment room. hen Topaz, when she had gone into another happy state d been rended out of that; she still winced even now om thinking of it. It was like breaking out of one egg-hell, into another, eggs and eggs, thought Caddie wearily. Then she remembered that moment in Milan, at La Scala, "the Gilda moment" as she called it in her own mind, which seemed to gild it forever like the angels' wings, when, as a frightened little chick might in a maelstrom, she, Caddie, had lifted her head—and seen, with sudden clarity. That, she thought was the most important mo-ment of my life, "And I have known moments," she could have said, "though I'm still not twelve." Now, in this one, frightening as it was, she was not afraid. She recognized it. It was only another breaking; some more growing. In this one day she, Caddie, had been rent, hurt, betrayed, yet here she was in the evening, sitting in the kitchen, still me, thought Caddie.

There were even compensations: the kitchen was vivid with life and there was a sense of drama as if she were a heroine. Beppino and Gianna had brought over the bill for the broken plates and bottles, and stared at her with round eyes. The fame of her going to the arciprete had spread now to the village, the trattoria knew that Rob and Fanny were leaving, and Beppino and Gianna, in admiration and sympathy, had brought a bunch of oranges and lem-ons as well. Celestina squeezed two of the oranges for her; "Gandhi, he live three weeks on juice." The oranges were blood ones and the juice was pomegranate red. "Red for

She could, too, hear Rob's voice, s[...]
seemed he was guarding Fanny. Even [...]
papers in the study, and that took som[...]
there with him. Perhaps, thought Cad[...]
be with Mother again. It was melodram[...]
be the truth.

Hugh and Pia had disappeared. As fa[...]
concerned they could disappear. She did [...]
either of them again and, sitting at the new[...]
it came to her that she had lost everything no[...]
lost Hugh, lost the battle; in a few minutes s[...]
Fanny; everyone, everything, she really cared[...]
Caddie alone, with nothing and no one to hol[...]
would always be alone now and it was then t[...]
made a startling discovery: she was alone, de[...]
had lost everything—and she was still herself, C[...]
all right. Then, it doesn't matter what happen[...]
thought Caddie. You go on.

Again it felt as if a tight skin had parted in her[...]
tight skin that had been fear, or anger, jealousy,[...]
Now it had broken or dissolved, letting her escape[...]
new dimension, bigger than herself; the same bigne[...]
had glimpsed that night in Milan; love, music, tro[...]
they all seemed to give you this power.

As if she were an old, old lady she seemed to look [...]
down the years; well, I have grown a lot in these [...]
weeks, thought Caddie, more, she could guess, than so[...]
people do in their whole lives. It had been painful but [...]
was a steady growing, and it seemed to her there had a[...]
ready been milestones: when Hugh went to school and she[...]
was rended out of their happy unconsciousness—I was a lit-

martyrs," Pia would have said. Caddie also had some salami
on a slice of bread. In Celestina's opinion she should have
been fed every few minutes, and instead of Fanny's paltry
toast and egg, Celestina would have given Caddie and Pia
a good hot plateful of pasta to lay the gas. It stood to reason,
thought Celestina, that an empty stomach must be full of
gas.

She was shocked to her simple soul by Rob's and Fanny's
leaving. If they had to go, why not the children with them?
Celestina had always taken it for granted that the more
children there were the better, but, as she said to Giulietta,
the English were unnatural: sending their children to bed
early as if they were ill when they were perfectly well: to
boarding school as if they were orphans—*questa povera
piccola* Caddie went to boarding school!—not allowing
them a glass of wine or martini. Celestina, from her year
in London, knew the habits of the English and she was
full of pity for Caddie.

A gust of wind shook the house with a drawn-out whining; the shutters rattled. Next moment a scurry of drops
hit the window panes.

"*Il mio bucato, i miei panni, le mie lenzuola!*" Giulietta
cried. "My washing!" With Beppino and Gianna she
rushed out to the garden. Caddie ran after them, but such
a wind met her on the terrace that she could hardly stand
up. Her hair was whipped into her eyes, her skirt wrapped
round her. The whole lake and sky were changed; the
mountains blotted out by driving cloud and rain, the sky
dark. Then there came two such thunderclaps that Gianna
shrieked and she and Beppino cowered down with their
hands over their eyes.

"*Stupidi, paurosi, vigliacchi.* Help me!" screamed Giulietta.

As Caddie ran to the washing line she could see that far over the lake the water was rough and white, the wind whipping it up into waves; their spray was flung high above the rocks. A gust came from the other side as the wind hit the mountain, a blast that caught Caddie and almost spun her round. With it came more thunder, so close that it might have been in the garden itself and each clap seemed to roll from mountain to mountain across the lake. Caddie helped Giulietta to struggle with the billowing sheets, with pillowcases full of wind. Wet towels lashed their faces, tablecloths were torn out of their hands. By the time they had gathered up all the washing they were breathless, sweatingly hot, their faces smarting from the driving rain, their hair and clothes wet. As they reached the kitchen door they saw Mario, his coat over his head, running up from the boathouse.

"We must wait awhile," said Rob.

"I don't want to wait," said Fanny. "I can't."

"It will be over in a few minutes. It always is," said Rob. "It would be silly to go now. You would get blown and wet, all the luggage soaked."

They were both ready, the cases packed. Fanny was in the travelling suit she had worn when she came, the small soft hat. Her bag and gloves were on the bed, and, "Don't let's wait for anything," she begged. The hand on which Rob's ruby shone was clenched so that the knuckles stood out.

"Darling, don't be so tense. This will all soon be as if it had never happened."

"I can't believe that."

"It will."

"Listen to the wind," said Fanny and shuddered.

"It's only wind," said Rob. "A storm; it will blow itself out—so will this. Let's be sensible. They put up a brave fight. Well, they have lost, that's all. When we are married everything will settle down. Stop thinking," he commanded. "Come. I'm going to get you a drink," but there was a clap of thunder and another so near it sounded over the bedroom. Then the window burst open, letting in a gale of wind and rain, as Celestina wrenched open the door. Fanny sprang to close the window, *"Che cosa succede?"* said Rob sharply. *"Cosa?"*

Celestina stood against the door panting for breath. She must have run up the stairs, thought Fanny trying to hold the window, and for Celestina to run was no light thing. Behind, on the landing, was Giacomino, Giacomino who never came into their part of the house, and Mario, and Giulietta, whose dark eyes were frightened. Beppino and Gianna wriggled themselves under Celestina's arm and Fanny saw Caddie pressed against the wall.

"Ma che diavolo succede?" said Rob again and in English, "I told you, the Signora was not to be worried."

"Signorino Hugh" Celestina managed to get out, and behind her Giulietta shouted above the wind, "Hugh! Pia!"

"Hugh and Pia. What about Hugh and Pia?" Rob had reached behind Fanny, pushed and bolted the window shut. "What about Hugh and Pia?"

Mario's deep voice spoke from the landing and Fanny saw Rob's face change.

"What is it? What *is* it?" Her voice screamed like a sheet tearing. "What is it?" and Rob said, "Hugh and Pia have taken the *Fortuna* and gone sailing."

XVI

"They will come back," said Rob.

"In this?"

"They may have been carried over to the opposite shore. They are probably in Limone by now. They are all right, Fanny. I'm sure they are."

"Why didn't Mario stop them? Go after them?"

"He didn't see them go. He had taken the outboard motor to the garage. Even if he had seen them, even if the outboard had been working, a sail in this wind would be faster than any motor; but Hugh would have got the sail down," insisted Rob. "He would have had that much sense."

"If he could get it down." Fanny's lips were as stiff as if they were frozen. "Listen to the wind." With her hands over her ears, she tried to shut out its whine but she could feel the whole villa shaking.

They had all come down to the drawing room. Celestina, with Giulietta, Giacomino, Mario, and the trattoria children, stood a little away in a silent group. Gianna was crying against Celestina's apron. Celestina and Giulietta were both praying. The arciprete had told Caddie to pray and now she tried to, looking up at the angel she had given to Hugh; its wings shone in the gloom, but of course it still had its painted smile on its face.

Rob was walking up and down. "Damned young fool! Couldn't he have *seen?* Mario was away for just half an hour. Half an hour! God! When they get back, I will beat the life out of them."

Fanny gave a little moan. Rob came to her, knelt beside her, and took her hands down from her face. "They are all right, Fanny. I know they are," but she could feel him trembling. "Give it a few minutes," he said. "If we can't sight them then, I will start the alarm."

In those first days at the villa, when she and Rob were alone, Fanny had welcomed the wind—though perhaps I should have welcomed anything, she had to admit. Then, its blustering and shaking had only made them seem more shut away and safe, made this room, with its books and flowers, gilt and paintings, the big olive fire seem more theirs and they more close. Now it seemed they were paying the price of those days. It was as if the whole villa were exposed to the storm, beaten under the wind, forcing her and Rob apart.

"I want Father," said Caddie suddenly. The whispering prayers, Gianna's snivelling, above all Rob's pacing were too much for Caddie's nerves. Father would not have let them behave like that. "I wish Father were here."

"Hush, Caddie," but Fanny, too, wished there were someone rock-like, somebody English, thought Fanny instinctively, not sharing but in command. Darrell would not have trembled, she thought and hated herself for that; she pushed the thought away. Rob was doing all that he could.

"We shall have to wait until it clears. Nothing could put out in this," he said again and again, but after a few minutes he could not wait. He fetched a coat and put it over his head and shoulders.

"But where will you go? Where can you go?"

"At least I can get to Malcesine. Fanny, when it drops, go over to the Hotel Lydia and wait. I will ring you in half an hour to see if there's a sign."

"And if not, what can you do?"

"Get boats out. Tell the police. Mario, Giacomino, come and help me with the garage doors."

"*Signore, la* Fortuna *è una piccola imbarcazione, un semplice dinghy.*"

"*Sta zitto, chetati,*" said Rob.

"What does he say?" Fanny's eyes went from Mario to Rob, to Mario.

"What we know already: that the *Fortuna* is only a small dinghy."

"*Non è possibile che possa sopravvivere a tutto ciò.*"

"*Basta,*" said Rob curtly. "Come along."

Fanny ran to the upstairs windows, Caddie after her. They stood at one window after another, trying to see through the rain, looking at the threshing sea of olives, the cypresses almost bent double. The storm in La Scala *wasn't* real, thought Caddie. The waves on the rocks sent up clouds of spray and as far as their eyes could see was tumbling water.

"You would never find a sail in all that white," said Caddie.

"There wouldn't be a sail by now," but Fanny did not say it.

The wind dropped. Abruptly, as if someone had reached out a giant hand and turned it off, it ceased to blow, the rain to flail. The cypresses stood erect, the olives ceased to thresh, though they quivered and dripped. Low down, in the sky above the mountain, the sun sent a watery beam among the clouds before it sank out of sight. Fanny and Caddie came out on the landing balcony. The garage doors were open, Rob had gone. Mario had run to the village, Giacomino was out on the headland scanning the lake. Fanny and Caddie came down, and with Celestina and Giulietta, stood out on the terrace. In the growing dusk they could see that the white crests of the waves were flattening out into giant rollers. They strained their eyes, Giulietta shading hers with her hand, Fanny and Celestina alternately using the binoculars. Once Celestina shouted and pointed to a dark blob in the water, then they saw it roll. *"Una latta di benzina!"* cried Giulietta. It was a petrol drum. There was no sign and, "I'm going to the hotel," said Fanny. "To telephone. *Vado a telefonare.*" That was an Italian phrase she had learnt in the days of *Saladin*.

"*Sì. Sì.*" Fanny made Celestina understand that Mario was to go down the lake road, Giacomino up.

"Look. Ask. Everywhere."

"*Sì. Sì,*" said Celestina.

The news had run like wildfire through the village and now the couple from the alimentari came running in to tell that two carpenters, working in a half-finished lakeside canteen, had seen a sailing boat just before the storm, making towards Riva.

"They could never reach it," said Fanny.

"On Garda many, many peoples drown," said Celestina with gusto, and she went on in her mixture of broken English, German, and Italian with tale after tale.

"Five fishermen," said Celestina. "Village fishermen, drown fifty metres from the villa. Here in the villa we hear their cries for help, '*Aiuto! Aiuto!*' and we can do nothing. Nothing! It grow dark, the cries go fainter, then only the women, praying in the garden, sobbing. All drown," said Celestina.

"If go down three times, never come up," said Celestina. "*Nulla risale a galla.* Never come up. A boat with German officer, he think he can sail, one little dinghy at night. They find him boots in empty boat. Boat lost mast. He think he can swim. They find his body. No head," said Celestina, drawing her hand across her throat.

"I want Father," said Caddie again.

Often no bodies were found. "In lake middle, *deep, deep,*" said Celestina plunging downwards with her hand. "Three hundred metres down, caves, big big caves. Water strong, sweep them like that. . . . Never find," said Celestina. She came closer. "Lastest year, three doctor, three in motorboat. Gone. *Kaput.* A little girl. Papa see her kneel to look big feesh. Never find."

"I'm going over to the hotel," said Fanny. "Caddie, come." She was holding Caddie's hand in a grip that hurt.

Though it was of little use, the local boats had put out. They saw Mario and Giacomino in the rowing boat, other fishermen in theirs. A crowd was standing round the alimentari and there was no need to explain in the Hotel

Lydia. The hotel guests had gathered in curious groups and the German manager, Herr Untermeyer, came out himself to meet them.

"They will find them. Certainly they will find them," Herr Untermeyer kept on saying soothingly, but he looked appalled. He took Fanny and Caddie into his office, away from the people, and they waited in silence until the telephone rang. Fanny was there before Herr Untermeyer. Rob's voice said, "Any sign?"

Fanny told him of the carpenters. "They think perhaps Hugh tried to make Riva, put in there."

"I doubt it. It would be too far, even if that boat was the *Fortuna*. They probably tried to turn and run before the wind. They may have been blown a long way. Very well. You had better go back to the house. If you see or hear anything, come back to the hotel and telephone the police, the carabinieri, here at Malcesine. If I hear anything, I will telephone Herr Untermeyer. We shall have news soon," said Rob. "They are alerting every town and village on the lake."

"Have they thought . . . ?" began Fanny, but Rob cut her short.

"They know how to deal with it. They have these accidents often."

"Do you think they will find them?" but Rob would not answer that.

It was almost dark now, a jewel evening. The water still heaved and rolled, splashed on the rocks, but the lake was the darkening blue of a sapphire, hardly broken by white. The mountains stood out, their outlines sharp against the sky which had taken opal colours and, higher tonight than it had been, was the evening star; as Fanny and Caddie watched it was drawn down, as if by its invisible thread, to fall behind the mountain. Soon the lights of Limone glittered and now they could see lit sparks like fireflies on the water. Fishing boats putting out with their lamps.

"But the lake is so big," said Fanny.

"Thirty-two miles long, eleven across," said the exact Caddie.

There were scores of fishing boats.

"The Signor has offered a reward of a million lire," said Celestina.

"A million!" said Caddie.

Police had come along the road, stopping at every village, and the hornet noise of their scooters was matched by the zooming of speedboats, criss-crossing the lake.

"Tre, three," said Celestina. They were all the speedboats in Malcesine. *"Tutti i motoscafi a Malcesine,"* said Celestina.

One turned south, another, driving a course up their side of the lake, headed north, "That's the *Nettuno* with Salvatore"; the third cut a zigzag across to Limone. More boats, Celestina told them, would be putting out from Riva.

"Vi sono palombari, squadra di soccorso. Divers mens, rescue mens, afterwards they search caves."

Fanny shivered.

She was called once to the hotel. Rob was on the telephone and, with a beating heart and a dry throat, she took the receiver from Herr Untermeyer, but Rob was only saying, "The police want to know what they were wearing. Can you endorse what I said?"

On the terrace they still strained their eyes to see. "But it's too dark now," said Fanny and her fingers closed on Caddie's shoulder, holding it so tightly that she bruised. Caddie tried to comfort her.

"Perhaps they are all looking in the wrong places. Hugh and Pia may not be on the lake at all. They may have been washed ashore. They may."

Now the boats showed more definitely on the water than they had in the twilight; some bigger boats were there; one looked like a ferry steamer, its lights showed green or red as it turned. Searchlights shone their beams, white, this way and that, picking up a length and breadth of water.

Just before ten o'clock they heard Rob's step. Its slowness and heaviness made Fanny stand up, holding to the back of her chair, Caddie beside her. Haggard with tiredness, his shoulders sloped, he appeared in the doorway.

"Yes?" whispered Fanny. "Yes?"

"They have found the *Fortuna*."

Fanny's throat moved but she could not speak.

"She was drifting down, just off Campagna, the village below Limone. Hugh didn't get the sail down; the mast must have snapped because it was over the side. She was capsized."

"And them?"

"No sign. They may have been picked up. They may have got to shore somehow."

"Hugh could swim." That was Caddie. "He could life-save. He would life-save Pia." But she was talking against that tide of knowledge: no one can swim in a storm like that; the third time they go down they never come up: the undercurrent takes them: caves three hundred metres down: but, "He would life-save Pia. I know he would," said Caddie.

"We can hope," said Rob to Fanny. "We must hope but I'm afraid, dear, they want you down at the police station. I have come to fetch you."

Children, thought Caddie, are always left out. In any crisis of fear or sorrow they are treated as outsiders, left to wait without news, not told. With scarcely a glance at her, Rob had taken Fanny down to Malcesine. Caddie was left on the terrace alone again.

If Hugh had taken her as his first passenger, the first sail on which he had taken anyone, as he *promised,* thought Caddie, she would have been at the centre of this drama, instead of Pia. She would have been a real heroine. I wish, thought Caddie, as the wretched tears pricked her eyes again, I wish . . . yet even as she wished she knew it was not quite honest. It was better to be Caddie left alone but alive, than to be drowned in that great waste of lake. Once, when swimming in the baths at school, she had gone down too deep and she remembered how she had fought for breath, her chest feeling as if it might burst, a raw hurt in her nose, mouth, ears. It was better to be alive, even if you felt half dead. With dragging steps, she went back into the empty drawing room and stood at the window, watching the lights dotted over the lake.

Celestina came in with a tray of soup, soup with the

pasta in which she so much believed, but she did not stay—
there was too much talk and excitement in the kitchen.
"Cerca di mangiare qualcosa," she said encouragingly.
"You try eat." She patted Caddie's shoulder and disappeared. Caddie could have gone with her. In the kitchen
she would have been a near heroine, but she was too tired.
This endless day seemed to have worn holes in her, as the
waves had worn holes in the rocks; she was worn out.
Suddenly she did not care any more and suddenly, too, she
could not bear that angel's smile. She got up on a chair and
turned them both with their faces to the wall. Then she
took two or three spoonfuls of the soup, put down her
spoon, staggered over to the sofa, and lay down.

Giulietta found her there when she came for the tray.
She tried to rouse her to take her upstairs but Caddie was
too fast asleep. Giulietta put a cushion under her head,
took off her sandals, and fetched a blanket to put over her.

"Poverina. Poverina," murmured Giulietta as she
tucked Caddie in. All at once she noticed the angels.

"Tchk! Che diavolo," said Giulietta. Scandalized, she
fetched a chair and turned them back again.

XVII

<<———————————————————————>>

I T W A S the strangeness that woke Caddie, or perhaps
it was the hardness of Madame Menghini's sofa, she had
dreamed she was back in the train again, or perhaps it was
the chill; she had only one light blanket over her and her
knees were bare. I'm asleep in my clothes, she thought, still
half in dream, in my best jerkin. Her skirt was twisted
round her waist, its pleats crushed, and instinctively she
thought, What will Pia say? She rubbed her feet together
and found her socks were round her ankles. No wonder
her knees were cold. Then the fact that she was in the
drawing room began to dawn on her; the angels glimmered golden in the pale light. But I turned them with
their faces to the wall. Who had turned them back? Was
it an omen? but the memories of the night came flooding
in. How could I have gone to sleep? What had happened
while she slept?

She sat up. There was a wry taste in her mouth that,
experienced now, she knew came from not having brushed
her teeth. Someone had set her sandals side by side, covered her with the blanket, turned out the light, put back
the angels. Celestina? Giulietta? Fanny? Caddie swung her
legs down, pulled her socks completely off and stood up.

The floor was so chill that it made her toes curl away from it and gave her the same shock of reality that her bedroom tiles had given her long ago, so long ago that it was another Caddie who had felt them. She left her sandals where they were, shook her skirt straight—Pia would indeed have been shocked at its crooked pleats—pulled down her jerkin, smoothed her hair and stood listening. The villa was silent, it was too early even for Celestina's birds, there was no sound but the lapping of the lake, gentle now. Caddie tiptoed into the dining room.

The clock here said twenty to six. The shutters were down, but the terrace door was open and she went out.

Outside it was full daylight, though the sun was still behind Monte Baldo and the sky was pale, the mountains dim, their rock steeps not yet turned rosy. As she walked down the garden, the grass was dry under her bare feet. She kept a look-out for her dear snakes but it was not warm enough yet to tempt them onto the rocks; they were all in the lake, and that made her think horrifyingly of Hugh and Pia. She saw them floating, bobbing, with the live snakes swimming round them and she remembered how Pia had always shrunk away from them. "How can you like them?" she used to say and shudder. Now they could touch her, twine all round her, thought Caddie.

It was easy to imagine Pia dead; her small pale face could easily look shut and wet, the black hair plastered down; but Hugh . . . To Caddie he remained obstinately himself and alive.

"Full fathom five, my father lies," Caddie tried to say, tormenting herself with the thought of those caves. "Of thy bones are coral made. . . ." but there wouldn't have been time, she thought. Coral takes ages and is there any in the lake? "Those are pearls that were his eyes," but she saw them rather as dead fishes' eyes, white because they would be rolled up . . . and she had hurriedly to go into the house.

It seemed to be wrapped in sleep. Would they sleep when Hugh and Pia . . . ? It seemed odd, but then Caddie herself had fallen asleep on the sofa and stayed asleep all night. After all, if Hugh and Pia were drowned there was no sense in the rest of them staying awake. Perhaps it was only Celestina, Giacomino, and Giulietta who slept. The other Italians would all have gone home: Mario to the boathouse; Beppino, Gianna, the trattoria mother and father, to the trattoria; the alimentari couple to the alimentari; villagers to the village. Perhaps Fanny and Rob had not come home, perhaps they had found . . . Here Caddie's stomach gave a strange heave, and she began to shiver. She was cold and still weak and she thought it would be wise to go into the kitchen and find something to eat.

Her bare feet made no sound as she went across the dining-room tiles; if it had not been for their coldness she would have felt as if she were floating on air, but when she reached the foot of the staircase, she forgot about going into the kitchen; she seemed to be drawn upstairs, past the brocade door, up to her own room. There was nothing to see there The two beds were empty and smooth as Giulietta had made them in the morning, yesterday morning, thought Caddie, yesterday, an aeon ago, twenty-four hours that seemed to stretch into infinity. The sight of Pia's table, the missal, the vase, the photograph of "my friend" made Caddie's heart stop again. Will Rob take her body to Rome if they find it? And at that, Celestina's stories came vividly alive. Probably there would be no body; the German officer had lost his head; that other little girl never been found. By now Pia probably was in the caves and even with divers they would not find her, even though Rob had offered that million lire. The highly coloured phrases made Caddie's head swim so dizzily that she ran cold water into the basin and doused her face. As she dried it and combed her hair she was surprised to see her hand was trembling.

Still feeling as if she were floating, she went out of the bedroom onto the landing. She was remembering the first evening when she and Hugh had explored the empty villa, seen Rob's shirt drying on the balcony, gone into his study and read the notice, seen the signs of Fanny's bath in the bathroom, the big bed turned down. Once again Caddie listened: Celestina's birds had begun to chirp now, a few sleepy trills, answering the birds outside. A shutter gave a small clatter, and even here came the quiet sound of the waves against the rocks. She peeped into the study; the table was cleared; there was only a litter of paper on the floor. She withdrew onto the landing, turned, went into the dressing room where Hugh had slept—and stood rooted on the rug, wide awake as if life had suddenly been poured back into her bones. Hugh was lying in the bed.

Dead? thought Caddie. But if he were dead, surely they would not have brought him back to the villa? Nor covered him up in blankets? She had an idea that dead people were covered with a sheet, and then she saw that, unmistakably, evenly, the blanket was moving up and down. Hugh was breathing.

She crept nearer. He was asleep, perhaps too much asleep, because he was breathing in a strange way; young people did not breathe as heavily as that. The ear nearest her had a grazed edge, rimmed with a dark red crust of dried blood. She could see another graze on his cheek and a bluish swelling. Tentatively she touched him, putting out a finger as nervously as if a snake might come out of the blankets—she too had a horror of them now—but the spot of skin she touched was damp and warm. Hugh was alive. But how? thought Caddie. How?

Filled with wonder she gave a loud and unexpected sneeze.

"Caddie?"

It was Fanny's voice, but not Fanny warning Caddie off as she usually did when Hugh was ill. It was like a stifled cry, asking, pleading for help? thought Caddie. That was what it sounded like, but she must be wrong.

Yet, "Caddie," it came again, more urgent. "Caddie."

The door between the dressing room and the bedroom was open. Instinctively the children had avoided that side of the landing at night or in the early morning; a bar of shyness had descended when any of them had to pass that bedroom door to go to the lavatory or bathroom, especially if they heard voices inside, or saw Rob come out in his dressing-gown. Caddie and Pia had not been old enough to understand, but they understood all the same and they all kept away, did not listen or look, but, "Caddie." Again that voice, mournful and hollow, as if it were Fanny, not Hugh or Pia who had been drowned.

Caddie went to the door, listened again, and then went in.

Fanny was sitting by the window, dressed as she had been the night before, for travelling, thought Caddie. Only her hat had been taken off and was where she had thrown it last night on the bed. The bed, like Pia's and Caddie's, had not been slept in.

Though Fanny had called her, Caddie had to stand beside her for perhaps a minute before she turned her head.

"Caddie?"

Caddie did not say "Yes?" but answered, for what reason she did not understand, "I'm here."

"You . . . woke up?" That was obvious but, in this new awareness, Caddie treated it gently.

"Yes. A little while ago. Hugh's not drowned."

That was obvious too but Fanny only shook her head.

"Is Pia?"

"No. She has a broken leg."

Fanny spoke as though from a long way off, through veils, thought Caddie.

"Pia is in Riva hospital but Rob is taking her to Milan. Her grandmother is coming. They are both safe."

"But how?" asked Caddie. "How?"

"Hugh knew when he went out it would be rough, that a storm was coming, but he didn't care. That was our fault." Fanny's voice trembled. "Then, when it grew so dark and thundered, he got frightened. He tried to get up to Riva, then to put in to a beach, but the storm broke before he could; you know how sudden it was. He struggled to get the sail down but he couldn't. He said Pia would cling to him and they were swept across the lake towards Limone." The words came out slowly as if jerked from a machine. "The mast broke and the *Fortuna* went over. He held Pia and clung to the side. They were swept still more towards the shore. A duckboard floated up. He managed to catch it and push Pia half onto it, and he held on above her, trying to swim."

"Then the current did not take them down?"

"They were close inshore. The *Fortuna* was clogged by her sail but, as soon as they left her, they were swept onto the rocks. That's where Pia broke her leg. She was knocked unconscious. Of course the boat was not far out but in those waves . . . It couldn't happen. They all say it's impossible, but it did." A little life came into Fanny's voice. "Celestina says it's a miracle. Hugh was brave, Caddie. They say as brave as a man. He pulled Pia up from the waves. Then he said he fainted. When he came to, he found a . . . cleft." Here the voice tailed off and Caddie caught only the words, "Grass tufts . . . oleanders . . . climbed up to the road. One of those double lorries . . . two men . . . one stayed with Hugh, the other went to Limone. . . . They got a doctor with a boat and took Pia off . . . sent for us."

"Is Hugh hurt?"

"Bruised and cut and shocked. Doctor Isella put him to sleep."

Only bruised and shocked. There was a silence, then Caddie asked the question she had to ask.

"Where's Rob?"

"Rob's gone."

"Gone!"

Caddie was right. It had been a cry.

Fanny put out a hand, groping as if she were blind.

"Caddie. Help me. Help me."

XVIII

<<———————————————————————>>

In the old days, when a battle was won, the conquerors brought their defeated enemy home, a prisoner. That was how it felt to Hugh and Caddie.

"Will we go back to the flat?" asked Caddie.

"I suppose so. I had better send a telegram to Father." Hugh was as slow as he had been quick before. Every thought seemed an effort.

"Will Mother come to the flat?"

"I don't know. I should think it depends on Father."

"Where else could she go?"

"We can take her to a hotel," but Hugh sounded as helpless as Caddie felt. They neither of them knew what was to be done with this shell of Fanny.

They had had to wait twenty-four hours. It was only towards the afternoon that Hugh had opened his eyes.

He opened them wide as if he had not seen the room or the villa before but, as a matter of fact, he had been awake a long time. He had woken first about ten o'clock and lain listening to the silence in the house, a silence that was echoed in himself. There was no struggle in him now, no torment. When Fanny, brought in by Doctor Isella, bent over him, it meant nothing at all. When Giulietta came, closing the shutters against the sun, bringing a fresh glass of water, he did not even have to turn over on his other side. They were only Fanny and Giulietta. Why? Why suddenly? thought Hugh. Was it, as some people said such things were, from having been so close to death? For the rest of his life, in Hugh, would be the remembrance of the death drag of that water; its coldness was in his bones, but no, it was not that that had changed him. It was mysteriously something to do with Pia. He kept seeing a nightmare glimpse of her unconscious face as she lay on the rocks. "I thought I had killed her."

He had been brave, they told him and he had said brusquely, "It wasn't brave. It was instinct, and training," but he lied. It was this odd way that Pia had of making him do things better, be stronger than he was, and he knew he could never have let her go, even if he had drowned with her. "I would rather have drowned with her," he said in surprise, surprise because he did not remember anyone before who had been more important to him than himself, Hugh. Fanny, Caddie, he loved them, of course, but, little old Pia! Funny, I didn't know I really liked her, thought Hugh. The liking, indeed, seemed to have let him into this curious freedom from Fanny and Giulietta—and from Raymond? he could have asked. Then he knew that was not true; he would never be free of Raymond but mysteriously Raymond was in his proper place, in perspective. It was all puzzling, perhaps because his head hurt so much and, "I don't understand *anything*," said Hugh.

There was, he felt, one person who could have explained—this was towards evening when his head was more clear—one person who would have talked, not preached and when Caddie next came in—she was acting as liaison between upstairs and downstairs, between the bedroom and dressing room—Hugh croaked, "Caddie."

"Yes, Hugh?"

"I want to see Rob."

"You can't. He has gone."

"Gone?" With Hugh's cut lips and swollen face it was difficult to talk. "Why has he gone?"

"Because we have won after all," said Caddie, and burst into tears.

If Rob had gone, that meant Pia had gone too, taken out of their lives just when . . . Hugh lay very still. Would he ever see Pia again? Perhaps not. Perhaps when they were grown up. He toyed with that a minute and saw himself a young man, Pia a foreign elegant girl; he could guess how elegant she would be; but that time was far away, years, thought Hugh; though Italian girls were said to grow up quickly, look at Juliet, Pia was only ten, and now he saw her and himself, and Caddie of course, and Rob and Fanny, as little figures looked at through the wrong end of a telescope, dwindling, getting smaller, and panic set in. This was the juggernaut power of adults, crushing what they did not even see, and for the first time Hugh was close to tears; not bitterness, ordinary tears. "I won't let them," he vowed. "I will go to Rome and find her"—he who had detested Italy—"there can't be two Pia Quillets." Then he remembered she would be living with her grandmother, the Nonna she talked about, and he did not know even Nonna's name. Write to Rob? Rob could be found through his pictures, but he could not write to Rob. Ask

Fanny if she knew Nonna's address? Hugh knew he could never ask her now.

Renato sent a car to take them to Milan. It brought their air tickets and a note which Caddie read. "Everything is paid. If the boy"—"That's you, Hugh"—"is not well enough to travel tell the chauffeur to telephone me and I will book you on another day. Keep the car," but Hugh, though stiff and sore, covered with bruises and still shocked, insisted on going.

The villa, too, was already clearing them out. It seemed Madame Menghini had dismissed them. During the morning, Celestina was sent for from the Hotel Lydia to telephone Milan. The villa was let, or lent, again.

"So soon?" asked Caddie.

It seemed callous even to Celestina but Madame Menghini's husband's niece was coming on holiday, "And why should she go into a hotel when the villa will be empty?" said Celestina.

The niece was coming tomorrow with her husband and five children. "All rooms! All beds!" *"Fünf Kinder!"* said Celestina, "Everything be put away."

The villa began to be as it had been; the little curtains went up again on every window, mats were put back under every vase and ashtray. The chairs were arranged round the centre table, the plant pots set in rows. Rob's study was a bedroom again. As soon as Fanny came out of her bedroom, the necklace and cross would be put back over the bed. The only thing altered in the villa would be that Celestina had two kitchen tables.

Yet there were traces: Celestina found Caddie's panama

behind the chest of drawers. It was squashed so out of shape that Caddie said she did not want it. Celestina gave it to Gianna, who wore it to Mass; its St. Anne's crest looked incongruous but it made Gianna very proud. Celestina found too the picture of Saint Sebastian where Pia had left it on the window sill; as Pia and Rob had gone, Celestina gave it to Beppino for his First Communion. In the bathroom Fanny had forgotten her soap, bath salts, and Jicky powder. Giulietta asked her if she wanted them, but Fanny only turned her head away and Giulietta gathered them up to keep for her wedding.

When Hugh and Caddie brought Fanny through the sunk garden on the way to the car, she stopped by an old olive tree. It seemed she wanted to touch it. "Well, she always does that when she's in trouble," Caddie whispered. Fanny's hand came down its trunk, feeling the dry wood and she looked at Hugh and Caddie with eyes that were suddenly awake.

Hugh had not been there that early morning when Caddie had had to stand by, inadequately trying to pat away that terrible grief, but now tinged with it himself, he could not bear those eyes, "Come, Mother. Mother, come," but even Hugh could not reach Fanny now.

Just before that dawn, "When the stocks smelled so strongly in the garden," whispered Fanny, "and it was so wet and chill," she had been sitting by Hugh's bed, as Rob, she thought, was sitting by Pia's in the hospital— each of us alone, with our own child, utterly separated. Separated, not only by this division of children but because she too, in those hours, had echoed Caddie's cry "I want Father." "I want Darrell." Hugh was Darrell's child. "We should telephone him," said Rob.

They could not do that, not while this agony was going on. "Not until we know," and then, "Wait until the morning," said Rob.

The morning.

Perhaps she had dozed in her chair because she seemed to be woken suddenly by a sound, a feeling, she did not know which. Light was in the room, the first light, dawn light, colourless and with it a coolness that touched her cheeks and eyes. She was conscious of her clothes, the tightness of her girdle, an ache in her back, her feet aching too from wearing shoes all night, and I had a feeling of stifling, thought Fanny, of terror. The terror of the night had not happened—miraculously, as Celestina said—but this terror was a terror to come. It was as if we had traded, Rob and I.

"If that hope had really been the beginning of our baby, Rob's and mine . . ." That brought such a wave of longing that she had almost cried out. We should have been safe, thought Fanny, bound, as children do bind you, but now, all the old teachings of Aunt Isabel had woken in her mind. If you do wrong, you will be punished, terribly punished.

Hugh was asleep. Fanny got up and when she came out on the landing, Rob's study door was open and he was at the table with the light still on; he had not noticed the daylight and he was writing.

For one moment Fanny had thought it was *Saladin*; *Saladin,* after that night! Writers are like locusts, she thought. They feed on the moment and pass on—then she saw it was a letter.

"Rob, what are you doing?"

He looked up. "Writing to Darrell."

"That's unpardonable." She seemed to be struggling for breath.

"I know, but you don't want to have to explain."

"Explain? I . . . I . . . I must go out into the garden," cried Fanny. It felt as if she screamed.

"Fan—" Rob had got up.

"Don't, Rob. Don't call me that." And she had cried, "I can't breathe."

The ground floor of the villa had been shuttered as Celestina thought it should be, even on that night. Rob opened the door from the dining room to the terrace; by mutual consent they had avoided seeing the lake, and walked round the house, down the steps, past the geraniums colourless in the half-light, and through the sunk garden to the olive grove where the grass was grey still, and the twisted stems of the old trees loomed and retreated into shadow as they passed. The olive leaves glimmered, the wisteria arch was grey. It is filled with ghosts already, thought Fanny. The flowers were still half hidden in darkness, still wet from the storm; only the rocks smelled strong and powerful, making wreaths of darkness or white round the olives. Fanny's shoes and stockings were wet but her face had cooled and she could breathe.

"We have given in," she said.

"Yes. Given in," said Rob.

"I am calm now," said Fanny and she lifted her face to Rob. "I won't make you a fuss."

The bell began to ring from Malcesine.

"It must be twelve o'clock," whispered Caddie. The

arciprete will be pleased when he hears, she thought; at least one person could be wholeheartedly pleased.

Twelve o'clock.

"Mother, you must come," said Hugh. "The car is waiting."

No answer.

"Mother, we have to get to Milan," but Fanny still stayed, pressed against the olive tree.

Caddie looked at Hugh, Hugh at Caddie. Then Caddie went to Fanny and took her by the hand.

"Come, Mother."

She came obediently and walked with them to the car, one of them each side of her.

Celestina and Giulietta had broken off their work to see them off. Giacomino had come to the steps, Beppino and Gianna were there. *"Arrivederci,"* they called, *"Arrivederci,"* but they were so busy they could not linger. Celestina shut the car doors briskly and stood back to wave.

As the car drove out of the gates, Caddie noticed what she had not seen before; that the whitethorn flowers had dropped, their petals were scattered in the road. The hedges now did not disguise their pricks and, almost before the car turned up the road, Giulietta ran and shut the gates. The last thing Hugh and Caddie saw were the gilt letters, VILLA FIORITA, as, with Fanny sitting between them, they drove away.